Three Can Keep a Secret

To receive a free catalog of Poisoned Pen Press titles, please
contact us in one of the following ways:

Phone: 1-800-421-3976
Facsimile: 1-480-949-1707
Email: info@poisonedpenpress.com
Website: www.poisonedpenpress.com

Poisoned Pen Press
6962 E. First Ave. Ste. 103
Scottsdale, AZ 85251

Three Can Keep a Secret

Judy Clemens

Poisoned Pen Press

Poisoned Pen Press

Poisoned Pen Press
6962 E. First Ave., Ste. 103
Scottsdale, AZ 85251
www.poisonedpenpress.com
info@poisonedpenpress.com

Printed in the United States of America

For Phil and Nancy Clemens
my parents, my friends

"It is our fixed principle rather than take up Arms to defend our King, our Country, or our Selves, to suffer all that is dear to be rent from us, even Life itself, and this we think not out of Contempt to Authority, but that herein we act agreeable to what we think is the Mind and Will of our Lord Jesus."
—Thirteen Mennonite Ministers of Pennsylvania, May 15, 1755

"Three can keep a secret, if two are dead."
—Hell's Angels motto

Chapter One

Dr. Rachel Peterson stepped back and shook her head. "I have to tell you, Stella. I'm concerned."

I glanced down at my arm where my tattoo, which used to say, "To thine own self be true," lay disfigured by unadorned skin taken from my back. My leg, previously unmarked, would forever sport white patches of scarring after the motorcycle accident five weeks earlier had thoroughly scraped the skin off the entire left half of my body. It also itched like hell. I looked up at the doc. "I thought you said the road burns were healing nicely."

"They are. It's the rest of you I'm worried about." She picked up my chart. "Your complexion is gray, you've got circles under your eyes the size of hoofprints, and you've lost thirteen pounds in five weeks. Not to mention your ribs aren't healing."

"I'm sorry."

She let out a laugh. "You're *sorry*? I don't want an apology. I want changes. You can't go on like this."

I eased myself off the examining table and started pulling on my clothes, not trusting myself to speak.

"Stella," Dr. Peterson said, "please. Sit down for a minute."

I turned around, my shorts in my hand, but didn't sit. It would take too much energy to get back up.

Dr. Peterson's eyes glowed with kindness. "It's not just the physical exertion, I know."

I fiddled with a belt loop on my shorts.

Her voice was soothing, and soft. "Grief can tear you apart, if you let it. Do you have anyone to talk to?"

I shrugged, not wanting to be thinking about this. Around the same time I wrecked my bike I also lost my long-time farm-hand and mentor, Howie Archer. My dairy cows didn't seem to notice the difference, but my dog Queenie and I felt Howie's absence every day.

"I'm talking to you," I said.

"No, Stella. You're not."

I turned back around and resumed putting on my clothes. The doctor sighed. "Can you find someone to listen? Someone you trust. A friend, your minister."

I closed my eyes and breathed through my nose. I had friends. Friends who cared, who would be there for me. I supposed I could talk to Ma Granger's minister, if I wanted to go the church route. The problem was, I didn't want to talk. To anyone.

"Okay," Dr. Peterson said. "You know how I feel about that. And about the farm work you've been doing."

"Find me a competent employee, and I'll start taking it easy."

"Stella—"

"I mean it. How am I supposed to get my cows milked twice a day and maintain the rest of the farm without working twenty-four seven? I have Zach Granger helping, but he's only fourteen. I can't expect him to work full-time. And he heads back to school next week."

"You are looking for someone to hire?"

"The farming grapevine is alive and hopping, well aware of my needs. Plus, I've got ads in the local papers and in *Hoard's Dairyman*."

"Which is…?"

"The national magazine for dairy farmers."

"Ah. Any calls yet?"

"So far, I've had two very un-recovered alcoholics, one seven-teen-year-old, a chick who'd never seen a cow in real life, and a guy who assumed I was the farmer's wife."

"Uh oh."

"He stayed as long as it took for me to personally lift him back into his truck."

Dr. Peterson laughed, but shook her finger at me. "Exactly the kind of activity you shouldn't be doing."

"Plus," I continued, "I've had several kids from the Delaware Valley College Ag program, but they can only promise a year or two, and only part-time."

"Which would be better than nothing till you find someone else."

I ran my fingers through my hair. "I know. I was just hoping to find a hand who would stick around a while. I don't want to go through this hiring thing again anytime soon."

She patted my good arm. "The right person will show up before you know it."

I grunted.

"And until then, you need to get some help. Even if it's just temporary."

"I have someone coming to apply this afternoon. Probably'll turn out to be a serial killer or religious fanatic or something."

She laughed again and led me down the hallway toward the reception area. "I want to see you again next week. No excuses."

I saluted weakly. "Yes, sir, ma'am."

She stopped at the desk and handed the receptionist my chart. "And until then, you can call me if you need someone to talk to. Now go get some supper. And eat it all."

I left the office, holding my ribs as I walked down the stairs outside. The sky was a vibrant blue, spotted with puffy white clouds, and the sun beat down on the blacktopped parking lot with ferocity. I opened both doors of my truck to let it air out before climbing in.

It was a beautiful August day.

And I was miserable.

Chapter Two

On an average day the traffic on Old 309 is so bad I want to swerve around traffic and speed by on the gravel shoulder. That day, on the way home from Doc Peterson's, there wasn't even room to do that. I took deep breaths to calm my rising blood pressure and craned my neck to see what was holding us up. Couldn't see a thing.

Fifteen minutes later I finally got a glimpse of the traffic light at Bethlehem Pike and Route 113. The changing of the light's colors made no impact on the flow of traffic, since a police officer stood in the intersection directing vehicles around an accident. As I crawled by I did my share of rubber-necking, but couldn't see anything other than a pickup with a bashed-in front end. The ambulance must've already left, since the only people I saw were emergency folks trying to rid the road of glass.

It brought back way too many memories of my accident just weeks before.

Finally free of the worst of it, I drove the remaining distance to my house and pulled into the lane, parking in the shade of a maple tree. A well-used Ford Taurus sat in the drive, and a woman stood leaning against the door, her face turned toward me. I stepped down from the truck, careful of my sore ribs. The woman stood up straight, her expression anxious.

I walked toward her. "You must be Lucy."

She scrutinized my clothes and tattoos—especially the one of the cow skull emblazoned on the back of my neck that peeked around underneath my ears. "And you must be the boss."

"Name's Stella." I stuck out my hand, and she shook it firmly. So far, so good. In the next few minutes I was sure she'd do something to disqualify herself, but until then I'd hope for the best. She looked the most promising of the candidates I'd seen so far, even if she was a bit small.

"Your last name's Lapp, right?" I asked. "Sounds Mennonite."

She smiled slightly. "It is. I'm Mennonite to the core. Is your next question going to be why I don't look Amish?"

"Sorry to disappoint you. Living around here, I know plenty of Mennonites who wear jeans." Such as the entire clan of Grangers, including Abe, my best friend since I was ten. "Not too much about the Mennos could surprise me anymore. Now, if you don't mind waiting a few minutes, I'll change my clothes and we can get to work."

"All right if I walk around a bit?"

I pursed my lips, not sure I wanted some stranger snooping around. I finally decided she couldn't do too much harm in such a short time. "Suit yourself."

I started jogging to the house, slowing to a walk when my ribs protested.

In my bedroom I took a second to roll my neck and ponder the woman outside. Physically, we were exact opposites. At five-nine, I could look straight over her head. Bulk-wise I could throw her down and truss her up in a matter of seconds. Not that I'm fat. My body is basically one big muscle. No curves, no softness, just angles and bones. Especially now I'd lost that weight the doctor was complaining about.

Lucy was built more like a cheerleader—short, with curves in all the right places. But older. Her skin tone and the lines beside her eyes said she definitely wasn't in high school anymore. And the look in those same eyes was tired, and hard. Had to be a story there. I wondered if she'd be around long enough for me to learn what it was.

Once I'd donned my barn boots, jeans, and T-shirt, and had popped one of my Motrin, I found her outside, checking out the site where my heifer barn had burned to the ground a little over a month before.

She turned when gravel crunched under my boots. "Electric?" she asked, indicating the barn.

"Arson."

That sparked some interest, but I wasn't ready to fill her in until I knew she was staying.

"Ready to milk?" I headed toward the milking parlor, and she soon followed.

Zach was guiding the cows into their stalls when we arrived. My collie, Queenie, lay in her usual corner. She got up and trotted over to me, ignoring Lucy, which meant she must've checked her out already and decided Lucy was okay. Score one for Lucy.

"Hey, Zach," I said. "This is Lucy Lapp. She's applying for the farmhand position."

He clipped a cow into her stall and came over, wiping his hand on his jeans before offering it to her.

"Hi, Lucy," he said. "Don't let Stella intimidate you. She's not as scary as she looks."

"Gee, thanks, Zach," I said.

Lucy's lips twitched, but the impression of humor was fleeting. Gee, this one was a laugh a minute.

"Why don't you help Zach get the girls in," I said to Lucy. "I'm going to go see about my temporary help."

Zach grinned, knowing I meant Abe.

"Did you check on Poppy?" I asked Zach. To Lucy I said, "We have a cow soon to calve, and Zach and I have a bet going as to when she'll produce. The sooner the better, for my wager."

Zach's grin grew. "She's still huge."

"Don't count your calves before they're hatched," I said, and left Lucy in his capable hands.

When I got to the office I peered through the window in the door to see if Abe was there. He sat at the desk, chin on his fists, staring at the computer screen. He worked weekdays at Rockefeller Dairy, doing their books, and spent every other available moment doing charity work for me. I was surprised he wasn't asleep.

I took a moment to study him and wonder where our relationship was headed. He had brought home another woman the month before, and I had finally admitted—to myself and to him—that I wasn't sure I liked it. He didn't like it either and was eager to pledge me his unending devotion. I wasn't quite there yet. I had suffered through a quick and painful romance with a barn painter at the same time Abe had brought the city gal home, so I wasn't sure I was ready for just one man, no matter how much I cared about him.

I pushed open the door, and he jumped. "Geez, you scared me."

"Sorry. Didn't mean to."

He spun his chair around. "What did the doctor have to say?"

I raised an eyebrow at him. "And that's your business because…?"

"Because I care about you. And your health."

"Oh." I considered that, and felt Dr. Peterson's presence beckoning me to share my feelings. She might be right, but that didn't mean I had to like it. "Let's just say I'm not her model patient."

"Surprise, surprise."

"I told her if she found me a farmhand I'd slack off a bit."

"Then let's hope today's the day. Lucy Lapp should be here any minute."

I cocked my head. "She's in the parlor, helping Zach."

"Oh. I guess I missed her driving in."

"That's unlike you. What's so fascinating on the computer?"

He looked at me warily. "You sure you want to know?"

"Oh God, Abe, not girlie sites?"

Red rushed to his face. "You know me better than that."

I laughed. "And I know you'd never stray off the straight and narrow. So what was it?"

"Well…."

"Come on."

"Okay. You know your finances aren't any too hot right now."

"Tell me another one."

Since the shit hit the fan a month before, I'd been lucky to keep my phone and utilities paid up, and food on my table. It had been discovered that my cows were producing tainted milk because of their food, so besides having my feed stores cleaned out and new feed brought in, I'd had to milk my cows for several days and watch the milk get carted away for destruction until the FDA had proclaimed my herd "cured." Needless to say, the government wasn't giving me any help with the money, and insurance interpreted the situation as an Act of Terrorism and was therefore denying reimbursement. After September Eleven insurance companies had to rethink their stance on terrorism claims, but so far their policy changes hadn't done me any good. Thank God for the free help I'd been getting from Zach and Abe, along with some charity from other folks. Not that my farming friends have much to give—time or money.

"Anyway," Abe said, "I've been thinking about some of the extra expenses that have come up lately. Your truck has been giving you problems, you'll need money to hire a new farmhand, and of course there's the obvious project of the heifer barn."

"I can fix the truck myself, I was paying Howie anyway, and insurance will pay for most of the barn."

Abe ignored me. "I've been studying some possible sideline incomes."

"Oh, great. Waitressing in between milkings? Bagging at the grocery store?"

"Something here at the farm. Did you know the Hoffmans are considering an ice cream parlor?"

"What?"

Marty and Rochelle Hoffman were other small-time dairy farmers, good friends of mine.

"They haven't mentioned it to me," I said.

"You have enough to think about these days. They didn't want to burden you worrying about them. Anyway, there are all kinds of things to do. Run a vegetable stand, sell flowers, let a phone company build a cell tower on your land, rent out one of the barns for parties—"

"For Pete's sake, Abe. Next thing you'll be wanting me to give hayrides and have Easter egg hunts."

He shrugged. "Why not?"

"First off, I scare children."

He grinned. "Only ones who don't know you."

"Second, we have no barn to spare at the moment."

"That will change as soon as we get the heifer barn rebuilt, and you said insurance will be paying for it."

"Third, what should I tell Jude when he wants to plant my back acreage and he can't because the phone company's erecting a permanent eyesore?"

"All right, I understand those problems. But what about the other stuff?"

"Which?"

"Flowers and vegetables. Basically no contact with the public if you use the honor system, and it would take up lots less land than a phone tower."

"And I'm going to tend the plants with what time?"

He looked at me steadily. "How about the time you're putting into fixing up the bike that almost got you killed?"

I stared back at him. "That Harley is all I have of a life outside this farm, Abe. And most of my friends are bikers."

"I've offered you another way."

I stifled a groan. "Marry you and become the perfect yuppie wife?"

"Is that so unattractive?"

I pushed myself out of my chair. "Abe, you know you're one of my favorite people, and I appreciate all the work you've done for me. But this farm is all I have left of my parents. Of Howie. No matter how I feel about you, I'm not ready to abandon it."

He studied me. "Well, then, isn't it worth it to consider one or two of these other options? I want to help save the farm. You know I do."

I jammed my hands into my pockets and looked out the window at my house. I did love the place. But how much more sacrificing was I going to have to do for it?

"So leaving my bike behind and tending a garden has become my only option?"

He tapped on the computer screen. "I'm doing my best to come up with others. None of them leave much room for joy-riding. But look at what it means in the end."

I turned slowly toward him. "What it means is I lose one more part of my life that brings me happiness. I don't have too many of those left."

He seemed about to say something, but I couldn't listen any-more. I left the room, closing the door a little harder than I meant to. I leaned against the wall and pushed on my temples with my fingers. It had been five weeks since my life had changed irrevo-cably, and I wasn't in a place to be adding more responsibilities to my already overflowing plate of chores. Let alone manage the stress that comes with trying out a new take on an old relationship.

I shoved myself away from the wall and went to check on my farmhand hopeful.

The cows were hooked into their stalls and Lucy was placing the milker on the first one when I got back to the parlor. Zach caught my eye over a cow's back and gave me an enthusiastic thumbs-up.

I stood and watched Lucy work. Seemingly oblivious to my presence, she projected an understanding of cows, unlike some of my loser applicants. She was gentle, patting their rumps and talking to them, but not so delicate she wouldn't put a knee in their leg to move them over, or prod them awake with her boot. Her hands on the milking apparatus were sure and steady, and she moved like she was at home.

Hope began creeping its way into my chest, and I had to work hard to stifle it, afraid of yet another disappointment.

I steeled myself and went into the feed room to get the cows' grain. There was no way to tell it anymore, but that little room was where I had found Howie, my beloved farmhand, taking his last breaths. I couldn't even look at the doorway to the room without feeling queasy.

I made it out to the parlor just in time to see Lucy avoid getting peed on by a cow. She waited for the river to stop, then stepped beside the cow to wipe off the teats with a paper towel. Another good attribute for a farmhand. Cool in times of excrement.

Zach was busy in his row with the same routine as Lucy— wiping off the teats and hooking on the milkers. I had just started filling the feed trays when Queenie growled a low, bone-chilling rumble. From where I stood I couldn't see her, but I could see Lucy, who had frozen.

"What?" I asked, and took a step.

"Stop!" Her voice was a forced whisper.

I stopped.

"We've got a problem," Lucy said.

By shifting my weight I could get my eyes around the cow blocking my view, and I sucked in my breath. Queenie crouched low on her haunches, her teeth bared. About a foot from her face a beautiful black and bronze snake lay at attention, its eyes locked with Queenie's. A copperhead. Venomous and not at all friendly.

"Holy crap," Zach said. "Where did that come from?"

"Stella," Lucy said. "Do you have a rifle?"

"In the office, but there's no way—"

"Somebody bring it to me."

I took a deep breath and let it out. She seemed to know what she wanted, and I was no expert on snake extermination. "Okay. Zach, you're closest. Go—"

"Slowly," Lucy said.

"—and get it. You know where it is. Grab some ammo, too."

Lucy, Queenie, and I stood stock still, keeping our eyes straight ahead, while Zach made a slow and quiet exit. Once he was gone Lucy's shoulders relaxed a little.

"Keep him far away," she said. "Copperheads can be lethal to kids."

"What about you? You're smaller than Zach."

"It's not necessarily your size that matters."

"Here it is," Zach said from the doorway.

Lucy angled her eyes toward him. "Okay." Her lips barely moved as she talked. "I want you to hand the gun to Stella without taking another step, then the ammo. Then get out of here."

Zach stretched his arm out, and by leaning slightly to the side I could reach the gun. He was too far away for me to reach the bullet, so I wiggled my fingers and he gave it a gentle toss. I closed my hand over it, then watched as Zach took a backward step and retreated into the hallway.

Lucy's arm was already stretched over the cow between us. Her eyes, focused on the snake, were cold and hard. By standing on my toes and balancing against a cow I could just get the gun to her fingers. She transferred it slowly to her left hand, swiveling her eyes toward me. I said a small prayer, then repeated Zach's process of tossing the bullet, which fortunately found her hand.

All of this seemed to be taking an eternity, but in reality it must have only been about five minutes. It took another year for Lucy to get the bullet into the twenty-two and rack it. A tremor shook my chest as she raised the gun to her shoulder. There was no way she'd hit the snake from where she stood. She was much more likely to hit Queenie or ricochet the bullet around the room, killing a cow or one of us.

"Lucy," I said.

She slid her eyes toward me impatiently, and the look in them silenced me. I shook my head and she went back to taking aim.

The shot pierced the air in the concrete room, and I recoiled violently, slapping my hands over my ears. Lucy's ears had to be ringing, too, but when I straightened she nodded and walked carefully toward the snake. I stepped out from behind the cows and watched as she scooped up the dead serpent with the barrel of the gun.

"Good grief," Zach said.

I stared. "Lucy. We need to talk."

"I hate snakes," Lucy said.

Chapter Three

"What the hell was that?" I asked.

Lucy and I sat in my office, where a little air conditioner chugged away in the window. My sweat, arising from both milking and the snake confrontation, chilled my skin, and my arm itched like mad.

After the snake had been properly disposed of behind the feed barn, Lucy, Zach, and I had finished the remainder of the milking before we women left Zach to clean out stalls and scrape the walkways. Now I needed a few answers.

Lucy shrugged. "I grew up on a farm. I've known how to shoot a gun since I was twelve. One time I shot a bat out of the sky."

That seemed a bit unbelievable, but then, she had just shot a snake.

"What's a good Mennonite girl like you doing with aim like that?" I was only half joking.

"We Anabaptists may resist hurting other people, but we can handle killing snakes."

"Which you do very well. You stayed calm under life-threatening pressure today."

"Not really." She leaned back in her chair. "You most likely won't die from a copperhead bite unless you're a kid or old or unhealthy. But the pain is almost worse than dying."

"You've been bit?"

"Once. Hurt like the dickens."

"I bet. So you grew up with cows?"

"And pigs. And chickens. And sheep. Whatever my dad was into at the time. The pigs didn't stay long. Mom finally said it was her or the oinkers. Couldn't stand the smell." She lifted a shoulder. "But there were always the cows."

I looked her over from where I sat behind my desk. She really was small, but she'd proven she was no weakling.

"So where were you before and why did you leave?" I ask 1.

She stiffened slightly and looked down at her hand, he fingers picking at the arm of the chair. "I've had several long-term jobs at farms, but not for a few years now. I...took a break. My husband was ill, and I stayed home to care for him."

Suddenly I understood the dullness in her eyes. "And your husband?" I asked quietly.

She swallowed, a tightness forming around her mouth. "He's been gone a little over a year and a half. He died the day after Christmas."

"I'm sorry."

"You can call my last employer if you want. He'll tell you how I did." She scribbled down a name and number and I took it and smoothed it on the top of my desk.

"Why get a job now?" I asked.

She cocked her head. "It's a combination of things. The main reason is I miss it. I miss the cows, the routine. Believe it or not, I miss the smells." She angled her face away. "But other things have been sneaking up on me. A year and a half is a long time to be grieving a lost husband while living with my parents and my in-laws right down the street. To be honest, they're driving me crazy. I mean, I love them, but—"

"You don't have to explain. I'm a great believer in personal space."

"So you understand. I cut out your ad in *Hoard's* two weeks ago, but have been holding off on any decisions." She gazed at me with what looked like desperation, and something deep inside me reached out to her.

"The job is yours if you want it."

Her mouth quivered, and I wasn't sure if she was getting ready to laugh or cry. "You mean it?"

"One thing you'll learn quick is I don't say things I don't mean."

She looked away for a long moment, and when she turned back, determination showed on her face. "I'll do a good job."

"I know. When can you start?"

"Today."

I smiled. "How 'bout tomorrow. I'll do the morning milking—that's always been mine. Why don't you come whenever you want and move into the apartment...."

The apartment. The space above the garage where Howie had lived. Now Lucy would be living there, and I needed to clean it out. Not that there was much to move. I'd put it off as long as I could, and I certainly wasn't looking forward to facing Howie's ghost.

"So I'll see you tomorrow," I said.

I suddenly felt emotional, realizing this person was here because Howie was gone, so I stood up. Lucy clasped her hands and peered up at me like a nervous high-schooler.

"What?" I said. "You don't see another snake?"

"Oh gosh, no. It's just...I have a couple more things to talk to you about."

I sat back down. "You're not an alcoholic, are you?"

"No." She let out a surprised chuckle.

"Use drugs? Been convicted of something?"

"No."

"Are you a serial killer? Escaped convict?"

She held up her hand. "Can't claim either."

"Okay. Good. So what is it?"

"Is the apartment big enough for two?"

I blinked. "Two?"

"I'll be bringing my daughter, Tess. She's eight."

I thought about this. I liked little girls okay, I guessed. I wasn't used to having them around the farm, but I could handle it, if it meant having Lucy.

"She's a good girl," Lucy said, "and she'll be in school starting Monday, as long as her registration goes through." She flushed. "I stopped by the administration building this afternoon, just in case...well, in case it worked out here. School's the main reason I finally took the plunge and came to apply. I realized it was starting next week, and if we were going to be here I wanted Tess to be able to start on day one. She deserves that chance." She hesitated. "I promise she won't be a problem."

"Why would she be? I'll be glad to have her. Sorry you can't stay tonight."

"I have to go back to Lancaster, anyway. Tess is with my folks. I'll bring her tomorrow. By the way, is the apartment furnished?"

"Got all the necessities. You want to see it?"

"That's all right. From your expression I can see it would be better to wait. A good number of my things are in storage, anyway. We'll just bring a few personal items, until we see what we need."

"Fine. Was there something else you needed to discuss?"

She winced. "We can work around this issue, of course, with whatever your wishes are, but I want to at least mention it."

I waited, expecting the worst.

"Might it be possible for me to have Sunday mornings off, so Tess and I could go to church? I mean, unless you go, then I'm willing to miss it."

I leaned back, relieved her request was innocuous. "I'll do morning milkings, anyway, so I can't see why that would be a problem. And I try to keep Sundays relatively free. Sunday could be your day off. That doesn't seem unreasonable."

Her eyebrows lifted. "Wow, that's just...that's great. I'll make it up to you the other days."

I flapped a hand at her. "Gotta have time off sometime. I should know. I haven't had any lately, and it's killing me. I can even point you toward a good church, unless you already have one in mind. Some of my closest friends go to Sellersville Mennonite. Been going there for years."

"Sellersville?" An expression of amusement flashed across her face. "That might work out very well." She stood up. "I'll be here to relieve you tomorrow. Unless you really would like me to stay for this evening. I can."

"No, go home to your daughter. I'll survive a few more hours by myself." I could practically feel Dr. Peterson's presence slapping me on the forehead, but I ignored it.

Lucy walked toward the door before stopping and looking back. "What happened with your last farmhand, anyway?"

I concentrated on my breathing. "He died."

"I'm sorry." She didn't push for a further explanation, perhaps recognizing the grief on my face. For the same reason, I didn't probe into her husband's illness and death.

She turned the doorknob. "I'll see you tomorrow, then."

When she'd gone, I picked up the paper where she'd scribbled her reference's name and number. Looked like he lived in Morgantown. It was a little late for a referral, seeing as how I'd hired her already, but I called the guy—Martin Spunk—anyway. He answered, and his voice made me want to laugh. All heart and no bite.

"Stella Crown?" he said jovially. "As in the farm with all them troubles last month?"

"That's me."

"I read about that. I was real sorry to hear about Howie."

"You knew him?"

"From way back. Worked together at a big farm in Wisconsin in, oh, sixty-two or thereabouts. Good hand. Good friend."

"The best."

We had a moment of silence.

"So what can I do for you?" Spunk finally asked.

"Wanted to check with you about a former employee. Lucy Lapp."

"Lucy?"

"I hired her today, and I'm calling to make sure I did the right thing."

"No doubt about it."

"She did well for you?"

"Best farmhand I ever had."

"So how come you let her go?"

"Had no choice. Her husband got hurt and she decided he was a bigger priority than me. Course that's the way it should be."

"I thought he was sick. She called it an illness."

"I guess you could call it that. Fell down the basement stairs. Paralyzed from the neck down. Nasty business."

Nasty, indeed. "And he died about a year and a half ago?"

"Yeah, real sad thing. She came back looking for a job a month or so ago, but I didn't have nothing to offer her. I was right sorry about that. How's that pretty little girl of hers? Tess?"

"I haven't met her yet, but she'll be coming tomorrow."

"You tell her hello from her Uncle Marty, will ya?"

"I'll be glad to, Mr. Spunk. And thanks so much for the reference."

I hung up and sat for a moment, wondering if I should consider the small discrepancy in Lucy's story. Would I call being paralyzed an illness? Perhaps if I didn't want to explain things. Made sense to me. And she seemed prickly enough I wasn't about to ask her. At least not till she'd been around a while.

I put that aside and tried to digest the Howie connection I had made. Talking to Spunk I had found out things about Howie I'd never known.

Zach found me in the same position ten minutes later.

"You hire her?" he asked.

I shook myself out of my trance. "She's ours. Thanks for your input."

"She seemed to know what she was doing. And was a good shot, too."

"She's bringing her daughter with her."

He brightened. "My age?"

"Is that hormonal interest I'm seeing? Sorry. She's only eight."

He grinned. "That's all right. I haven't decided to sign my life over to girls yet. That can wait a year or so."

"Good plan. Besides, I thought I was your only woman."

"You are my only woman. High school chicks are just girls."

"As long as we're clear."

He laughed. "My dad's here. I'll see you tomorrow. Everything in the parlor's done."

"Thanks, Zach."

I walked to the window and waved to Jethro Granger, Zach's dad and Abe's oldest brother. His bulk filled the driver's side of his Chevy Dually, and his arm hung big and meaty out of the window. He waggled his fingers and they drove away, spitting up a cloud of dust.

I stood there, wondering what to do next. I considered going to find some supper, but the heat had pretty much sapped whatever appetite I'd rustled up. I pondered a few other possible activities, but when I actually considered counting hay bales in the feed barn I knew I was just postponing the inevitable.

I had to face my demons and clean out Howie's apartment.

Chapter Four

The dusk-to-dawn light flickered on as I made my way across the drive. Bad Company's song *Seagull*—an echo of my loss and sorrow flitted through my head, and I tried to shake off the eerie feeling enclosing my heart.

Queenie trotted after me, making playful leaps at the garbage bags draped over my shoulder. She had no idea they would soon be filled with Howie's belongings. I guessed technically his belongings were mine, now.

I stopped at the base of Howie's stairs and took a deep breath, hoping to fortify myself. It didn't work. I procrastinated more by looking in the garage to make sure the washer and dryer were ready for Lucy. They were a bit dusty, but usable. The cupboard above them even stored part of a container of detergent and some dryer sheets. Howie's gift to Lucy.

The garage held a lot of other odds and ends, including the generator Howie and I had pulled out of retirement during a power outage last month, but there was an empty space where my hog usually sat. Hog as in Harley. My beautiful black 1988 Low Rider was now recuperating at the Biker Barn, my friends Lenny and Bart's mechanical nursing home, reclining among other bikes that were in pieces.

Queenie jump-started me by sticking her nose in my crotch, and I gently pushed her away. "Okay, okay, I'll get to work."

Queenie followed me up the stairs and lay down on the landing with a huff, apparently not wanting to go inside. I couldn't blame her. I didn't want to go in, either, but the door was unlocked so I didn't have any more excuses. I braced myself for an emotional rush and eased the door open.

Surprisingly, the wave of grief I had expected passed me by. The apartment, devoid of Howie's presence, felt at first like what it was—an empty space. Sure, there were items of furniture, but nothing felt alive or even remotely as if Howie were lingering there. My headache started to go away.

It came back as soon as I realized I had to move. My first attempt at action was to flip on the main light. At least I'd accomplished something.

I tackled the kitchen first. If any room was in dire need of cleaning, that would be the place. I knew the worst would be gone because Belle Granger, Zach's mom, had come over after Howie's funeral to take care of things. The only items she'd left in the refrigerator were baking soda and empty ice cube trays. I filled the trays with water and stacked them carefully in the freezer.

The cupboards still held lots of Howie's stuff—plates, silverware, and such—and a stash of canned goods and other non-perishables occupied the pantry. More gifts from Howie to Lucy, if she wanted them.

Howie's little table sat bare, a chair at either end. Just right for Lucy and her daughter. I ran a cloth over the table, displacing dust, and allowed myself a small smile, imagining Howie's expression if he'd known a woman and girl would be living in his place. He loved women and kids, but, like me, would have blanched at having to share his space. Granted, I have a lot more space in my farmhouse than he had in this little apartment, but our feelings about cohabitation were the same.

Other than the dust and a few mouse turds I cleared away, the kitchen was ready to be occupied.

The living room didn't need anything, either, other than a light dusting. Howie had a sofa and a television/VCR combo on a stand as his main furniture, with a little desk and folding chair off to the side. On the desk was a blueberry iMac, complete with printer.

I sat in the chair and ran my fingers over the computer keyboard. It was hard to imagine Howie, in dirty overalls, pounding those keys, but I knew he had. It was partly his computer research that had gotten him killed.

Because of that, I considered the fate of Howie's second-most expensive possession, the first being his truck, for only a moment before deciding it would stay right where it was. I certainly didn't need to be looking at it every day. It was hard enough having the apartment looming over my shoulder. Besides, Lucy's daughter could probably use the computer for school, and I had no idea what Lucy did in her spare time. Maybe she was an eBay junkie.

"You okay?"

I twisted around in the chair. Abe stood silhouetted in the doorway, leaning against the jamb, his hands in his pockets.

"I didn't hear you come up," I said.

"Soft as a barn cat's feet. So are you?"

I shrugged. "I guess." I turned back to the desk and rested my face in my hands.

"I take it this means you hired Lucy?"

"Yup. She starts tomorrow. I think she'll fit in fine. Real quiet."

"You mean she'll let you get on with your life without interfering."

I didn't say anything. He knew me too well.

Abe walked across the carpet and I soon felt his hands kneading the steel plates that were my shoulder muscles. I closed my eyes and let the pain radiate from my neck to the top of my head. When I dropped my forehead onto my arms the pain dulled. After several minutes I even relaxed a bit.

"You done up here?" Abe said quietly.

I shook my head and my neck immediately tensed up again. "I have to do the bathroom and the bedroom yet."

"Want me to check them out?"

I sat up. "No, I should do it." I looked up at him. "Thanks."

He ran his hand over my hair and cupped the back of my neck. "How 'bout I come along for the ride?"

We made our way about fifteen feet to the bathroom door, and I switched on the light. Belle had been busy in there, too. Everything was clean under the light layer of dust, and the medicine cabinet held nothing personal. All that remained were Tums, a bottle of ibuprofen, and heavy-duty hand lotion. A small stack of towels and washcloths sat on the toilet, ready for use.

The bedroom was just as bare. The dresser drawers were empty of the most personal clothing, handkerchiefs, or anything else I might have found disturbing, for which I was thankful. The top drawer held a few white—or almost white—T-shirts and a package of socks that hadn't been opened, but the other drawers sported only lining.

The closet was completely bare except for one pair of fairly new overalls that brought my heart to my throat. The carpet had been swept, removing any trace of Howie's boots. A wave of dizziness washed over me, and I put out my hand to rest on the back closet wall.

"Stella?"

I shook my head and we stood quietly for a few moments, the crickets outside the only sound.

"What's that?" Abe finally said, breaking the silence.

I looked where he was pointing and saw a small keyhole hidden in the dark grain of the wood panel next to my hand.

"Don't know." I leaned closer and made out minuscule lines in the paneling, forming a square. "Looks like a hiding place."

"See any keys?"

I searched inside the closet, but didn't find anything.

"Could be in the living room," I said. "I forgot to even look in the desk drawers."

We traipsed back to the computer, where Abe pulled open the top drawer.

"Ta da." He held up a little key on a string. "How much you want to bet this is the magic opener?"

He was right, and a little door swung out from the closet wall as soon as he stuck in the key. It was a safe, about one and a half by one and a half feet.

Abe looked at me, and I shrugged. I'd had no idea it was there, and wondered if Howie had added it during his years in the apartment or if it had been built in originally. Right now, all that was in it was a flat, square box, which Abe carefully lifted out. He carried it over to the bed and we sat on the mattress. I moved a pile of clean, folded sheets to make room.

Inside the box was a stack of photographs. Not exactly what I'd expected in a wall safe, even if it was a flimsy hiding place. Abe tipped the box onto the bed, and out spilled a collage of color photos and black-and-whites, wallet-sized rectangles, and eight by tens that looked like they had at one time been in frames.

My throat tightened as I began to recognize faces in the pictures. My dad. My mom. Howie, of course. Dogs several generations before Queenie, and lots of the Granger clan, including Abe. From what I could see, the photos ranged in time from my birthday party last month all the way back to the year I was two, when Howie first joined our family. When both of my folks were still alive.

I could feel Abe's gaze on the side of my face. "Want some company while you look through these?"

I fluttered my fingers over the photos. Dr. Peterson had stressed the need to share my grief, and who better to do that with than Abe? No matter what the state of our romance, he'd been my best friend for almost twenty years, and that hadn't changed.

I stared at the bedspread, afraid to meet Abe's eyes for fear I might do something embarrassing, like cry. "Do you mind?"

He picked up a photo. "I'd love to."

We sat quietly for a few minutes, shuffling through the pictures, occasionally sharing a particularly special one. Abe finally spoke.

"I know I was a little pushy about your bike today. I'm sorry I can't feel more positive about it."

"Me too. I know you hate it."

"It's not the bike itself. It's just...I worry about you. There was another article in the paper today. Some poor guy—can you believe his nickname was The Skull?—got killed on his way home from work. Truck pulled out right in front of him. He was thrown a hundred feet. Happened right there in Souderton, at the intersection of Old 309 and 113."

My head snapped toward him. "Yesterday?"

"Yeah. In the afternoon."

"Oh my God. I drove by it."

"The accident?"

"The aftermath. The bike must've been hidden behind the truck. I didn't even see it."

He looked at me for a moment before picking up another picture. "That's why I wish you'd stop riding. Because bikers get killed. Not because I want to take something away from you."

I closed my eyes and took a deep breath. Guilt crashed into me. Guilt for worrying Abe. Guilt that I hadn't known a fellow biker had died just feet from where I'd driven.

"So now you know how I feel," Abe said. "I'll try to keep my mouth shut about it from now on."

I nodded, not sure what to say. I was glad he cared about me, but burdened by his anxiety

"So which dog was this?" Abe asked. "Any relation to Queenie?"

I shook myself out of my thoughts and looked at the picture he was holding of my very first dog—not actually an ancestor of Queenie, although Ringo had been a collie, too.

Life had thrust me into a horrible place during the past few weeks, but now I was here, with my best friend, looking at things that meant a great deal to me. I made myself as comfortable as I could on the bed, and let myself drift into Howie's compilation of his, and therefore my, history.

Chapter Five

"You ready for me?"

I pulled my head out from under the open hood of my truck to see Lucy standing in the doorway of the tractor barn. I leaned in the truck's window and turned down Stevie Ray Vaughan, right in the middle of the guitar riff in Jimi Hendrix's "Voodoo Child." Talk about sacrifice.

Queenie trotted over and Lucy put down her hand to be smelled and approved.

"Where's Tess?" I asked.

"Waiting in the car. She's a little nervous."

"She like dogs?"

"Loves 'em."

"Well then, come on, Queenie. Let's go meet our new neighbor."

Tess' eyes could just be seen over the dashboard of the Taurus, and they lit up when Queenie came into view. Lucy tapped on the car window, and Tess rolled it down an inch.

"It's okay, sweetie," Lucy said. "Why don't you come out and pet the dog?"

Tess' eyes slid to me, and I gave her my friendliest smile. I wasn't always at the top of my form with kids, but I'd do my best to overcome that and make this one feel welcome.

Tess finally stepped out of the car and giggled when Queenie snuffled around her. She leaned down to let Queenie lick her face, and giggled some more.

Lucy's eyes crinkled, and even I had to laugh at Queenie's enthusiasm. I needed to remember that accepting Tess wasn't a betrayal of Howie. Dogs can appreciate an infinite number of people, and just because Queenie liked the new folks, that didn't mean she had forgotten the old ones.

"Hello, Tess," I said. "I'm Stella."

She stood up, and Queenie flopped at her feet, panting happily. Tess peered at me from below blond eyelashes. "Hello." Her voice was quiet and sweet. Like a kitten.

"I'm really glad to have you and your mom here," I said. "I hope you love the farm as much as I do."

She nodded once, then bent down to Queenie again.

Lucy rubbed a hand across the top of her daughter's head. "She's a bit shy till you get to know her. She'll come around soon."

"No problem. We have all the time in the world." I paused and swallowed the lump in my throat. "You want to go ahead and move in? The apartment's all ready for you."

"Maybe you could take us up, show us around. But if it's all the same to you, I'd like to start working. With the dog here, Tess won't need much else to do."

I could deal with that.

The morning went quickly. After Queenie and I gave Lucy and Tess the grand tour, including a very brief look at their apartment, it was already eleven o'clock. Lucy seemed antsy to get going, so I set her up on the scraper, moving cow crap from barnyard to manure lagoon. I left her with a funny, pleased grin tickling her face.

After checking on Poppy—still big and uncomfortable with her impending calf, signaling the imminent loss of my bet with Zach—I tromped into my office to see if anything needed my immediate attention. The blinking light on my phone, indicating that I had voice mail, welcomed me. I punched the button to avoid looking at the box of photos I had brought down from Howie's apartment late the night before. The message was from Lenny. I picked up the phone to call him.

"Biker Barn," growled a voice.

"Bart, it's Stella. Got a message from Lenny to call him."

"Yeah, well good luck figuring him out. He's been acting damn strange today."

"Like what?"

"Like he's got a batch of Olympic ants in his pants."

I laughed. "Put him on, will you?"

I heard scraping, like he'd set the phone on the counter, then muffled yelling. A couple of bangs and clicks later, Lenny came on the line.

"Stella, thanks for calling back." His voice was quiet, like he didn't want anyone to eavesdrop.

"No problem. What's up?"

He muttered something unintelligible.

"Sorry, Len, I can't hear you."

He sighed loudly, then spoke up. "You're friends with that detective you met last month?"

"Willard? I don't know about friends, but sure, I know him."

He cleared his throat. "Think you could introduce me? I'd like to talk to him about something."

Taken aback, I said, "What?"

"I just thought...if you're not comfortable with it, you don't have to."

"No, I don't mind. You just surprised me. Sure, I can do that. You want to go today?"

"No, no." His voice rose. "Today's Saturday. I'm sure he's not in. How about Monday?"

"Monday's fine."

"And about tomorrow, should I pick you up?"

"Tomorrow?" I wracked my brain. "What's tomorrow?"

"Our club's annual pig roast."

I rubbed my forehead. "Oh, Lenny, I don't think I—"

"I can see why you forgot, with all that's happened," he said, "but you should go. It'll be good for you."

I slumped against the wall, defeated. Hadn't I just been complaining to Abe that I needed my biker friends in my life? "All right. What time will you come?"

We set a time for the morning, and I hung up. Why would Lenny want to talk with Detective Willard? I supposed he'd tell me when he was ready, but I was burning with curiosity.

I looked around the office, not quite sure how I felt about going out and having fun the next day at the pig roast. Until then, I supposed, I should earn my keep. No paperwork was waiting for me, since Abe had been doing most of it, so I gladly left all of my few administrative tendencies in the office and went out to do real women's work.

An hour and a half later Lucy was almost done scraping the paddock and I had fixed my truck and repaired some damaged boards on the main feed trough. I was famished, and exhausted. I waved to Lucy and she turned off the scraper.

"Come on in and have some lunch," I said.

She looked at her watch with surprise and jumped down from the machine. "I forgot how fast time goes. I would have guessed I'd just eaten breakfast." She gestured at her Taurus. "I can take Tess somewhere and get something to eat."

"Give me a break," I said. "It won't bankrupt me to feed you one time. Unless you need something gourmet."

"Gosh, no. Anything that keeps me going is fine by me."

Why didn't that surprise me?

We found Tess brushing Queenie by the side of the house, and she apologized to the dog for leaving her in the middle of grooming.

I shook my finger at Queenie. "Don't you go getting spoiled now."

Tess giggled. "I'll take care of her. She's nice."

"Yes," I said. "She's a good dog." I patted my good dog on the head while she gazed up at me with an expression of canine ecstasy.

Lucy and I left our boots at the door, checked our clothes for displaced manure, and found our way to my kitchen, Tess following closely. I pulled some shaved turkey out of the fridge, as well as whatever condiments I happened to have. Miraculously, I found a new bag of chips and had a full pitcher of instant iced tea, which I poured into three cups.

"You stick with the Mennonite brand of chips, I see," Lucy said, pointing at the blue Herr's bag.

I popped one in my mouth and talked around it. "I like them the best. And the guy on the back looks friendly."

"Like Grandpa," Tess said, and Lucy smiled briefly.

The Lucy that looked at me across the table radiated confidence and strength, and the satisfaction in her eyes had only increased since that morning. Nothing like pushing cow poop around to give you zest for life. If the amount of mayonnaise she put on her sandwich was any indication, the woman had a metabolism the size of my largest cow's—and cows have four stomachs. She ate half the bag of chips and asked sheepishly if she could have another sandwich.

"You been starving yourself?" I asked.

"Just tired of McDonald's."

"Not me!" Tess said.

Lucy made a face. "It was right down the road in Lancaster and way too convenient."

"Sure," I said. "Chips and processed lunchmeat are much better. Eat another sandwich."

Ten minutes later she was ready to get back to work. If she kept on like this, I would soon be able to take a week's vacation without anyone knowing the difference.

While Lucy finished scraping and Tess galloped around the yard with Queenie, I took some of the newspapers my neighbors had dropped off and ran them through the shredder. We were running low, and I was sure we'd get through our supply when we cleaned out stalls after the evening milking. Newspaper's cheaper than straw, and works almost as well. And if we can do a little recycling in the process, why not?

I was shredding the last batch when Lucy trotted over to say she was finished, and what did I want her to do next?

I wiped sweat off my forehead, suddenly aware how worn out I was. "Why don't you go ahead and move into your apartment. You want to feel comfortable sleeping there tonight."

She put her hands on her hips and stretched her neck. "I guess I could use a break. I'll find Tess and get our stuff up there. We don't have that much to move, but it would be good to get it done."

"You might've seen before, I left a bunch of stuff up there. Books, kitchen stuff. If there's anything you don't want, let me know and I'll take it out. And," I added, the lump back in my throat, "Howie's truck can sit out. I'll pull it into the drive and you can park your car in the garage."

She studied my face. "You sure? I don't mind leaving the car out."

I nodded. "I'm sure. Let's just do it."

I got the key to Howie's truck and parked it in the lane, trying to ignore the grief bouncing around in my chest. I contemplated what all I could do to distract me from someone taking over Howie's space, but couldn't come up with anything that would work.

So I swallowed my pain and offered to help carry things up to the apartment.

Chapter Six

Ten minutes later their car was unpacked and I felt like a third wheel. I walked down the apartment stairs and headed back to my house, where I could have a little time to sort out my emotions, which were being held tightly in check. I also needed to sit down and rest for at least a couple of minutes before my ribs came bursting out through my skin.

I'd just stepped inside when my phone rang. I walked carefully across the kitchen floor, hoping I wasn't tracking too much dirt onto the Linoleum.

"Royalcrest Farm," I said.

"Stella Crown?" The voice was a man's.

"That's me." I leaned down to take off a boot, my ribs protesting the position, and tossed it toward the door. Dirt splattered on the kitchen floor, and I swore under my breath.

"Am I to understand you hired Lucy Lapp to work for you?"

I stood up, my second boot in my hand. "Who is this?"

"A concerned party."

"Concerned? About what?"

"Your well-being and that of those around you."

I looked at my boot, then threw it to join the other one. "What's this about?"

"I suggest you check into your new hire's past before you let her get too involved in your business. Go back about two and a half years."

"Now look here," I said, but I was talking to a dial tone. I depressed the flash button and dialed star sixty-nine, but the number was described as a private one. "Dammit," I said out loud. What was that about?

Two and a half years ago. According to Lucy, and to Martin Spunk, her reference, that was when Lucy's husband took ill. Or had his accident. What exactly was the caller implying?

I thought back on the morning and my interview of Lucy the day before. The only thing that had thrown up a red flag was the discrepancy in what had caused her husband's death. An illness or a fall down some stairs. Other than that, Lucy was fantastic. A bit strait-laced and morose, but a hard worker. I sank into a kitchen chair. If only I had Howie to discuss it with. He'd be the voice of logic. But of course if I had him to talk to, Lucy wouldn't be on my property or my payroll.

I didn't regret hiring Lucy. It obviously would take a while to get to know her, but something about her felt right. And real. I couldn't imagine there was anything to this anonymous caller's warning. And how credible could he be, not even giving me his name?

But I went to the door and put on a clean pair of boots. I needed to talk with Lucy again, calm my doubts.

I knocked on the apartment door, and Tess yanked it open. "Mom! It's Stella!"

I stepped inside, and Tess bounded away toward the computer, where she was already playing a game involving little vegetables that talked. I closed the door behind me and looked at the items Lucy had placed around the room. Centered on the shelf above the computer was *Martyr's Mirror,* one of the thickest books I'd ever seen, which I knew compiled a history of Anabaptists killed for their beliefs. Ma Granger had one just like it on her coffee table. Leaning against the sofa, waiting for its place on the wall, was a hand-painted fraktur with a quote from Menno Simons—a founder of the Mennonite church. "We are people of God's Peace."

Lucy appeared in the doorway of her bedroom, a framed photograph in her hand. "You need me for something?"

Again I was struck with Lucy's air of sincerity, and I felt like a heel for doubting her. The last thing I wanted to do was question her about her husband's death, no matter what the cowardly caller had implied. I changed tacks.

"I was wondering if you want to know anything about the Mennonite churches around here, or if you've already decided where you'd like to go tomorrow."

She indicated the sofa. "Here, have a seat." She moved the fraktur to the side and sat on the opposite end of the couch. "You said you have good friends who go to Sellersville?"

"The Grangers. You've already met Zach and Abe. Their whole clan goes to Sellersville Mennonite, but I'm not sure if it's the kind of congregation you want."

Her eyes lit up, and again I wondered at the amusement. "I think it's exactly what I want."

"You know about it already?"

"Gosh, yes. It's quite the gossip back in Lancaster."

She placed the photo on the sofa beside her. In the photo were Lucy, a much younger Tess, and a man I had to assume was her late husband.

"Your husband?" I asked.

She touched a finger to his face. "Yes, that's Brad. Before he…. About three years ago. Handsome, wasn't he?"

He was.

"Anyway," she said, "the past ten years we've attended the Mennonite church where Brad grew up. My parents are Mennonite, too—my maiden name's Ruth—but Brad really wanted to stay where his roots were, and my family didn't move to Lancaster and attend a church there until I was already a teen-ager." She wrinkled her nose. "I didn't like his church all that much, but it was important to him."

"And his congregation doesn't like Sellersville?"

She laughed harshly. "If you want to put it that nicely. Yoder Mennonite is ultra conservative. Very traditional. The thought of a woman behind the pulpit gives them hives, and gay people? Might as well not even visit. No reason to get involved since you can't become a full-fledged member. The church seems to think once you put your mind to it you could stop being gay if you really wanted to."

I snorted. "There are plenty of those churches around here, too. Sellersville isn't one of them, which is one of the reasons the Grangers like it. As for the women, Ma's about as strong a one as you can get, and while she wouldn't want to preach a sermon herself, she's glad to hear a female up there once in a while. The minister is a man, but one who's open to women in ministry."

"And from what the folks at Yoder say, Sellersville accepts homosexuals?"

"They aren't officially a 'welcoming' congregation, seeing as how you get kicked out of the conference for that, but there are gay people who go there and who are members. It's one of those sad things that kind of gets swept under the rug. At least for now. I know Ma's doing her best on that front to change things."

I thought of Jordan, Granger son number three, who, in his late thirties, was still unmarried. Those of us close to him didn't care, or even think it was our business, but there were those in the community who seemed to think they needed to know why he was still a bachelor. Somehow, no one ever dared to ask Jordan or anyone else who might actually know.

Lucy glanced toward the computer, where Tess was driving a car around a town, picking up characters of the vegetable persuasion. Lucy stood and walked toward the kitchen, gesturing that I should follow. I did.

"And a single mother?" Lucy asked, her voice quiet. "Will there be lots of questions?"

"I doubt it. But if there are, can't you just tell them the truth?"

A shadow flickered across her face. "The truth. If only….I hate having to talk about it all the time."

Didn't I know it. The last thing I felt like doing was what the doc wanted me to do. Talking about Howie was like pounding on a continuously bleeding wound. But it had been a year and a half for Lucy, and I wondered why she'd hesitated when I'd mentioned the truth.

"I don't think you have to worry about nosy-parkers," I said. Other than myself, and I was already feeling creepy about it. "Ma will fend off the worst of them for you."

Again she looked amused. "I'm looking forward to meeting this paragon."

I headed for the door. "I'm going back to work. Come on out when you feel like it. Make yourself at home."

She stepped over and grabbed the door, holding it open for me. "We already have. Thanks."

I made my way carefully down the stairs. I hadn't gotten any answers, but I was even more sure of two things.

I liked Lucy a lot.

And there was something about Brad's death she wasn't telling.

Chapter Seven

We were in the middle of the evening milking when Queenie jumped up from her corner and ran outside, barking. I went to the window as a dark blue Buick pulled into the lane. Zach had gone to see a movie with his friends, and Abe was spending the evening with Ma, so I wasn't expecting anyone. I didn't recognize the car.

"Someone you know?" I asked Lucy.

She straightened up to look and flushed red at the sight of the Buick. She closed her eyes briefly and set her towel on the rim of her bucket. "Excuse me for a minute. Tess, stay where you are."

Tess, who had been sitting with Queenie and writing in a notebook, immediately disobeyed and ran to the door to see what we were looking at. Lucy gently pushed her back into the barn and walked outside.

A good-looking man, about Lucy's age, stepped out of the car and stood gazing around at the farm. He brightened considerably when he saw Lucy approaching him. His brightness dimmed quickly, however, once she got within spitting distance. I was soon convinced Lucy was okay, and while I really wanted to know who the guy was, I got back to work. If Lucy wanted to introduce me, or wanted my help, she would let me know. Besides, Queenie was out there, and I knew nothing would happen without her being in the middle of it.

Tess stood on a hay bale, watching through a window.

"You know that guy?" I asked her.

"Sure. He's from church. He and my mom are friends."

"They do things together?"

She plastered her nose to the glass. "A few times, I think. I didn't go along."

Hmm.

A minute later I heard raised voices, and when I glanced out the window Queenie was standing at attention. The man was leaning toward Lucy, his arms reaching for her. I didn't like his posture, even though Lucy was standing firm, and Queenie didn't seem to, either.

"Stay here, Tess." I set down my grain bucket and walked outside. "Is there a problem here?"

The man stopped talking and dropped his arms to his sides.

"No problem," Lucy said. "Noah was just leaving."

Noah and I took each other's measure, and while I didn't relish the thought of removing him forcibly from the farm, I figured I could do it. I guess he figured that, too, because he stepped back.

"Noah Delp," he said. His hand twitched like he wanted to hold it toward me, but a quick glance at Queenie kept him from following through. "There's no problem. I'm just making sure Lucy's okay here."

"I told him I'm fine," Lucy said. "He doesn't need to check up on me. And he won't again."

I looked at Noah. "I guess you got your answer. Anything else you need?"

"Is that dog going to do something?" He glanced at Queenie, who stood quivering next to Lucy.

"Does she need to?" I asked.

"Goodness, no. I only wanted to be sure Lucy was all right. Honest. And Tess."

"Then the dog will leave you alone." I looked at Lucy. "Lucy? What do you want me to do?"

She pinched her lips together. "Give me a few minutes, please?"

"Sure. We'll be right inside. Come on, Queenie."

Queenie reluctantly followed me into the parlor, where I went back to filling feed bowls. Tess still stood on the hay bale, but she was out of hearing range of the conversation outside. Noah and his Buick soon left, and Lucy returned.

"Mom," Tess said. "How come Noah was here? How come I couldn't say hi?"

"He came to see where we're living." Lucy's voice was tight. "If he ever comes again and talks to you, I want you to tell me right away, okay?"

Tess looked confused. "Why?"

"I just want you to. All right?"

Tess jumped down from the bale and settled in beside Queenie, who was back in her corner spot. "Okay. We'll tell her, right, Queenie?"

Queenie sniffed the girl's face, then looked at Lucy as if to say she needn't worry about Tess. Lucy walked over and patted Queenie's head.

"You okay?" I asked.

Lucy didn't look at me. "I'm fine."

"Noah's not a problem I need to know about?"

Lucy's back stiffened. "No."

I watched her for a moment before turning back to the feed cart. Lucy seemed convinced Noah wouldn't be bothering us anymore. I decided to take her word for it.

But if he did come back, I'd be ready for him.

Chapter Eight

"Hey Ma," I said when she answered the phone. Lucy and Tess were in their apartment, and I'd already brushed my teeth, taken a Motrin, and climbed into bed. "Got a minute?"

"I always have a minute for you, sweetheart. How are you? Are you sleeping? Resting those ribs? Abe told me your doctor wasn't pleased with you today."

Gee, thanks, Abe. "I'm fine, Ma. I hired a farmhand."

"Yes, Abe told me. And how do you feel about that?"

Typical Ma. Straight to the heart of it.

"It feels…good, I guess. Strange, and uncomfortable, if I let myself think about it. Which I don't."

"You like her?"

"I do. And I think you will, too. In fact, that's why I'm calling. She'll probably be coming to Sellersville tomorrow. I thought I'd give you a heads-up."

"What's her name?"

"Lucy Lapp. And she has an eight-year-old daughter, Tess."

"How wonderful. Should I pick them up?"

"Don't think you need to do that, but if you'd save a spot for them on your pew I'd appreciate it."

She was quiet for a moment, then thought aloud. "If I move Jordan and Abe to the row behind me, and Jethro doesn't whine about being a mite squished, I think that would work. The Bishops have been sitting in my row for thirty years, so I don't think they'd appreciate moving, but my boys can squeeze in with some of the others."

"Pew politics," I said.

"Oh, it's a serious business, and I try to abide by it. Don't upset the apple cart if you don't want apple butter, I always say."

"Something else, Ma. Lucy's a single mom. Lost her husband a year and a half ago, and doesn't want to have to explain it to everyone tomorrow."

"I hear you, and I'll take care of it. No one will bother her."

"Thanks, Ma. I knew you'd be up to the challenge."

"Now where is Lucy coming from?"

"Lancaster. Some church called Yoder."

Ma clucked. "Oh my. And she wants to come to Sellersville?"

"So you know it?"

"Yoder has been a thorn in the side of progress for years, as far back as I can think. Why, I remember Pa saying if he wasn't a Mennonite he'd go show those Lancaster Yoder folks a thing or two."

I laughed. Pa Granger had been the perfect complement to Ma—the last person who'd ever pick a fight. If even he had gotten his hackles up about Yoder I guessed they were a problem.

"Well, that's it, then," I said.

But Ma wasn't done. "Is Lucy all settled?"

"Just moved in today."

"So no groceries."

I smiled, knowing where this was headed. "I'm sure she'd be grateful for whatever you bring by."

"You leave that up to me, then," Ma said.

"Oh, I will."

"I guess this call means we won't see you at church tomorrow morning, Stella?"

I tilted my head back, stretching my neck. "Don't count on me, Ma. You know how it makes me feel to have all those people crowding me, telling me how sorry they are about Howie."

"They care about you, honey."

"I know. But I already promised Lenny I'd go to a club picnic with him." Thank goodness.

"In that case, we'll expect to see you at the hymn sing tomorrow night."

What? "I've never been a singer, Ma. You know that."

"All the more reason to come when there's lots of folks to drown you out. I'll see you then. Seven-thirty sharp."

She hung up on me, and I knew I was doomed to sing.

If I got lucky, tomorrow afternoon I'd come down with whooping cough.

Chapter Nine

"I never dreamed I'd be in this position," Lenny said.

He lay on top of me, fortunately taking most of his considerable weight on his elbows and knees. It was a beautiful afternoon, and Lenny's wild hair blocked the sun from my eyes as we reclined in the grass.

"Yup," I said. "You're a lucky man."

He smiled.

"The old man's home!" someone screamed.

Lenny jumped to his feet. I held still to keep from getting trampled by his heavy boots, then eased onto my stomach to watch him leap (well, as much as a full-grown, beer-gutted guy can leap) over our side of the fake double window sill and onto his Harley. He slammed his foot down to kick-start the bike and roared away, leaving an eight-foot skid mark in the lawn. He beat out the other biker by two seconds.

"All right!" I stood and held my fists in the air briefly, until my side shrieked a protest. Angry ribs aside, it felt good to be the "Old Man's Home" winners for the first time ever. Dr. Peterson would be proud I let myself be coerced into joining my Harley Owner's Group chapter for the annual pig roast. At that moment, I was glad I came.

Lenny came rumbling back and parked his bike on the opposite side of the double-sills.

"We are the champions," he sang, to applause.

We accepted our prizes (an outdated Harley-Davidson Christmas mug for each of us) and sat down in the grass to be spectators for the last field game.

"Hey, Stella!" Bart loped toward us. "Why don't you guys do the Weenie Bite? You'd win hands down."

I made a face. "You want to see me throw up?"

The weenie in question is a cold hot dog speared on a plastic fork, dangling from a string. The object is for the driver of the bike to go as slow as he can underneath said wiener so the passenger can get the biggest bite possible out of the dog. They'll spruce it up with mustard or ketchup—your choice.

"We can't take too many prizes," Lenny said. "It would look bad, me being a club sponsor and all."

Bart flopped down next to me, and I felt lopsided between him and Lenny. Bart is shorter than me, about five-seven, and about as big around as an exhaust pipe. His long brown hair is tied back in a single braid, and his snake tattoo travels from one arm to the next, around his shoulder blades, without a break.

Lenny, on the other hand, is big and burly. The red hair on his head is matched only by his beard, and lends him the look of an Irish bear. He's got tattoos, too, but they're more the individual kind—a cross, a heart bearing the name Vonda, a nasty skull with a clerical collar.

Tattoos were abundant that day at the picnic, mine included, and I looked around at the other club members with appreciation. Our group hosts the shindig every year to raise money, half of which goes to charity. This year it would benefit a local family who'd lost everything in a house fire two weeks earlier.

"Any luck with your ad for a farmhand?" Bart asked.

"Actually, I hired somebody yesterday. She's off to church with the Grangers this morning, so she should be getting a grand welcoming."

Lenny grinned. "Another woman on the farm, huh? And a Mennonite?"

"You know those Menno women," Bart said. "They come from good German stock. She'll pull her weight."

Lenny guffawed. "Or Stella will make her pull it."

"It'll be interesting to hear what the Grangers think of her." I tipped my face up and enjoyed the heat of the sun. "So Bart, what would you think if someone told you her husband died of an illness, but you find out from someone else that he wasn't really sick. He was paralyzed."

Bart looked at me, confused. "Well, I guess I'd figure some people have different descriptions for the same thing. And then I'd tell myself to mind my own business."

I thought about Lucy's evasiveness whenever Brad's death was mentioned. "You wouldn't think she's trying to hide something?"

Bart pulled a cigarette from his pocket and stuck it in his mouth, unlit. "Like what?"

"Well, the guy was paralyzed because he fell down some stairs."

"And?"

"What if it wasn't an accident?"

His cigarette drooped as he stared at me. "Oh, come on. What is this? She's evasive, so that means she pushed him?"

"I had a phone call, too, telling me to watch out for her."

"And who was this thoughtful person who called?"

I grunted. "He didn't say."

"So," Bart said, "your reasons for suspecting your employee of murder are a few ambiguous words about illness and an anonymous phone call?"

I shrugged. "You're right. It's ridiculous."

"Who's ridiculous?" Lenny said.

"Haven't you been listening?" Bart took his cigarette out of his mouth and held it between two fingers. "Stella thinks her new lady farmhand is a murderer."

"Wouldn't that be murderess?" Lenny asked.

"It's neither," I said, "because she didn't do it. So just stop."

"You're the one who brought it up," Bart said. "Don't snap at me."

Lenny leaned over and whapped Bart on the back. "Stella didn't come here to get talked smart to by you. I had a hard enough time convincing her to come at all."

"Then maybe she should've stayed home," Bart said cheerfully.

"What?" Lenny said. "With the murderer?"

Bart widened his eyes. "Murder*ess*."

"Okay," I said. "Why else would she evade my questions? Assuming she didn't really shove her husband down the stairs."

They thought, but had no suggestions.

"Okay," I said. "Seeing as how you guys are no help, I can think of a few things right off the bat. She's tired of talking about it. Someone else—my caller, perhaps—already suspects her of pushing him and she's sick of it. She doesn't like talking to relative strangers, which I am. I don't know, why else wouldn't she talk about it?"

They looked at each other, then at me.

"Come on, Stella," Lenny said gently. "You of all people should understand that."

A wave of comprehension rushed over me, and I bent my head toward my knees. Bart placed his hand lightly on my back, while Lenny leaned close enough I could feel the heat from his arm against mine.

They were right. My raw grief for Howie hadn't gone away in five weeks, and I wasn't anywhere near wanting to talk about it. I seriously doubted the pain would go away in a year and a half. Perhaps it never would.

"What the—?" Lenny's voice sounded like a growl, and Bart was suddenly on his feet. I followed the direction of their eyes and went stiff.

Across the way at a picnic table, a greasy-looking biker stuck out like a sore thumb. Making him even more conspicuous was the switchblade he had pulled from his vest and was holding at another guy's throat. Cowering behind the second man were a woman and a boy, who looked like he was about twelve.

I jumped up beside Bart and focused on the knife-wielder. Bart and Lenny's energy vibrated on either side of me as we marched toward the picnic table. The guy with the knife glanced up and froze when he saw us.

"Don't come any closer!" he yelled. "I'll cut him! I'll kill the bastard!"

We stopped.

"Come on, now." I held my hands out so he could see I was unarmed. "I'm not going to hurt you."

His wild eyes darted from side to side, but eventually settled on me. Lenny and Bart drifted away, Bart toward the woman and boy, Lenny toward the greasy guy's back.

"What's the problem here?" I took another step forward.

"Don't do it!" he screeched. "I'll cut him!" He jabbed the knife toward the man's neck and the man flinched backward, avoiding the point.

"Okay, okay," I said. "I won't come any closer. Just tell me what's going on. What's your beef with this guy?"

He grunted, a half-laugh.

"He steal your woman?" I tried to sound sympathetic. "She leave you to be with this creep?"

"Slut." Spittle flew from his mouth. "Didn't know good when she had it. Taking my boy and replacing me with this loser."

Out of the corner of my eye I could see Lenny getting closer to him. Bart was only a few feet from the woman and boy. Either the entire crowd had frozen in place and was watching in silence, or the pounding of my heart was drowning out everything except the guy's voice.

"He your son?" I asked. "Good-looking kid."

His chin lifted a fraction. "My son in name and blood. It's my right to have him with me. Not with the bitch's new fuck."

"That's right," I said. "So what's your name? The name the boy has?"

"Trey. Trey's me and Trey's the boy."

"Good name," I said. "So I'm sorry, Trey."

"Sorry?"

Lenny tackled him from behind, grabbing his knife hand as they went down. Trey only got to thrash for two seconds before my boot found his wrist and pinned it to the ground. He yelped, and his fingers automatically opened. I grabbed the knife and handed it off to Bart, who had positioned himself between Big Trey and the man he'd had at knife-point.

Trey didn't have a chance with Lenny's weight holding him down, and I leaned over to put my face a few inches from his. His breath was putrid, a mixture of smoke and whiskey, and I let the disgust show on my face.

"Yeah, I'm sorry, Trey," I said. "Sorry you're such a disgusting, filthy bag of shit. You're the reason regular American Joes are afraid of bikers. This here is a family picnic. Didn't you notice we've got children and babies? And the drink of choice is birch beer? There's no room here for slime like you."

He inhaled sharply and spat in my face. The crowd took a collective breath. After a tense moment someone hung a handkerchief where I could see it and I took it and wiped my face.

"Oh, Trey," I said. "I really wish you hadn't done that."

"Police are on their way!"

I looked up at Harry, our HOG club's director, and nodded. "You okay there, Lenny?" I asked.

Lenny's eyes narrowed. "I could stay here all day."

I patted Trey's cheek, none too gently. "Your friends, the boys in blue, will be here soon. Don't you worry."

I got up and walked over to where Bart now sat with the woman, man, and young Trey. "You folks okay?"

The man stuck out his hand. "Dave Crockett. Thanks a lot. You saved my ass."

"Davey Crockett?"

He sighed. "Yes, it really is."

I laughed. "Sorry."

"Me, too. This here's Norma. Guess you figured out this is Little Trey."

I shook hands with both. Norma's face was streaked with tears and mascara, and Little Trey looked like he was both thrilled and scared. He gazed up at Bart with something approaching adoration.

"He bother you a lot?" I asked Norma, jerking my thumb toward Big Trey.

She shrugged and looked away. Little Trey opened his mouth as if to say something, then shut it.

Crockett put his hand on Norma's leg and patted her thigh. "She sees him more than she'd like. Let's leave it at that. Sorry it had to mess up the time here today."

I gestured around. "Doesn't look like anybody cares too much."

The crowd had already returned to socializing and eating, and the Weenie Bite was back under way with some unfortunate woman getting ketchup all over her face.

"Huh," Crockett said. "I guess there's nothing more to be excited about with *him* sitting on Big Trey."

We looked over where Lenny sat, ankles crossed, hands planted on Trey's shoulder blades and butt. He wasn't sparing any weight, either, like he did when we were playing Old Man's Home. At least, Trey's face was red, and his eyes were more bugged out than they'd been five minutes earlier.

I heard sirens in the distance. A whole slew of them.

"Anything else I can do to help?" I asked Norma.

She looked intently at something on the ground, and Little Trey bit his lip and stared at me silently. Bart raised his eyebrows and gave a subtle hitch to his left shoulder.

"I think everything will be okay," Dave said. "Now that our problem is going to jail."

He tilted his head toward the parking lot, where a couple of police cars had pulled up. Two anxious looking cops got out of one, and one out of the other. Harry, ever the vigilant director, hustled out to meet them. As we watched, the parking lot filled with cruisers from every precinct within scanning distance. Hilltown, New Britain, Dublin, Souderton, Telford, Montgomeryville. Looked like they'd even called in Staties, as well as a K-9 unit. Probably scared of us mean bikers. Ha. We'd see what they thought once we hit them with our buffet.

A quintet of officers carefully made its way toward Lenny, scoping out the situation. Harry followed, insisting things were under control, but they only gave him half of their attention. The rest of their focus was on Lenny and what they could see of Big Trey.

Two of the officers looked like seasoned cops, allowing the humor of the situation to crease their faces with smiles. Two seemed a little tense, and the last, probably a youngster just out of the academy, acted like he was approaching the devil himself.

Once they were situated around Lenny he pushed his way to his feet, grunting, and Big Trey lay on the ground like a deflated tire. He didn't even try to struggle. I don't think he had the lungs for it. In less than thirty seconds two of the cops had him cuffed and headed toward a squad car. The others looked like they were going to hang around to get the scoop. Uniforms from other cars were fanning out to take statements from witnesses, too. I supposed my turn would come soon.

I made a thorough inspection of Big Trey's jacket while he was being led away. No gang insignias I could see, and no recognizable gang colors. I let out a sigh of relief. The last thing I needed was to have the Pagans or Warlocks on my ass because I helped to jail one of their own.

I turned back to Crockett. "So much for that."

He put out his hand for another shake. "Thanks again." He shook Bart's hand, too. "Either of you ever need anything, Davey Crockett's your man." He handed each of us a business card.

"David S. Crockett, Esquire," I said. "You're a lawyer?"

"Weekend warrior." He grinned. The Harley world is full of weekenders—folks who bring out their bikes and leather on the weekend, and look like normal folks the rest of the time.

"Gotta have 'em," I said.

"Lawyers?"

"Wanna-be's."

He laughed and saluted, and Bart and I made our way over to Lenny.

"Had enough fun for the day?" I asked him.

He stuck his hands in his pockets and turned away, almost into the face of an officer with a pad and pen. I raised my eyebrows at Bart, surprised at Lenny's snub.

Bart shook his head, then grinned. "Too bad Abe wasn't here to see this. Cause you're sure sexy when you're telling some poor slob where to go. Especially when you have spit on your face."

I couldn't help it. I slugged him.

Chapter Ten

Lenny and I roared onto the farmstead after being questioned by the police for what seemed like hours, and he stopped in the middle of the drive. Lucy poked her head out of the barn, where she was probably getting ready for milking. She watched us, her face betraying her curiosity.

"Thanks for the ride, man," I yelled to Lenny.

He peered at me from under a furrowed brow and jerked his chin in acknowledgment. His gaze traveled to Lucy. He nodded, she nodded, and he performed a tight U-turn and headed out the lane.

I squinted at Lenny's departing back. He didn't usually allow things to get him so rattled. Today, for some reason, had been an exception. He'd been especially fun at the beginning of the day, and happy about winning The Old Man's Home, but the fight had stripped all that away. I wondered again why he wanted to meet Detective Willard. I would've introduced him at the HOG club when all the cops showed up, except Willard was absent. He mustn't have been working the weekend.

Lucy disappeared into the barn, and when I found her she was distributing grain into the troughs. The cows stood in their stalls, munching contentedly on hay.

"I thought Sunday was going to be your day off," I said.

She glanced up. "I figured I'd at least get things started. Besides, I only began work yesterday. Seemed a little odd to have a day off already." She scooped another pile of grain and deposited it in a feeder.

"So how was church this morning?" I asked.

"Good."

"And the Grangers?"

She gave a little smile. "You're right. They're the best. Although I can't say I have them all straight."

"Kind of hard, when there are eight brothers to remember. Although I can't imagine you'll forget Jermaine."

She gave a quick laugh. "I'll say. It's not every day you meet someone who looks like the Refrigerator from the Chicago Bears. Especially in a family of white folks." Another scoop of feed clattered into a holder. "They had Tess and me over for a potluck lunch, which was really nice, seeing as how I didn't have any food to contribute. We met at Ma's and ate outside at the picnic tables. And she sent me back here with a couple bags of groceries and some leftovers."

"I knew she'd come through," I said.

Lucy's eyes angled toward me. "She asked me to remind you about the hymn sing tonight, and said you're not to make any excuses."

I groaned and patted Minnie Mouse, the cow closest to me. "Did Tess have a good time?"

"Couldn't help it with all those kids around."

"And did you meet Zach's sister Mallory? You ever need a baby-sitter, she's your gal."

"Yeah, she told me. Even gave me a little business card she made up."

I turned. "I'll go change and be back out to help after I check on Poppy and see if she's any closer to winning my bet for me." At the door I stopped. "Anybody ask too many questions about your husband? Make you feel uncomfortable?"

She didn't look up. "A few tried. Ma held them at bay."

I wondered if I'd ever have any luck getting answers, myself.

"Where's Tess?" I asked.

"In the apartment. Organizing and re-organizing all of her things for school tomorrow. The bus will pick her up at seven-thirty."

"She excited?"

Lucy nodded. "But nervous, too. She's only ever attended a small Mennonite school, so this big public one will be a change for her. But a good one, I hope."

"There are a couple of Mennonite schools here, you know. Penn View and Quakertown Christian."

Her eyes became veiled. "I know. But I can't afford it right now. And I wasn't all that thrilled with the school in Lancaster. It was the school my husband attended, but was way more conservative than I like. Some of the teachers…. Well, let's just say they asked Tess too many questions."

About Brad and his accident, I assumed.

"Lancaster Mennonite?" I asked.

She shook her head. "They don't have elementary, and they're not so conservative. This was a small feeder school." A scoop of grain almost missed its target, and Lucy stopped, her shoulders sagging. "We'll see how the public school pans out."

I walked across the grass toward my house. Seemed to me we were waiting to see how a lot of things panned out. Including my own questions about Lucy's past.

Chapter Eleven

The church parking lot was almost full when we pulled in at seven twenty-eight. I eventually found a spot in the row farthest from the door and Lucy, Tess, and I scooted into Ma's pew, where she was taking out her blue hymnal. Abe sat on the other side of Ma and smiled at me, his eyes warm and inviting.

"Number One," Ma whispered.

No time for dilly-dallying, or for catching up with Abe.

The song leader blew a note on her pitch pipe and the congregation flew right into "What Is this Place?," accompanied only by the other voices around them. I was glad to have Jethro's rumbling bass surrounding me from behind, which would blot out any attempts I made at participating. Lucy sang soprano on my left, while to my right Ma added a competent alto. Abe's tenor floated toward me from time to time, and even Tess joined in on the melody. This left me free, thankfully, to simply listen and hum along when the notes were in the right range.

I tried to take comfort in the familiarity of the sound and songs as the music took over the air. The four-part harmony of the Mennonites is something that should never be taken for granted. Ma has told me that unfortunately some churches are forgetting this rich part of their heritage, and can't sing a good unaccompanied hymn to save their souls. If you want to put it that way.

The little Sellersville church was plainly painted, the walls a light gray with shiny white trim. No ornaments graced the walls, and no flags. The only decoration was a banner in front with four differently colored hands grasping each other. "Members in Ministry," the banner said, proclaiming the congregation's belief that every person was meant as God's "vessel of healing and hope."

A few elderly women still bore the coverings Mennonites had worn for so long, a white mesh bonnet pinned lightly to the backs of their heads. Not practical for anything, the coverings are merely a symbol of submission to God. Ma had chosen long ago to stop wearing hers, but it was mostly because she was ready for a more stylish hair-do. She thought her hair would work better in a short cut, and once she got it done she decided the covering looked…well, a bit silly.

I think the whole idea of coverings is ridiculous, but then, no one cares what I think.

We slammed through "Come, We That Love the Lord," the chorus making me tired just to hear it—"We're marching to Zion, beautiful, beautiful Zion. We're marching upward to Zion, the beautiful city of God."—and "Joyful, Joyful, We Adore Thee," before the song leader finally gestured that we could sit. I was relieved, because holding the heavy hymnal was making my ribs ache.

"You okay?" Ma asked.

I nodded. I would be.

A small ensemble of instruments—guitar, violin, flute—joined the song leader up front, and we sang a few more hymns before being asked to stand again. The musicians sat, and, several a cappella hymns later, we were finally told to turn to number 118, to what's thought of as the Mennonite Anthem. Known all over the country as "606," the hymn's number in the former Mennonite Hymnal, it's a rousing tune able to shake the proverbial rafters. I was thankful not only that it was the last song of the night, but that it was okay to put away the now-leaden hymnal, since everyone knows the song by heart:

Praise God From Whom All Blessings Flow,
praise him all creatures, here below,

praise him all creatures here below.
Praise him above, praise him above,
Praise him above, ye heavenly hosts...

The song rose in volume and speed until we reached the "Hallelujah, amens," and I dropped out because the notes were clearly out of my range and league. When the hymn was finally over I sank down to the bench and took a deep breath.

"You all right?" Abe sat beside me, scooting behind Ma while she talked to friends in the row ahead.

"I will be. Now that I can sit."

He smiled. "Ma coerced you into coming?"

"She took care of Lucy all day. It was the least I could do."

Abe gestured to the aisle. "Shall we?"

We threaded our way through the people-crammed aisle to the foyer, where several tables were set up displaying plates of desserts. The MYF—the Mennonite Youth Fellowship, consisting of the church's high schoolers—was offering delicious snacks for a small donation, which would land in the coffer for their trip to the nationwide Mennonite youth convention the next summer.

"Stella! Uncle Abe!" Zach gestured wildly from his table, and we wandered his way.

"So what are these?" I asked him. "They look incredible, but sinful."

"Squares of shortbread with chocolate, caramel, and nuts melted over the top." Zach smiled and puffed up his chest. "Homemade turtle cookies. Mom didn't even help."

"You're amazing. And the calorie content of these miracles?"

His face fell. "You care about that?"

"Gosh, no. Just wanted to see your face when I asked."

He grinned. "So how many do you want?"

I dug in my pocket and pulled out a rumpled dollar bill. "This is all I've got. What will it get me?"

Abe put his hand over my money and gently pushed it down. "We'll take two plates."

Zach lit up. "You mean it?"

Abe handed him a ten.

"Geez," I said to Abe. "Your pockets are much more productive than mine."

Zach shoved the ten into his donation can. "Pick the ones you want."

Abe scrunched his forehead. "Stella?"

"I don't care. They all look good to me."

"Making lots of money, I see." Willie Alderfer stepped up to the table, laying his arm across Zach's shoulders. He'd been an MYF sponsor for at least five years and was as proud of the teenagers as any parent.

Zach peered up at him slyly. "Bet I've made more than anyone else so far."

Willie laughed. "Good going. I'd better grab one of those before Abe takes them all." He dropped some coins into Zach's tin and picked a cookie, popping it directly into his mouth. "Oh, wow."

"Told you," Zach said.

Willie slapped his back and moved on to the next table while Zach called to other church members to come check out his merchandise.

Abe picked a couple plates of the turtles while I searched the room. I finally spotted Lucy and Tess in the corner surrounded by Grangers, so I figured she was as safe from prying questions as she was going to get.

"So what do you think of her so far?" Abe asked, following the direction of my eyes.

I hesitated. "She's a great worker."

"But?"

I sighed with exasperation. "It's so stupid. And something I'd usually ignore. But it's my farm...."

"What?" Abe's voice sounded alarmed.

"Nothing that will endanger me," I said. "I promise. It's just...her husband died a year and a half ago, and there's some question, apparently, as to whether or not she killed him."

"*What?*" Abe sounded even more frantic.

"Nothing concrete. Just some vagueness on her part, and an anonymous call I received yesterday."

"What happened?"

I explained what I knew about Brad Lapp's accident and death, which wasn't much.

"Sounds like you need to do some checking," Abe said.

"But I hate—"

"Of course you do. But, as you said, it's your farm."

"Anywhere you think I should start?"

He pointed at someone across the room. "Right there."

I followed his finger to a couple sitting at a table with Abe's brother Jacob and his wife, Nina. "Who're they?"

"Jacob's roommate from the year he went to college, and his wife. Dan and Zelda Souder."

I looked at them. "And?"

"They're from Lancaster. They came up for the weekend, going back tonight."

"I get it. Want to introduce me?"

"Sure."

The two couples made room for us at their table, and Abe did the honors while unwrapping a plate of his cookies and passing it around.

"So how are you doing, Stella?" Nina asked. "Abe says your doctor wants you to take it a little easier."

I kicked Abe under the table, and he winced.

"I'm fine. Especially now I've hired a new farmhand."

"Which is the main reason we came over here," Abe said. "I thought Stella could ask the Souders what they know."

"About what?" Zelda looked surprised.

I explained who Lucy was and the questions that had come up, and our entire group turned to look at her, which of course she noticed. I smiled and waved, hoping she would assume I was simply talking about my new farmhand. I felt like a jerk.

"Well, sure, I remember that story," Zelda said. "It was the talk of the town—and of the Lancaster Conference. Remember Yoder

Mennonite about having a collective coronary, Dan? Everyone was convinced Lucy had done it."

"But why?" I still was at a loss.

"No reason," Dan said hotly. "People just wanted something to talk about. You know, Christmas spirit and all."

Zelda grimaced. "He's right. No one ever gave any good reasons. The most popular story was that she wanted his life insurance money to start her own dairy operation."

"Bunch of crap," Dan said. "Who in their right mind would want to run a dairy farm alone?"

Abe looked at me.

"But what happened?" I asked. "She obviously was never convicted of it."

"Or even arrested," Zelda said. "The police couldn't find anything strong enough to hold her, even though she and her husband had taken out new life insurance policies within the past year. Anyway, a fat lot of good that money would've done her, seeing how he survived the fall and she had to quit her farm job to stay home with him."

Dan grunted. "Bunch of gossipy biddies."

"Any other people involved?" I asked, remembering Noah, the guy who had come by the farm. "Men? Women?"

Zelda and her husband looked at each other. "I can't remember anything about that," Zelda said. "You, Dan?"

He shook his head.

"Not much help, are we?" Zelda asked. "Sorry."

"Don't be. I feel like an ass even asking about it."

"Check the Lancaster newspapers," Dan said. "The *Intelligencer Journal* and the *Lancaster New Era*. It was the biggest story they'd had in years, and they ate it up. If I remember right, it all came back again when he died. When was that?"

"Year and a half ago," I said.

Zelda nodded. "That's right. It was at Christmas-time again, wasn't it? A year after the accident? I remember feeling so sorry for that little girl."

Our group took another look over toward Tess, which luckily escaped Lucy's eye. I was feeling guilty enough without her assuming the worst.

A wave of exhaustion swept through me, and I glanced at the clock. "Well, it's past my bedtime. Thanks for the info. I'm sure it will turn out to be nothing. At least nothing for me to worry about."

"I hope you're right," Zelda said. "For your sake and for hers."

Abe and I stood, saying our good-byes.

"I'll walk you to your truck," Abe said as we moved away.

"I've got to snag Lucy and Tess. They came with me."

He looked uneasy. "Stella, are you sure—"

"—she won't murder me in my sleep? Quite sure. Besides the fact I can't believe the rumors, Queenie wouldn't let her get near the house without causing a ruckus. Queenie may like her, but she's pretty territorial, especially at night."

Abe still hesitated, holding my arm.

"Abe, let go. I'll survive the night, I promise. Now come and be your usual charming self to Lucy and Tess, or she'll know exactly what we've been discussing."

I managed to tear Lucy away from the friendly group surrounding her, and we made it out to the truck with only a few people stopping me to ask how I was doing. Luckily for Abe's health no one else mentioned my doctor's concerns. And I managed to grab the second plate of turtle cookies while Abe was busy studying Lucy.

On the way home, conversation was stilted. Lucy and I didn't have a whole lot to talk about yet, and Tess about fell asleep. By the time I parked the truck and we went our separate ways, I was feeling claustrophobic and crabby. Thank goodness Tess had to get to bed.

I liked Lucy and Tess, but God...

I missed Howie more than ever.

Chapter Twelve

Once Lucy and Tess had retired to their apartment, I headed to the office, even though I desperately needed to hit the sack. A welcome refuge from the heat, the office was also where I could do a little confidential detective work. If Lucy was going to hedge whenever I asked questions about her husband, I'd have to do some researching on my own, or I'd never get any sleep at all.

I logged onto the Internet, eating another cookie, and went to AskJeeves.com, my favorite site for finding out whatever I wanted to know. I typed in, "newspaper articles about Brad Lapp," and got quite an array of hits. I then spent at least fifteen minutes weeding out the articles about Brad Lapp the painter in New York City, Brad Lapp the actor in Philadelphia, and Brad Lapp the rodeo cowboy in Wyoming. I pared it down to articles in the *Intelligencer Journal* and the *Lancaster New Era*—the papers the Souders had suggested and which I should've checked to begin with—about the Brad Lapp I wanted.

Factually, there wasn't as much as I'd hoped for. As far as the actual event and physical trauma, it seemed Brad tripped at the top of the basement stairs and fell down the entire flight, breaking his neck and irreparably damaging his spinal cord. The newspapers didn't go much farther than that about the injuries, except to say Lucy quit her job a week later to stay home and take care of her now quadriplegic husband.

The motive angle was much juicier. Everything was suggested, from Lucy being angry over a lover to Brad indulging in drugs and mistaking the basement door for the bathroom. Insurance policies, past relationships, and disagreements over religious issues were all discussed, as well. But as the Souders had said, the most popular theory—strangely enough, considering the usual societal fascination with extramarital sex—was Lucy's desire to run her own dairy operation. There didn't seem to be much of anything supporting all the gossip, but that didn't keep the newspapers from speculating.

A few weeks into the investigation the articles petered out, and the most closure I could get was that the police were looking for whatever help people could offer. Didn't sound too promising.

A year later a new rash of articles appeared on the occasion of Brad's death. The whole sordid affair was brought up again, and several anonymous sources complained that Lucy had not been questioned more closely. It seemed someone at the paper wasn't afraid to damage Lucy's reputation. Perhaps it was already damaged beyond repair.

A note at the end of Brad's obituary mentioned that those who wished to contribute to a fund for the family could route it through Yoder Mennonite Church. I wondered if that was Lucy's idea, seeing how she didn't really like the church. It could've been a simple way for her to let Brad's family receive comfort from their congregation.

I sat back, halfway frustrated and halfway relieved. I had been hoping for better information about the extent of Brad's injuries and the event itself, and I sincerely wished there had been more of a sense that the investigation found the accident exactly that—an accident.

I also felt like a goddamned snoop.

I rubbed the back of my neck as I dealt with a very unwelcome reality. To satisfy myself I'd hired someone with true grief and clean hands, I'd have to go back to the source I should've stuck with from the beginning.

Lucy herself.

Chapter Thirteen

I was awakened by Queenie's frantic barking.

I slid out of bed and peeked through my blinds. A dark shape sat in the drive, close to the apartment. A car.

A glance at the clock told me it was almost two a.m. Not a time for visitors. Any visitors who were expected, anyhow, or that Lucy would want me to see.

I pulled on some shorts and went down the stairs as quickly as I could, seeing how my Motrin had worn off. By the time I got to the front door Queenie's barking had stopped, but I couldn't see her. I reached out and flipped the switch in the front hall that floods the yard with light.

One figure—face hidden by a ski mask—held Queenie at bay, a blanket over her head, while another stood poised at the front of the garage. Both turned to gape at me, shocked by the light. The one at the garage, face obscured by a Donald Trump mask, ran toward the car, while the one holding Queenie let go of the blanket. Queenie untangled herself and lunged at the fleeing figure. She sank her teeth into Ski Mask's calf, and a sharp cry of pain split the air as the person stumbled.

I ran into the yard, but when I got within twenty feet of Queenie, her victim kicked her in the face, dislodging her bite, and scrambled to the car. Spitting dust, the Grand Am, already pointed toward the road, raced away. There was no time to get a license number.

"Queenie, girl, you okay?" She danced around while I gripped her collar, her throat resonating with deep growls. A quick check of her face showed no injuries, and I breathed a sigh of relief.

The door at the top of the apartment steps flew open, and Lucy stood on the landing in an oversized T-shirt. "What's going on?" The harsh floodlight did her no favors, her face looking pale and haggard.

I glanced toward the garage and wished I'd been half a minute quicker to interrupt our visitors. Sprayed across the doors in a bloody red were the words "WHORE," "SLUT," and an incomplete "MURD—". I waved a hand toward the vandalism, and Lucy trotted down the stairs to see.

She stopped short at the sight of the graffiti, her hand flying to her mouth.

"Any ideas who would do this?" I asked. I had to assume the slurs were meant for her.

She remained still, staring at the garage. I turned toward the house. "I'm calling this in."

She spun around. "Do you have to?"

The desperation in her voice was clear, but I'd had enough. "I'm not letting this happen to my property without reporting it."

She looked at me for a few seconds before turning back to the garage. "Do you need me?"

"Don't know. I'll see what the cops say."

Slowly, she climbed the stairs to her apartment. At the top she glanced back over her shoulder. "I'll be waiting in here."

Within ten minutes a patrol car pulled into the lane. I recognized the officer from the month before when my barn had burned down, but couldn't place her name.

"Officer Stern," she said, holding out her hand.

I shook it, holding Queenie's collar with my left hand so she wouldn't go after the cop out of frustration. "Sorry to drag you over here again."

"No worries. Let me see what you've got."

I took her to the garage, Queenie at my heels, and she sized it up. "Nasty words. Any idea who did this, and why they would say this about you?"

"Not about me. About my new farmhand. At least, she just came yesterday, and I've never had trouble like this before." Besides, if I'd been sleeping with anyone, let alone multiple people, I sure didn't know about it.

"How about the vandals? Did you get a look at them?"

"They wore masks, so I couldn't see their faces. But they weren't huge. I mean, not fat, not too tall. Five-nine or -ten at the most. And the way they moved they weren't old. The one managed to get away from Queenie, and her teeth were well sunk into him."

"Him?"

I shrugged. "Wasn't much to the chest, as far as I could see, on either one, but it all happened pretty fast."

Stern scribbled on her clipboard. "What did your employee say?"

"Nothing, yet."

"Can I talk to her?"

"Sure. She lives up there."

Officer Stern trotted up the stairs for a short conversation with Lucy. I stayed away, figuring Lucy might say more with me out of the picture. Stern soon came down.

"I'll take a couple of photos and have you sign a complaint. If Detective Willard wants to take it further, he'll contact you tomorrow."

"Fine. They also left that." I pointed toward the brown wool blanket that had covered Queenie's head. "Don't know that it can help you, but I sure don't want it."

She grabbed a garbage bag from her trunk and carefully placed the blanket inside it. Next she got her Polaroid and snapped pictures of each offensive word.

"I guess that's it for now," she said. "Let us know if it happens again."

"I will. Thanks for coming out."

"As I said, I'm glad to do it. Sorry it happened to you."

"Can we paint over it?" I asked.

She considered it briefly. "It's not like we'll lift any finger-prints. And I've got photos. Should be fine."

Her taillights disappeared down the lane. Lucy's door remained closed, and I thought it best if I didn't go up. If she wanted to talk, she'd be down there with me, not shut in her apartment. And I was angry enough—at the vandals and at her for bringing this to my farm—that I knew I'd say something I'd regret.

"You're a brave girl," I told Queenie, rubbing her back. "You done good." She panted and sniffed my face, her eyes still sparkling with anxiety. I left her on the front step, her ears perked, eyes dart-ing toward every tiny movement. She wouldn't sleep tonight.

I snapped off the floodlights, immersing the yard in dark-ness. Then I went to bed, where I soon realized I wouldn't be sleeping any more, either.

Chapter Fourteen

I sat in my kitchen the next day, my feet up on a chair, trying to cool off. Lucy and I had put in a full morning's work—the garage was now completely white again, thanks to her heartfelt efforts—and I was hot, sweaty, and exhausted. Crabby, too, seeing as how I had a new employee who just might be a murderer and have some major issues with men.

I finished my scrambled egg sandwich and checked the clock. Lucy had left for the hardware store, and I decided I could use a break. Lenny had never gotten around to setting a time to meet Willard, so I thought I'd drive over to the Barn and see if he was ready to go. I hadn't heard from Willard yet that morning about the graffiti, so taking Lenny to the police station would give me a chance to tell the detective firsthand about our night visitors. I drained my glass of milk, dumped the dishes in the sink, and went out to my truck.

Queenie hung her head out the window on the way to the Biker Barn, her drool splattering onto the extended cab's window. She loved having an outing now and again, and the guys always liked seeing her.

Well, they liked seeing her when they were in good moods. This time, the door's bell jingled and they yelled at me in stereo to keep the damn dog out of the store. After recovering from shock, I called to her and told her to stay outside. She acted a bit offended, so I assured her it was them, not her.

"Geez, guys," I said, returning to the showroom. "What's up with the attitude? You act like Queenie's got mad cow disease."

Lenny sat on the stool in front of the counter, his head in his hands. Bart stood behind the cash register, a smoldering cigarette threatening to dump its ashes down his shirt. Lenny didn't even look up when I spoke.

"We had some visitors last night," Bart said.

"Yeah?"

"The unwelcome kind."

"Rats?"

Bart rolled his eyes. "This ain't a barn, no matter what we call it."

"So who?"

"Thieves. Burglars. Assholes."

My eyes darted to the cash register. "They take much?"

"Never made it in the door."

"So how do you know someone was here?"

"Back door's a mess. They tried to break open the locks, but either the new ones we got are too strong, or the burglars didn't have the right tools."

"Didn't the alarm go off?"

Bart shook his head. "Doesn't sound unless someone actually opens the door or breaks a window."

Lenny stood up abruptly and disappeared into the repair shop.

"Did you call the cops?" I asked Bart.

"And tell them what? Our locks worked great and nobody got in?"

"Your property was violated."

"Like cops would care."

"Why wouldn't they?"

He squinted, annoyed. "Look at me. Do I look like someone the cops go out of their way for? Do you happen to remember how many squad cars showed up at the picnic yesterday when 911 got the call about that dumbshit Trey? Our club might as well have been a terrorist group."

"Come on, Bart. It's not like you're a one-percenter."

His eyes widened and he glanced toward the shop door, shushing me with his hand.

"What?" I said.

"Don't talk about one-percenters around Lenny if you want to keep your head on."

A one-percenter is something the AMA—the American Motorcycle Association—came up with. They published an official statement proclaiming that ninety-nine percent of the nation's bikers are law-abiding citizens, while only one percent are the outlaws everyone is so scared of. Shows you how paranoid the average person is.

"What's Lenny's problem with them?" I asked.

"Seems to think they have something to do with this break-in."

"Oh, come on. There would be a hell of a lot more done than just a messed-up door. The place would be burned to the ground. Or we'd be outside with gas masks cleaning up piss and vomit."

Bart rubbed a spot off the glass counter with his finger. "I told him the same thing, but ever since yesterday, Lenny's been acting weird. It's like his former life has snuck up on him."

I raised my eyebrows. "What's that supposed to mean?"

Bart looked surprised, then embarrassed. "Sorry. I'm shooting my mouth off where I shouldn't be. Forget I said anything."

It was my turn to be annoyed. "Okay. I thought we were friends, but if you can't trust me more than that, I'm outta here." I slid off the stool and headed toward the door.

"Wait, Stella." Bart scurried around the counter, reached out to touch my arm, then thought better of it. "I'm sorry. It's just, it's Lenny's issue here, and I'm not sure what's going on. It's driving me crazy, too."

I sighed, rubbing my forehead. "All right. I'll go talk to him myself."

"Be careful."

I swung the shop doors open, and Lenny jumped up from behind the Electra-Glide he was working on. "Geez, woman, don't you ever knock?"

I gave a half-laugh. "You just saw me in the store."

He pierced me with an irritated look and hunkered down beside the bike again, muttering under his breath.

Thinking he might talk if I gave him a little time, I wandered over toward my poor Low Rider and took in the sad specimen. Five weeks ago it had been a beautiful, shiny black machine, thundering around with the best of them. Now it sat mutilated and crumpled, sporting quite a list of injuries: bent fork, broken headlight and turn signal, bent front rim, dented and scratched tank, demolished saddle bags, and numerous other scratches and dings.

Actually, the dented tank was no longer in evidence, as my buddies at Granger's Welding (Jethro, Jordan, and Jermaine), were giving it a fix-up for me. Only reason I could afford that treatment was because they would extend credit. They assured me they knew where I lived.

Other than that, only small things had been repaired since I didn't have money to pay for anything bigger. I'd buffed out the polished aluminum as well as I could and detailed away dirt and spilled oil left over from the crash. Right before my wreck, Lenny had given me a great timing cover with a skull whose eyes actually lit up. Fortunately, it survived the crash. Unfortunately, it now looked like it had been thrown under the hooves of stampeding cows. My saddlebags were at a leather shop, where the guy was deciding whether they would be worth fixing or if I should just give them up and invest in a new pair.

Ugh

I turned back to the part of Lenny's head visible above the bike. "So did you want to go meet Detective Willard? You have a good excuse now, with the Barn being broken into."

He peered up at me over the Electra-Glide's seat. "Forget it. He wouldn't do anything about it, anyway."

"He's a good guy," I said. "He'd listen."

"I said forget it! I don't want to go."

"Oookaaay," I said, mostly to myself. "I guess I'll be going, then."

He grunted, not lifting his head, and I went back into the salesroom.

"Wow, Lenny's really freaked out," I said to Bart.

He threw me a "shut up" look, his cigarette losing ashes at the sudden jerk of his head. A customer stood at the counter, and we didn't need to broadcast the Barn's or Lenny's problems. I shut up.

Not wanting to turn the knife in my biker heart by looking at parts, I studied the customer Bart was talking to.

He was bald, and since he was white you could see where his receding hairline ended even though he had recently shaved his head. You could also see every bump in his skull. It seems to me white guys should just stick to keeping whatever hair God gives 'em.

His face, at least, had a little fuzz. A closely trimmed goatee surrounded thin red lips and complemented the heavy eyebrows riding over his dark eyes. I shrugged to myself. I guessed a little hair was better than none.

He wore black riding boots that looked like they'd seen about everything, which matched the tattered black jeans worn tight on his almost non-existent butt. A black T-shirt with the sleeves cut off covered his chest where his leather vest wouldn't have. I was glad about that, seeing as how his upper body was just as skinny as his lower. I would've bet my best milker his chest was the sunken kind that makes a person appear like they're always stooping.

One item of his person I could appreciate was a fancy tattoo of a snake coiled around his right biceps. The snake was red and black and held its mouth open to reveal an extra-long forked tongue. Well done, but kind of nasty. I liked it.

The guy finally reached into his pocket and pulled out a wallet attached to his belt with a chain. He slapped a couple of bills on the counter and claimed whatever it was they'd been haggling over. Looked like a gasket kit, but I couldn't quite tell from where I was standing.

The bell dinged on the door as the guy let himself out, and I went up to the counter.

Bart held up his hands defensively. "I'm sorry. This whole break-in thing has us both rattled."

"But Lenny's not acting himself at all." I sat on a stool and leaned on the counter. "He seemed a little strange when he dropped me off at home yesterday, too, but nothing this aggravated. And he'd started out yesterday so relaxed, winning The Old Man's Home and all."

The repair shop door slapped against the wall and Lenny came barreling into the store.

"Are the people who own that bike complete idiots? Their oil is practically coal and they apparently haven't even heard of air filters. Why don't they just drive it out in front of a semi and be done with it?"

He disappeared back into the shop, but immediately returned, pointing at me.

"And what the hell are you still doing here if you're not going to buy something? Bart has better things to do than stand around yapping all day."

He marched back into the shop and we stared after him, dumbfounded. I'm pretty sure if a fly had come by right then it would've had no problem setting up housekeeping in my mouth.

"This is getting beyond weird," Bart finally said.

I tore my eyes off the shop door. "What should we do about it?"

Lenny suddenly stalked out of the shop again, bellowing to Bart that he was going out. The little bell on the door smacked against the wood. By the time I got to the window, Lenny's bike was racing out of the parking lot.

I looked at Bart. "What the hell was that about?"

"You think I know?"

I stared out where Lenny had disappeared, then shook my head. I guessed I wouldn't be taking him to meet Willard that day.

"You sure you don't want to report the attempted break-in?" I asked.

Bart nodded. "I'm sure. Lenny would probably kill me, and then the business would go down the tubes, anyway, so what's the point?"

"You want me to stick around, in case the burglars come back?"

"Nah. They're long gone. I'll be fine."

"All right. But give me a call if you need me."

Queenie and I got in the truck, Queenie back to her usual happy self. My nerves were shot, and I was concerned about the break-in, but at least the guys' problems had made me forget my own for a while.

Chapter Fifteen

A stop at the police department proved useless, since Willard was out somewhere, so I went home. I rummaged through the fridge, feeling suddenly hungry, and pulled out an apple. As I ate, I stared out the window above the sink and wondered what to do with myself. Lucy was repairing a stuck auger, and Tess was at school. Once Abe got to the farm I'd talk to him about getting Lucy's payroll and benefits started, but that wouldn't be till he was done at Rockefeller's at five-o'clock.

I threw the apple core into the sink and watched it disappear down the disposer. If Abe's gardening ideas were going to take off, I might have to start saving some of my castoffs for compost. Like I wanted a mound of rotting food for Queenie and her various rodent friends to root through.

At that moment, Queenie herself starting barking as a car drove into the lane. I ran outside, my adrenalin rushing at the memory of last night's visitors. With surprise, I realized it was the minister from Sellersville Mennonite. Peter Reinford stepped out of his ancient Corolla and waved. I'd known him for years, having attended church with Ma many times as a kid, and he'd always seemed like a good man. His hair, now a lot grayer than when I first met him, was windblown, and his face glowed red.

I told Queenie to stay and stepped forward to shake Peter's outstretched hand. "You look hot, Pete."

"That's because I am. Dumb AC busted on this heap. Costs too much to fix it."

"I can relate. Want a glass of water or something?"

"I'm okay. Thanks, though."

"So what can I do for you? Or are you here to visit your new flock recruits? Lucy's around somewhere, and Tess should be coming home on the bus any minute."

He smiled, but a wave of concern washed over his face. "I wanted to talk with you first, if I could. Then, if it's not too much trouble, I'll have a word with Lucy."

"Sure. Why don't we step into my office?"

He followed me in and gratefully took a seat in my air-conditioned office. "Now that's much better. Until I have to get back in my car, that is."

"Enjoy it for a few minutes. What's up?"

He ran his hands through his hair. "I got a phone call from Lucy's old minister in Lancaster. He seems concerned that Lucy could cause some trouble at our church."

I sat back, shocked. "What?"

"I know, it's really irritating, but I didn't want to ignore his warning just because he's a self-righteous jerk." He grinned. "If I'm allowed to say that about a fellow pastor. You've known Lucy a few days now, and I assume you checked her out before hiring her. Anything you see that gives any credence to his tattling?"

"What kind of trouble is he afraid of?"

He blew air out through his nose. "Claims Lucy likes to challenge the status quo and question authority."

"Isn't that good in a church?"

He nodded. "Sure, to some extent. But not if it's someone who just likes to make waves. You know what I mean. So what do you think? Anything strike a nerve with you?"

I thought about the questions I had about Brad, the Lancaster hype, the graffiti, and the anonymous phone call. But it didn't feel right spreading what amounted to gossip. Even to a well-meaning minister like Pete.

"She's been nothing but hard-working so far," I said. "Hasn't questioned anything I've asked of her, and has stayed way out of my personal business. And her daughter's a great gal."

"That sounds right, from what I observed. And I couldn't help but notice they already have the Grangers in their corner." A smile flickered on his face. "Thanks to Lucy's benevolent employer, I'm sure."

I lifted a shoulder. "The least I can do. You want to see Lucy now? There's really not much more I can help you with."

"Sure. And I'm sorry. Normally I wouldn't talk with someone else like this, but I've known you since you were a kid and figured I could take you into my confidence. Especially since I was pretty certain it wasn't true, anyway."

"You figured right. I'm not about to go spreading rumors about my employee. Now, let's go find Lucy."

But we didn't have to. At that moment, Lucy came barreling into the office, her face white.

"The school bus just slowed down at our lane, then left without dropping Tess off. I have to go after her."

"Did you see her on it?"

"It went by too fast. There was no way I could check all the windows."

"Go ahead, chase the bus. I'll call the school and see what they have to say."

She ran out, not even noticing Pete, and I grabbed the phone book.

The secretary at the school knew nothing about where Tess had gone. She remembered her, sure, since Tess had just registered for school on Friday, but she had no idea what happened to her after the bell rang and the buses dispersed. She hung up after saying she'd contact the bus driver. She'd call me back in a minute.

"Anything I can do?" Pete asked.

"Wouldn't know what. Unless you want to pray."

"I've gotten pretty good at that." He rested his forehead on steepled hands and went to work.

The phone rang, and I snatched it up.

"The bus driver says Tess isn't on the bus," the secretary said. "Apparently never got on."

"Aren't they supposed to check this sort of thing?"

She made an exasperated sound. "It's close to impossible. With all the after-school activities and such, there's no way to keep track of who's getting on and who's not. And with the chaos of the first day...."

"So there's nothing you can do?"

"Not really. If she didn't get on the bus and she's not here, there's no telling where she is. Might someone have picked her up?"

"Can't imagine who. She doesn't know anybody."

"I'll get on the phone to the police," the secretary said.

Lucy's car skidded into the driveway, and she jumped out.

"Hang on," I told the secretary. "Tess' mother is here. We'll call you back."

I met Lucy outside.

"Is she here?" she asked. "Have you heard anything?"

I shook my head. "The school has no idea where she is. They're ready to call the cops."

Lucy burst into tears of frustration, and I stood beside her awkwardly. Pete came out of the barn and laid his hand on Lucy's shoulder. She looked up at him, shocked. "But, what are you doing here? Did Stella call you?"

He smiled gently. "No. I came by to welcome you to the neighborhood, and happened upon this crisis. What can I do to help?"

Just then, a powder blue Chrysler rolled in the lane. From Lucy's widened eyes, I gathered she recognized it. She bolted toward it and flung open the rear door. "Tess!" She pulled the girl out of the car, tangling them both in the seatbelt. Finally free, Lucy turned on the middle-aged man and woman who climbed out of the front seats. "What are you *doing* here?"

They looked stunned. "What do you mean? We're here to see where our granddaughter is living."

Lucy closed her eyes, her hands clenched. When she opened her eyes her voice was calmer, but she spoke through her teeth.

"You can't pick Tess up at school without telling anyone. We have people all over town trying to find her!"

The woman clicked her tongue. "But we were always allowed to pick her up from the school in Lancaster."

"Of course you were. They know you there. And I arranged it ahead of time. You can't just come here and grab her off the sidewalk! I've been in a panic!"

The man raised his hands in front of him. "Sorry, Lucy, we just wanted to be with Brad's only child. And we were bringing her right home. Figured we'd beat the bus."

"Well, you didn't."

Tess squirmed, and Lucy released her from her arms. The movement reminded Lucy that other people were present.

"Oh, Stella, these are my in-laws. Thomas and Elsie Lapp. This is Stella Crown, my new boss." I couldn't help but think Thomas didn't look nearly as cuddly as the man on the Herr's potato chips bag. Perhaps Tess had meant her other grandpa when she'd made that comment.

Lucy turned to Peter next, almost as if she was surprised to see him still there. "And this is the minister at Sellersville Mennonite, where we attended yesterday. Peter Reinford."

Thomas Lapp looked at Lucy. "Sellersville. We'd heard you went there."

The Mennonite grapevine was apparently just as lively as the farming one.

"And liked it very much," Lucy said.

Thomas' face remained blank as he stepped forward to shake Peter's hand. Elsie didn't move. Peter, I could see, was trying not to grin.

"Since we're here, Lucy, can we at least see the place?" Thomas said.

Tess gravitated back to her mother's side and peered at her grandfather from behind Lucy's arm.

"Sure, you can see it," Lucy said calmly. "Since you're here." She turned to Pete. "Did you stop by to visit Tess and me?"

He smiled. "That's okay. I'll come another time, when you don't have company. But we did enjoy having you at church yesterday, and hope to see you again."

Lucy glanced at her in-laws. "We'll be back."

"Wonderful. I'll be going then. Unless you need me for anything."

"We're okay now. But thanks. Oh, I guess I should inform the school."

"I'll take care of it," I said. "You go ahead and give the tour."

Lucy took a deep breath, then turned toward the garage. "Why don't we show you our new apartment first?"

Peter and I were left looking at each other.

"Oh boy," he said. "Glad they aren't my in-laws."

"And I wish they weren't hers." I sighed. "Guess I'd better call the school to let them know it was an overzealous grandparent problem."

"Yup, you'd better. And I'd better get back in my heat trap and make some more rounds."

"You still worried about Lucy?"

He shook his head, grinning. "Never really was. Besides, if she stands up to her own relatives like that, I'd guess a minister more conservative than I could easily deem her a troublemaker."

"Are there any ministers *less* conservative than you?"

He laughed. "Certainly not at Yoder Mennonite."

After he'd gone I made the embarrassing call to the school, then found more than enough to do until Abe arrived to talk about Lucy's salary. A dairy farm is a no-fail source of never-ending chores. I took a trip to see the heifers down in the lower pasture, made sure there was enough hay and straw for the older calves, and found Poppy, our soon-to-be-mother, in the pasture with beginning signs of labor. Too late for me to win the bet with Zach, unfortunately.

There are several ways to tell if a cow's time has come to give birth, and Poppy was exhibiting a few of them. She had removed herself from the rest of the herd, finding a lonely corner of the pasture; her vagina looked swollen; and her udder was extremely full—more so than usual.

Cows don't like to be watched when they're giving birth. They would be appalled at all of the people who take video cameras and such into the hospital for that pivotal moment. I've never understood that myself, but then, I've never had my body split apart to admit a new person into the world, either.

Anyway, I left her alone. I'd check on her in a few hours to see how things were progressing.

Time flew, and soon Abe's Camry was pulling into the drive. I glanced at my watch and was surprised to see it was almost five-thirty. The Chrysler that belonged to Lucy's in-laws was gone.

"You're a little late," I said when Abe got out of his car.

"Yes, ma'am. Sorry, ma'am. Please don't beat me."

I grinned. "Got a minute?"

"I always have a minute for you. And I have something to show you."

He hesitated, then draped his arm over my shoulder. I considered his arm, as did he. He removed it.

His eyes fell on the garage. "How come the garage is so white?"

"Painted it this morning."

"May I ask why?"

"Vandals. Sprayed some nasty words on the doors."

His face clouded. "About you?"

"Nope. Lucy."

"About her husband's death?"

"That, and some references to her lifestyle."

He stared at the garage. "Stella—"

"I called the cops, okay? They're on it. Now come into the office."

"All right. Just a minute." He went back to the car and pulled out a bag, which he brought with him into the barn.

Inside, I sat down and watched as he lowered himself into a chair, looking smug.

"What's up with you?" I said. "You win first prize in an accounting contest?"

"You want me to go first?"

I gestured for him to go ahead.

Standing up, he stuck his hand into his bag and pulled out three frames. He set them one by one on my desk, facing me. At the sight of the first my stomach tightened, and it got worse with each photo that followed.

The first was of my folks and me, which meant I was just a little thing, since my dad died when I was three. We were sitting in the living room of the farmhouse, on the sofa, wearing matching overalls and white T-shirts. I sat on my mother's lap, and Dad had his arm around her shoulders. We looked healthy and happy and without a clue as to the sadness soon to come.

The second photo was of my mother, me, and Howie, leaning against one of the fences in the barnyard. I was about ten or so. After Dad died, Howie stayed on as my mother's hired hand, helping her keep the farm amid financially and emotionally trying times. He became like a second father to me, and more than once I wished Mom had had the guts to bring him into the house as a real one. It wasn't to be, although I always had the feeling Howie wished it, too.

The last photo was from several weeks ago, soon before Howie was killed. It was a snapshot taken at the birthday party Ma had thrown for me, and Howie and I were sitting side by side at a picnic table, grinning like fools. Howie had barbecue sauce on his chin, and I was holding a spoonful of what looked like potato salad. Happy as can be.

I sat back in my chair and looked up at Abe, who was smiling in a concerned kind of way.

"Where did you get these?" I asked. "The first two look like ones I saw in Howie's box." I kept my eyes from moving to the box itself, which sat at my elbow.

"That's where I got them. I sneaked back here yesterday while you were gone and got them blown up this morning. Here are the originals. The last one Zach took at your birthday party."

He tossed an envelope onto the desk, and I stared at him. "I don't know what to say."

"I hoped you wouldn't mind. I always wondered why you didn't have some pictures of your folks around and decided it was time." He squinted at me shyly. "Do you like them?"

I stood up slowly and put my arms around his neck. He looked me in the eyes, almost fearful, until I leaned forward and kissed him. He stood still for a moment, then slid his hands around my waist. I reached up into his hair and was pulling myself closer to him when I heard the door open.

"Oh, geez, I'm sorry." Lucy slammed the door behind her.

"Wait, Lucy!" I pulled myself from Abe's arms and ran into the hallway.

Lucy stood outside the door, mortified. "I am. So. Sorry."

"It's okay. Really."

Abe stuck his head out the office door. "Geez, Lucy. Your timing really sucks."

I burst out laughing, and a small smile finally made its way to Lucy's face. Abe grinned at her, then ducked back into the office.

"You need something?" I asked.

"Just wanted to apologize about my in-laws and the trouble they caused today. They're good at that."

"Hey, I'm just glad they're not mine."

"Yeah, you should be." She looked like she was going to say something else, but turned, instead, and headed toward the parlor.

When I got back in the office Abe was already sitting behind the desk, had booted up the computer, and was looking through a manila folder, avoiding my eyes. I was glad he wasn't standing there waiting for more kissing, because I was embarrassed I'd done it at all.

"There was something you wanted to ask me, right?" he said.

"Um, yeah. I wanted to make sure we got Lucy's paycheck and benefits started. You on top of that?"

"On my list to do today."

"Wonderful. Need me to do anything?"

He looked at me strangely, and heat swept through my body. I cleared my throat. "I'd better get to the parlor. It's only Lucy's third day and already I'm leaving her to the milking alone."

"Stella," Abe said as I opened the door. I looked back. "Any chance we could continue our earlier conversation sometime in the near future?"

I gave him what felt like a very shaky grin, and shut the door.

Chapter Sixteen

Lucy and I were forking the last shredded newspaper into clean stalls when a Harley rumbled up the lane. I could tell from the timbre of the roar that it was Lenny's bike.

"Uh oh," I said.

Lucy straightened abruptly. "What?"

I waved my hand. "Oh, nothing. It's just Lenny, and he was in a hell of a mood when I saw him today."

Abe had already gone to supper, taking Zach away with him, so Lucy, Tess, and I were the only ones around. I leaned in the doorway of the barn and stared at Lenny. He stared back.

"Hey, Len," I said.

He looked out at the field behind my house, then back at me. "Sorry."

I walked toward him and he swung his leg over his two-toned green Wide Glide. When I got close, he offered the meaty part of his arm and I gave it a light punch.

He rubbed his shoulder. "Are we even?"

I grinned. "Sure."

"Kind of you. And I haven't even told you what I found for you today."

"What?"

"How 'bout a new fork for a little birdie's song? Be a big step to getting your bike back on the road again."

"Really? That's great."

"And I've got another surprise I need you to come by the Barn for. Tomorrow?"

"What is this? Christmas?"

He shrugged, and I saw in his eyes he was still haunted by something.

"All right," I said. "Thanks. I'll swing by tomorrow. How'd you manage to get the fork?"

Some emotion flitted across his eyes then disappeared just as quickly. "I've got my sources. Don't—"

He cut off abruptly and glanced toward the barn. Lucy stood in the doorway, looking anxious. I waved her over.

"Lucy, Lenny. And vice versa. You saw each other yesterday when Lenny dropped me off. She's my new farmhand, Len. And Lucy, you know how Zach told you not to be scared of me? It's the same with Lenny. He's only half as bad as he looks."

They looked at each other rather seriously and shook hands.

"Actually," Lenny said to Lucy, "I was here to make amends with your boss lady, here, and take her out to supper."

"Wow," I said. "Taco Bell again?"

"Want to make it a party of three?" Lenny asked Lucy.

"Oh, thanks," Lucy said, "but I've got my daughter to feed. And it's getting late, so we'd better stay here."

Lenny brightened from his somber mood. "A little girl? Well, bring her along."

"Really?"

"I love little girls."

"Well, okay," Lucy said, a smile finally beginning. "Let me change out of these clothes and we'll be right down." She trotted off to the garage.

"Nice little lady," Lenny said.

"I'll let you get by with that," I said, "because she really is little."

"And how else would I have meant it?"

I grunted. "I'll go change, too. Want to come in?"

"Naw. I need some attention from this other little lady here."

Queenie sat patiently at his feet. Lenny lowered his bulky self to the ground and Queenie immediately attacked him. I left them rolling around like two kids.

Five minutes later I went back outside and Lenny seemed even more relaxed. I guess it's hard to be uptight when you've got grass clippings and dog slobber on your jeans.

Soon we were caravanning down the road, Lenny leading and the three of us gals in my truck. Tess had her hair tied back in a ponytail, and I could've been wrong, but I thought maybe Lucy had swiped a little mascara on her eyelashes.

Lenny led us to Zoto's, a family restaurant down on Route 309. Tess' face lit up, and she jiggled with excitement in her seat.

Lucy met my eyes over the girl's head. "I told you we'd eaten at McDonald's too many times."

I made a disgusted face and pulled in beside Lenny. While we hopped down from the truck, Lenny turned off his bike and sat. If I hadn't known better, I would've thought he was casing the place. He seemed very interested in the other vehicles in the parking lot and took a lot of time locking up his bike. He also took a long look at Suzy's Lounge across the street.

"Everything okay, Len?" I said.

He shot me a startled glance but ignored my question, gesturing toward the restaurant's door. "Shall we?"

Lenny had quite a discussion with the hostess, a chunky little thing who looked like she was barely sixteen. She wanted to seat us in the back part of the restaurant, but Lenny told her if we couldn't be in the front, we were leaving.

Lucy looked a question at me.

"He's a biker," I said. "He'll feel a lot better if his scooter's where he can keep an eye on it."

Lucy nodded understanding, and the ditz hostess finally led us to a booth overlooking the parking lot.

After a little awkwardness, Lenny and I squeezed into the same side of the booth so Lucy and Tess could sit together. I hoped we wouldn't have to argue too much about whose elbow was bumping whose, because Lenny had some big elbows.

After we ordered, Lenny unwound enough to help Tess figure out the maze on the back of the placemat, and Lucy watched with sadness in her eyes.

"Do you have children, Lenny?" Lucy asked suddenly. "You seem so comfortable with Tess."

He avoided her eyes by looking out at his bike and then at the ketchup on the table. "No, ma'am. It's just me. Well, me and Bart, but that's different."

She wrinkled her nose at him, confused.

"I mean, we're not family or anything, but he's the closest thing I come to it. I mean...never mind."

I wondered what on earth made him so jittery about a simple question, but I soon figured out, from the blush creeping up his face, that it was the person asking the question rather than the question itself. His eyes darted toward Lucy, who was acting weird and self-conscious herself, picking at something non-existent on the table. Lenny's leg started jerking up and down, shaking the floor.

"Good lord, Lenny," I said under my breath. "You trying to start an earthquake?"

His leg stilled. "Sorry. I'm not used to people actually caring about my personal life."

"Come on, Len," I said. "You know I'm only interested in you for your body."

He blinked, then finally laughed, and the tension at our table dissipated. Tess had been oblivious all along.

The rest of the meal passed in stilted but friendly conversation about bikes, Mennonites, and Lucy's farming experience. Lenny somehow picked up that he shouldn't ask anything about Tess' father, and we were soon pushing our plates toward the waitress. We all declined coffee, Lenny paid the bill, and Tess and I clambered into the pickup after thanking Lenny.

Lucy stayed outside to talk with Lenny while he unlocked his bike. I turned my radio on low so Tom Petty could drown out whatever conversation they were having, but I didn't need to hear anything to see that Lenny was giving his bike a more thorough than necessary inspection, and that once again he was studying Suzy's parking lot across the street.

It was also apparent that Lucy was feeling awkward and shy. If the words written on our garage had any truth to them, I'd be incredibly surprised. She looked like a teen-ager, not sure how to stand or where to put her hands while she was talking. If she was as promiscuous as the graffiti indicated, she'd have no such problems.

Finally, Lenny straddled his bike and Lucy slid into the truck. She belted herself in and gazed straight ahead, an ambiguous expression on her face.

Lenny waited with a concerned expression until the truck came to life, then started his bike. I gestured for him to take the lead. He rode ahead of us for a few miles before we parted ways, him toward his home in Perkasie, and us toward the farm.

I swear Lucy's eyes never left his taillight.

Chapter Seventeen

The first sound I heard when I stepped down from my truck was the high keening of labor pains. This is unusual, so I knew something had gone wrong with Poppy's delivery.

Lucy caught my eye over the hood of the truck. "Let me get Tess to bed, and I'll be right out."

I looked at Tess, rubbing her eyes, sleep lines on her face from dozing on Lucy's shoulder. "Take your time. I've seen it all before."

While Lucy led her sleepy charge toward the garage, I dodged Queenie's excited jumping and jogged inside—slowing to a walk when my ribs reminded me of their existence—to change into delivering clothes. Most likely everything would go smoothly and Poppy was just being a baby, but no matter what happened I was bound to get splashed with blood, urine, and an ungodly amount of other bodily fluids. That didn't bother me, but there was no reason to get one of my two pairs of nice jeans stained. I wasn't going to have money to buy new ones in the foreseeable future.

The light on my phone was flashing when I got into the kitchen, but I didn't feel like taking the time to listen to any messages. The clock on the oven said it was already close to my usual bedtime of nine-o'clock, so whoever it was could just wait till morning. Or at least till Poppy had delivered her calf and I'd taken a shower.

Decked out in old jeans, a ratty T-shirt, and work boots, with a fresh Motrin coursing through my bloodstream, I found Poppy standing and breathing hard in a secluded corner of the pasture. After ordering Queenie to sit and stay, I turned on my flashlight, checked Poppy's hind end, and saw tell-tale signs of labor—her water had broken, making a messy circle in the grass, and there was other discharge leaking onto her legs and the ground.

But no hooves were sticking out where they should have been.

When you have a mature cow calving, it shouldn't take more than two to four hours for labor and delivery to be complete. Since Poppy had been showing signs before dinner, her present condition had me worried. The front hooves are supposed to be the first thing to show, with the nose coming next. With nothing showing after all this time, it could mean the calf was breech, coming nose first, or in some other bizarre or crooked position.

I stroked Poppy's face while talking soothingly to her, and tried to decide which approach to take to figure out what was wrong. In a couple of minutes her breath started coming faster, and she was soon moaning again, straining and pushing.

"Sorry, old girl," I said.

I rubbed her side until the contraction was over, then went to her rear and lifted her tail. Still nothing.

I rummaged around in the first aid kit I'd brought and found a rubber glove that fit over most of my arm. I smeared a little KY jelly on my fingers and inserted them into Poppy's vagina to feel around a little.

"Damn," I said.

"That doesn't sound good." Lucy stood a few feet away in the semi-darkness.

"Feels like the calf's trying to come out head first," I said. I pulled out my hand and rested it on Poppy's bony pelvis. "But at least it's not breech. We just have to get those hooves in front of its head."

Lucy's face lit up, reminding me of Queenie when she wanted me to throw her the remains of a sandwich.

"You want to do the honors?" I asked.

She looked for a moment like she was going to do a cheer, but immediately became all business, finding one of the gloves and moving to Poppy's behind.

"It's been a while," she said, looking anxious.

"You'll be fine."

She took a deep breath and moved her hand slowly, finagling her way deeper into Poppy's insides. I could tell when she felt the calf's nose by the dreamy look that came into her eyes.

The nostalgic expression was replaced almost instantly by one of surprise when Poppy went into a contraction. Lucy gritted her teeth and smiled tensely.

"Forgot about the pressure, huh?" I said.

She gave a quick laugh and closed her eyes. Soon the contraction was over and Lucy was able to move her arm around, feeling which direction the calf needed to go.

"I think I just need to—"

Poppy suddenly dropped onto her front knees, and it was easy to see the rest of her was going down, too. Lucy extracted her arm and stepped back to let the cow get comfortable on the ground. While this would make Lucy's job more difficult, it's very normal for cows to get up and down a lot during labor, and it just might jostle the calf into a better position.

"Well," Lucy said.

"Maybe she'll get up soon," I said. "That would be a lot easier than trying to do this lying down."

We sat where Poppy wouldn't see us, hoping it would allow her to relax. As I mentioned before, mature calvers don't like having people around during labor. Maybe she could forget we were there for a few minutes if we stayed out of sight.

We watched her suffer through a few more contractions before she lumbered her way upright again, swaying a bit until she got all four feet under her.

"Let's see what happens with a couple more pushes," I said. I was hoping the up and down had moved the calf to a better place. We waited, but no hooves made themselves evident.

"Guess I'll go in again," Lucy said.

This time her expression was one of satisfaction.

"That really did help," she said. "Look at this."

Lucy's tongue stuck out between her teeth as she gently tugged and a perfect, shiny little hoof poked out. She reached in again, and the next thing we knew, both hooves were out and Poppy was pushing. Lucy grabbed hold of the hooves and pulled while Poppy strained, and the feet slid out several more inches. After a quick grin from Lucy, I lay back on the ground to relax while she worked. Queenie came over and licked my face.

"Stella," Lucy said a few minutes later.

I gently pushed Queenie away and was happy to see a little nose coming out in between two well-formed front legs. After a couple more contractions with Poppy pushing and Lucy pulling, the entire head slipped out.

The head is the biggest obstacle—literally—when a calf is being born. Once that's out, the mother can breathe a little easier—not quite literally. The next feeling of success comes when the calf's shoulders emerge, and then, finally, the hips. Once they're through, it's pretty much a done deal.

"Good girl, Poppy," Lucy said. She gave the cow, who had decided to lie down again, a final pat on her rear and came to sit by me.

Normally I would go away and let the cow do the rest of the work, but since Poppy'd had so much trouble this time, I thought I'd stick around and make sure she wasn't too exhausted to finish it out.

"You can go back to the apartment, if you want," I said to Lucy.

She shook her head. "I don't want to miss my first calving in three years."

The look of contentment on her face prodded me to try to remember the last time I felt inspired by the birthing of a calf. Probably not since I was about ten. Starting almost from my own birth I'd seen hundreds, maybe thousands, of calves born, and while it was still satisfying to have a new calf, it wasn't earthshaking. I guess that's okay, but Lucy's enjoyment made me feel I might be missing something.

As we watched, the calf's shoulders emerged and came through, and soon the hips, and before we knew it the calf had slipped onto the ground and Poppy was standing up, cleaning it off.

"Looks like a nice little heifer," I said. Heifers—girls—are always hoped for, since they can be added to the dairy herd and will be milk producers by the time they're two. A male is just another animal to sell to the neighbors for fattening.

In a natural setting, the calf would be standing and finding her way to her mother's udder in a short couple of hours. In a farming situation it's a bit different. We'd let Poppy do some of the cleaning, but give her help with drying, using a pile of towels I had brought with me. As soon as the calf was dry and a bit more accustomed to being in the outside world, I would carry her to a private hutch, where she would sleep on clean, dry straw, and drink Poppy's colostrum as soon as we got it.

As far as Poppy was concerned, the placenta would soon be delivered, and—sorry—she'd probably eat it. I've never learned why cows do this, but there must be some reason since it happens almost every time. Poppy would forget about the calf by this time tomorrow, not having bonded with it, and would be back in her usual routine, being milked twice daily until she recovered enough to be bred again.

It may sound cruel to you, taking the calf from her mother, but I run a business, and things have to be done a certain way. And the animals certainly don't suffer under my care.

Besides, when you're going through the grief of losing someone you loved like a father, it makes you wonder if you'd be better off never bonding with anyone.

Chapter Eighteen

We finally got the new calf settled in its pen, and I was turning toward my house and bed when Lucy cleared her throat.

"What?" I said.

"Can I ask you something?"

I stopped. I knew we needed to talk. We hadn't spoken at all about the events of the night before, and I'd felt the tension all day. Now all I really wanted to do was sleep, but I waved at her to go on.

"Is Lenny as good a guy as he seems?"

I should've known he'd be the subject, rather than her wanting to actually clear up other issues, but I'd already forgotten the look in her eye at supper. I sighed. I didn't feel like I could blow her off, even though I was about dead on my feet and the farthest thing from a matchmaker. Perhaps if I stuck it out I could get in some questions that might throw some light on her husband's death.

"All right," I said. "Come in for a minute. I need a drink before bed anyway."

"Oh, no, I don't need to come in."

"If you want to talk to me, you do. I've gotta sit down."

She hesitated, looking toward the apartment, but eventually followed.

We got settled in the living room, me on the sofa with my head resting on the back and my feet on the coffee table, and

Lucy sitting forward on the matching chair. I had heated up a mug of milk and honey for myself, but Lucy refused anything. She looked down at her hands and I wondered if she was regretting her impulse to talk.

I took a sip of milk and enjoyed the warmth as it traveled down my insides. "What do you want to know about Lenny?"

She didn't look up. "I just want to know if he's a good guy."

I took another swallow. "He's a great guy and an even better mechanic. He'd give you the shirt off his back if he didn't think you'd suffocate in it."

"And Bart?" she said.

"Bart?"

"What was all that about Bart being Lenny's only 'kind of' family?"

I laughed. "I think that was about Len being nervous talking to you. But Bart is his closest friend and his business partner."

"They own the Biker Barn equally?"

"Don't know for sure. I actually think Lenny has the money and Bart has the business sense, but I could be wrong. It's just the impression I've always had."

"Do they live together?"

"You're not asking if they're gay, are you?"

That made her look up. "Goodness, no."

"Because I don't think they'd make that great a couple. They argue too much. Anyway, Lenny has his rowhouse in Perkasie, and Bart rents an apartment in Quakertown. Bart's also a church-goer, while Lenny chooses to practice his religion on his own. Definitely not Mennonite background."

She almost smiled at that. "Has Lenny always been a good guy?"

"Does it matter?"

"It does to me."

I studied her for a moment. I don't talk about my friends to just anybody. But she looked sincere enough I knew she wasn't asking just for kicks.

"I don't know the details," I finally said. "But he changed from bad guy to good guy about twenty years ago or so. From things he's implied or things I've guessed, he rode with an outlaw club before getting out and going straight. He's been Joe Good Citizen as long as I've known him." I took a sip of milk. "I do know he has a nickname from the old days he doesn't like. Hammer. Don't ask me what it's from. He doesn't like to talk about those times, and I don't ask. Doesn't mean anything to me."

Lucy sat back in her chair, and I unbent a little more. "Look, I know you're attracted to him. That's pretty obvious. Don't you want to find out some of this stuff on your own?"

She was quiet for so long I thought she'd gone to sleep with her eyes open. Finally, she said, "I haven't dated much—at least, not seriously—since Brad died. It still feels like a betrayal. And there is Tess to think about."

So who was Noah? It didn't seem like a casual relationship the way he'd lit up when he'd seen her. Or the way she'd reacted to his appearance on the farm.

"Tess seemed to like Lenny," I said. "And he was super with her tonight."

"Sure. I saw it, too. But what if it wouldn't work out? I'd hate to break her heart, along with my own."

I took a deep breath, wondering if now was the time to get some answers. "It's been a while since Brad died, right? A year and a half?"

She nodded. "Feels like a lot longer, sometimes. And then other times it feels like yesterday."

She went quiet again, and I realized I'd just heard more in the last five minutes than I had in the entire time she'd been on the farm. In fact, she was being downright chatty.

"Lucy," I said, "I really hate to ask this, but what exactly did Brad die of? You had said he was ill, but Martin Spunk told me he was paralyzed. That must've been a terrible burden, taking care of him."

She stared into space for a moment, and I wondered if she was going to answer at all. "Yes," she finally said. "He was paralyzed. A quadriplegic."

"An accident?" I asked, even though I knew he had fallen down stairs.

She looked at her lap. "An accident. Look, can we talk about this another time? I'm....My brain doesn't function too well after midnight."

"Good grief, is it that late?"

The clock on the wall said twelve-thirty. I shuddered. Five-o'clock was going to come mighty early.

"All right," I said reluctantly. "We can talk about it another time. And we need to discuss your salary and benefits, too, but that definitely needs clear heads."

She walked toward the door.

"Sorry there's only one bed in the apartment," I said.

She waved me off. "Don't worry about it. If Tess starts kicking me in the kidneys, I'll move to the sofa. Besides, I'm so pooped from today I don't think I'll move an inch once I hit the pillow."

I knew what she meant. The way I was feeling I might not even make it out of my chair.

Chapter Nineteen

My alarm clock might as well have punched me in the head, the way I felt when it went off.

By the time I got to the kitchen my eyes were staying open without too much extra effort, and I noticed the blinking light on my phone. In all the excitement and exhaustion last night I had forgotten about it.

I pushed the button and listened to Abe stumble through a message at about eight-o'clock the night before.

"Stella, it's…it's me. I just wanted to talk. Can you call me when you get in tonight? It doesn't matter how late it is. Well, that's it. Talk to you soon. Bye."

I closed my eyes. He was probably all worked up about that kiss I'd given him that afternoon. Maybe I would have been, too, if I'd had the time or energy to think about it. Perhaps the fact it hadn't even entered my dreams should have told me something.

Another message came on, from two hours later. Abe again.

"Stella? I guess you're not in yet. I hope everything's all right. Call me, okay?"

I sighed and rubbed my temples. Five-fifteen in the morning was too early to be worrying about whether or not I should have kept my hands—or lips—off of him. I wasn't going to roust him out of bed before dawn to discuss our relationship. And I certainly wasn't going to call him at work and have him talking about personal stuff where everyone in the Rockefeller

Dairy community could hear him. I hoped he would be okay with waiting till the afternoon to hash it over. I was sure I'd be hashing it over myself until then.

After chugging a glass of orange juice, I went to work and got through most of the milking on autopilot. By the time Temple Radio had played through several symphonies and the cows were meandering out of their stalls, Lucy was walking Tess to the end of the driveway to wait for the bus. Lucy looked as bushed as I felt.

I had switched the radio to WMMR, and Aerosmith was singing "Walk This Way" when Lucy made it into the barn.

I handed her the pitchfork. "Can you finish this? I need some food. And the calves haven't gotten their colostrum and formula yet. If you wouldn't mind...."

"Glad to. That way I can check out our baby."

"She's all yours."

I was almost to the door when she stopped me.

"Stella?"

I turned around.

"You were asking me some things last night. About Brad."

"Yeah," I said.

"Do we really need to talk about it? I mean, for me to keep my job here?"

I studied her expression. Worried, and hard. What was she hiding?

"Look," I said. "I need breakfast. How about I come back out in a half hour? We can talk then."

Her lips formed a grim line, and she bent over the pitchfork.

The milk truck pulled in as I walked toward the house, and I waved to the driver. We had a new guy as of a month before, and while I liked him okay, I didn't feel like getting to know him. Call it paranoia, call it snobbishness, I don't care. I was too hungry to be nice, anyway.

A bowl of oatmeal with raisins later and I felt like a new woman. Well, almost. A nice slab of scrapple with apple butter would have tasted mighty good, but there wasn't any in the fridge. Big surprise.

Lucy was still working in the parlor, and I had some business phone calls to make, so I went out to my office. It was now after that magic hour of eight, when most regular people are on the job, so I hoped I could catch a few of them. As soon as I opened the door I noticed the frames from Abe sitting on my desk. Damn. Without looking at the pictures I stacked them face down in Howie's box, where I wouldn't have to see them. I supposed I'd have to do something with the whole stash soon, but it was too early in the morning for that kind of emotion.

Lucy was in the milkhouse chatting with Doug, the new trucker, when I found her twenty minutes later. Doug gave me what I guessed was a smile if I could've seen it under his huge mustache. He was a middle-aged guy, dressed in white pants and a red shirt with the truckline's emblem on the chest.

"I take it you met my new hire?" I said.

He nodded. "Good to see you have some help. Can't say I was worried about you, but everybody can use a hand now and again."

"I'm beginning to realize that, myself." I turned to Lucy. "You want to come talk for a minute?"

Looking grim again, she said her good-byes to Doug and followed me back through the parlor to my office, where I sank into my chair. I'd start with the easy stuff. "Ready to talk about finances?"

"Sure." She sat on the edge of the chair in front of the desk. "Abe got my particulars, so I think the details are taken care of."

"The salary and benefits sound good to you?"

Lucy turned pink. "I felt pretty dumb when I realized I'd left our interview on Friday with no idea what I'd be making. I was just so glad to have the job. But yes, everything sounds fine."

"Mennonite Mutual Aid is our insurance. You're okay with that?"

"I think it's great. I've always wished I could go with them, but Brad's employer only offered Blue Cross, and that was the one we used."

The Mennonite Church's insurance carrier, MMA, is a bit different from most, their premiums actually going to pay for other members' claims. Thus the "Mutual" in the name. You end up in the hospital after a heart attack, it's my money that's partially paying your stay. While the cost is sometimes a bit more, MMA makes up for it with friendly service and the feeling that if I need help, the other members will back me up, too.

"Good," I said. "Now, are you okay for this month money-wise, or do you need an advance on your salary?"

"Actually...." She wrinkled her nose. "Brad's life insurance has kept us pretty well, so I haven't had to worry. Thanks, though."

I hesitated, then asked casually, "So in other words, you're not working for the money, but for the love of cows?"

She grunted. "Can't say that. I want the money left over from Brad's insurance to go right for Tess' college account, and if I wouldn't work, that would disappear quickly into the black hole of living expenses."

How well I understood. "Do you have a house in Lancaster you'll be selling?"

She shook her head. "My brother is living in it for now. He got married last spring, and it works out nicely for them. Why do you ask?"

I hated to say I was checking up on her, so I said, "Just curious."

I mustn't have been too convincing, because her face darkened.

"So now we're getting to the things you really want to know?" Her voice was tinged with anger.

I sat forward and rested my elbows on the desk. "I'm sorry, Lucy, but I'm feeling a little nervous. You probably think there are things that aren't even close to being my business, but I have to take care of my farm."

"And my personal life is threatening it somehow?" She crossed her arms over her chest.

I stared at her. "Have you forgotten what happened the other night?"

"It was just graffiti."

Just graffiti. "Lucy, in all my life I have never had anyone paint obscenities on my buildings. I can't believe it's because of anything I did."

"So you believe what it said?"

"I didn't say that." I closed my eyes and took a deep breath. Looking at Lucy again I said, "Just tell me something to ease my mind. Besides the graffiti, I've had an anonymous phone call warning me about you—"

"*What?*"

"—been told Lancaster rumors, and have seen an unwelcome visitor here at the farm."

"You mean Noah?"

"Yes."

"For heaven's sake. He's harmless."

I studied her, wondering why she'd been so worked up when he'd come if he was as harmless as she asserted. "What it comes down to," I said, "is that I need some assurance you're the honest, dedicated worker I've thought from the beginning, and that my farm isn't in danger."

Her jaw tightened and she looked like she was holding in angry words. Not that I could blame her.

"So please tell me something," I said. "Anything."

"Like, 'No, Stella, I didn't kill my husband'?"

I shrugged. "That would do."

She bent her head to her chest. "Perhaps I should just leave. Take Tess back to Lancaster."

"Right back where the rumors are coming from? Don't be an idiot. If you tell me my instincts are right-on, I'll be more than happy to hear it. And I won't ask again."

She sat silently.

"Come on, Lucy. Don't let this end already."

She thrust her chin out. "You got a *phone call?* Saying what?"

"That someone was concerned for my well-being, and the well-being of my farm."

I could see the war being fought behind her eyes. Does she throw a fit and storm out, ripping herself and Tess from what had seemed a great situation, or believe in my integrity and tell me something? I held my breath, hoping she'd decide to trust me. I really didn't want to lose her.

Finally, her mouth twitched. "That call was pretty ridiculous. Like you're not way tougher than me."

Relieved, I smiled. "I don't know. You're much better with a gun. Even though you are a pacifist."

I waited, but she didn't share any more. Dammit. But I decided I'd done enough pushing. For now. "Okay. I have something else I want to run by you, as we're figuring out what exactly your job description will be."

Still a bit wary, she cocked her head. "What's that?"

"Abe's trying to talk me into sideline incomes, and I'm wondering if that's something you and Tess might want to take on. I know some folks who run a vegetable stand during the summer that pays for their taxes. Some others are opening an ice cream parlor. The garden would have to wait till next year, but Abe also suggested some fall family activities. You want to think about that?"

Her expression relaxed a bit. "Sure. Do you care what kind of thing I come up with?"

"Nope. As long as I don't have to be in charge of it. Why don't we just make it part of your job description?"

She stood up. "Sounds good to me. That will leave you free for other things. I'll get right on it."

I waited, but she didn't move.

"What?" I asked.

"We're okay? You don't want to know anything else?"

"Not right now," I said.

She hesitated, obviously not knowing what to think of that, but finally left the office. I tilted my face down to rest my head on my hands. I'd be free for other things, Lucy had said.

The conversation had taken what little energy I'd had, and I still wasn't satisfied with what I'd learned.

I let my head drop down on my desk, and took a nap.

Chapter Twenty

A half hour and a new ache in my neck later, I opened heavy eyes. In my mind I knew there was a lot to do around the farm, but my body was obviously telling me I needed to take a break. And with Lucy around to work, my body was able to win this round.

Remembering Lenny's invitation to stop by the Barn and get a surprise, I decided to take him up on it. I figured I should let Lucy know where I'd be, and found her on the back side of the house, checking out the yard.

"What'cha doing?" I asked.

"Thinking about the addition to my job description. If we use this back part of the yard, we could have a little fall festival here. Games for kids, hayrides, nothing that would have too many out of pocket expenses. We could sell cider and—"

"Luce," I said, "it sounds great. Go with it."

"For real?"

"If you can make some extra money and I don't have to do the planning, I'm all for it. I'd better check with my insurance guy, though, just to be sure everything's okay on that front. Now, I'm heading over to the Biker Barn. I'll be back in a little while."

She licked her lips. "You going to see Lenny?"

"Yeah, he asked me to come by. Want me to tell him something?"

She turned away. "No. No thanks."

"Okay, see you later."

I whistled for Queenie and was at the Biker Barn in fifteen minutes. I thought I'd prevent any offense and just had Queenie stay outside this time.

Bart was sending another HOG club member away with some parts as I pushed open the door.

"So what's my surprise?" I asked.

Bart grinned. "Come with me."

We barged into the shop, where Lenny was at the sink, cleaning his hands with Fast Orange.

"Stella's wondering about her present," Bart said.

Lenny grunted, then gestured at me to come closer. When I got within reach, he spun me around.

"Okay," I said. "I'm looking at a piece-of-shit bike. What about it?"

Lenny glowered at me, but Bart laughed.

"It's for you," Bart said. "Until we get yours running again."

"Yeah, right. Like this thing runs."

"Don't knock it till you've tried it," Bart said.

I looked at Lenny, who gave me a half-hearted nod. I moved closer to check out the bike.

It was an old Sportster, if one could see through the battle scars. Some wanna-be mechanic had made a hash of it. The tank was a nice combo of rust, dingers, and ugly brown paint, while the fenders were painted a cross between green and puce. The front fender, in addition, had been chopped in half in the hopes it would look more bad-ass. Instead, it looked stupid. The seat was a two-person affair, one of the big blocky seats Harley tried that never caught on, and a nice mix of regular bolts and spike bolts held the bike together. A couple of chrome covers had been added, sporting bright gold, flashy skulls in stark relief. The rest of the bike doesn't need detailed description. You just need to know it was ugly as hell.

"Don't bother thanking me or anything," Lenny said.

"I'm not sure if I should thank you or curse you."

He shrugged. "Doesn't make much difference at this point."

I swung my leg over the seat and got my bearings. The seat sat like a lumpy rock, but the bike fit me just fine. I turned on the fuel, made sure I was in neutral, and looked for the starter button.

"Kick start," Lenny said.

I grimaced. "Bully for me."

I slammed my foot down on the starter and got it going on the second try. No matter how the bike looked, it sounded fine. I gunned the throttle, tried the turn signals and the horn, and decided it would work for now. I just hoped nobody saw me on it. I cut the engine in order to save our eardrums.

"Thanks, Len," I said.

"Hmpf."

"Where'd you get it? How much do I owe you?"

"Same place we're going to pick out your fork. And you don't owe me anything, other than your undying gratitude. I just want it back when you're done with it."

"No argument here. It would spoil my reputation to be seen on it too often."

Bart let out a short bark of laughter, and Lenny allowed a small smile.

"So let's go pick up your part," he said.

As soon as we wheeled the hideous contraption around to the parking lot I sensed trouble. Queenie was no longer sitting where I'd left her, and ominous sounds were coming from the far side of my truck. I took off running toward the growling. Lenny was on my heels, letting the bike fall to the ground with a nasty crunch. I rounded the truck's hood to find two people plastered up against the passenger door. One of them was the bald guy who'd been at the store the other day buying the gasket kit. His hand was reaching into his vest, and I was worried about what might come out.

With him was a woman, probably about twenty, looking righteously pissed. Her dark hair was pulled back into a tight braid, and flattened helmet hair wisps stuck to her forehead. She wasn't wearing any makeup except thick black eyeliner, and the color in her face looked like it was fighting a losing battle with cigarettes and bad nutrition.

"Down, girl," I said to Queenie.

Her growling cut back a notch, but she remained tense and focused, her tail still and solid against my leg.

"Help you folks?" I said. "Got an interest in my truck?"

The woman glared at me and ran her tongue over her teeth. The guy looked at Lenny, then at me.

"We got off our bike, there," he said, pointing at a ratty Big Twin. "The dog backed us up against here when we was trying to get to the store."

I put my hand on Queenie's head. She didn't like these people, and I wondered why. I assumed it wasn't the bad grammar—Howie's had been lousy at times, and the Grangers weren't known for their stellar use of the English language. Something else must have triggered this attack. It was strange, because usually if I had to scold her, it was for being too friendly.

I glanced at Lenny and was curious to see surprise on his face, if not shock. He stared at the woman while she looked at everything but him. Her jaw was tense and she crossed her arms over her chest defensively.

"Well, sorry if the old girl here gave you a scare," I said to the guy. "You can forget whatever you're going for."

He looked down at his hand as if it were acting on its own and removed it, empty, from his vest.

"S'okay," he said. "Who knows what turns dogs on sometimes?"

Giving Queenie a last nervous glance, he edged back toward his bike. The woman hesitated long enough to give me a poisonous glare, then followed Skinny Buns.

"Who the hell are they?" I said. "Lenny?"

He didn't hear me, because he was looking after the woman like she was something he'd last seen in a nightmare.

Chapter Twenty-one

Lenny ran and jumped into my truck like his pants were on fire.

"Follow them!" he yelled. He slammed the door, and I sprinted around to the driver's side.

"C'mon, Queenie!" I said. She dove in ahead of me and I cranked the key, bringing the truck to life.

The skanky guy and gal, not bothering to stop for helmets, had already gotten a jump on us, having kick-started the bike and skidded out of the parking lot. I gunned the engine, but had to stop to let several cars go by before heading out. By the time I made it to the first traffic light the bike was already too far ahead of us and turned off onto another road, disappearing altogether.

I glanced over at Lenny. His face was so ashen I was afraid he was going to puke, so I quickly pulled into the Clemens Market parking lot and turned off the truck.

"You okay?"

He sat silently, blinking, his mouth hanging open.

"Len?"

His mouth closed, and he swallowed. "Yeah, yeah, I'm okay."

I squinted at him. "You don't look it. What was that all about?"

He blinked some more.

"Lenny!"

"I don't...I don't think I want to tell you anything right now."

"Oh, really."

He turned his head slowly toward me. "Please, Stella? Don't push."

I breathed in through my nose. "Okay. But are you going to be all right?"

"I'm not sure."

At least he was honest.

"Okay. I won't push. For now. But I want to help."

He looked out his side window. "I know you do. But not yet."

"Does this have something to do with the break-in yesterday?"

He chewed on his mustache. "I don't know."

He sure didn't know much. Or wasn't saying.

I turned on the truck. "Okay, tell me where we're going. If we're still going."

We left the parking lot and drove, Lenny not uttering a word the entire trip except to tell me where to turn. Queenie sat between us, her front paws on his lap, her drool going all over his jeans. His big, oil-stained fingers were buried in her fur as he mulled over whatever was preoccupying him. That nasty chick, if I was right. Although it could also have been the break-in or whatever he had wanted to talk to Willard about. It seemed he had plenty on his mind. I sat quiet while he pondered.

We arrived at a huge garage about a half-hour later and drove into the empty gravel parking lot. Lenny opened his door and let Queenie jump out ahead of him, then lumbered to the ground. I locked the doors and followed.

I hadn't known who or what to expect at this place, seeing as how Lenny was being so secretive, but the guy who showed up was far from whatever I might have imagined.

He came to the door of his gigantic warehouse, a cigar in one hand, a bottle of Jack Daniels in the other. A grin lit up his face. He looked about a hundred and fifty years old and had approximately one tooth sticking out from his upper gum. Sparse gray hair was combed to give minimal coverage to his scalp, allowing liver spots and old scars to shine right on through. He wore camouflage pants and a black T-shirt so thin I could just make out a faded skull with flames tattooed across his chest. Holey untied combat boots covered his feet.

Quite a sight.

"Hammer," the guy said, his grin widening. "Don't tell me this is the little woman."

Lenny reddened, but I wasn't sure if it was because of the use of his old street name or the thought that I could have romantic attachments to him.

"Name's Stella," I said, holding out my hand. "Can't say I've ever let anyone call me their little woman. Even Lenny here."

The guy laughed, and instead of taking my hand he reached out and squeezed me in a big hug. I was so surprised I stood frozen until he stepped back.

"I'll remember that," he said. "Shoulda thought how my old lady about decked me whenever I called her that. If I was smart I woulda just called her General."

"This here's Mal," Lenny said, hooking a thumb toward his friend. "Mal Whitney. We go way back."

"You can call me Sweetheart," Mal said.

I gave him a level stare.

"Everybody does," he said. "Believe me."

"It's true," Lenny said.

Mal wiggled his eyebrows. "Ladies can't leave me alone."

Lenny snorted. "Fifty years ago, maybe."

"I think I'll stick to Mal, if that's okay," I said.

"Suit yourself."

"Anyhow," Lenny said, "you got a bowl we could give the dog? I don't want to let her out in the heat without any water."

"Hell, bring her in here," Mal said. "I got a nice big fan she can sit in front of. Come on, princess."

I started, wondering how he knew Howie's old nickname for me, but quickly realized he was talking to Queenie.

Shaken, I followed Mal—who veered to the right as he walked but somehow avoided running into anything—into his domain, Lenny clumping along behind me. When I got through the door

I stopped in my tracks so fast Lenny gave me a flat tire. As I fixed my shoe I gazed at the room, awestruck.

The garage was as big as my largest barn, about eighty by a hundred twenty, and was filled end to end with bikes. Old, new, in pieces. Harleys, Indians, piles of parts, unidentifiable wrecks. I'd never seen so many bikes in one place in my entire life.

"Kinda makes you want to pray, don't it?" Mal said.

I turned to Lenny. "I take it this is where that heap back at the Barn came from."

Mal laughed again. "Ain't pretty, is she? But she'll get you where you need to go until yours is back on the road."

"Lenny told you my story?"

"Enough of it." He gave me what I interpreted as a sympathetic look, but it was so quick I could've been mistaken. He veered farther right, gesturing me forward. "Here's what you came for."

Two perfectly straight and relatively unscathed forks lay on a work table. Mal flicked a rag over them and stood back. "Not show pieces, but as good as they come health-wise."

I checked them out. Nothing a good buffing and a coat of polish wouldn't fix. The one on the right had one small dinger I didn't like, so I pointed at the other.

"I'll take that one. What do I owe you?"

He gave me a figure and I pulled out the cash I'd gotten at the ATM on the way. It hurt to part with the bills, but the pain dwindled when I reminded myself I was one big step closer to having a ride-able bike. Besides, there was still a chance insurance would come through for it, seeing how the accident wasn't my fault.

Mal reached over to grab a receipt from a drawer and the sleeve on his T-shirt rode up, exposing his biceps and the diamond-shaped tattoo emblazoned there. I blinked with surprise, wondering if Lenny had known about it. Any self-respecting biker would recognize the tattoo—a diamond surrounding the number one. If Lenny and Mal had been friends for so long, I figured Lenny'd have to know Mal was, or had been, a one-percenter. I also wondered why, if Lenny was so against one-percenters, he was doing business with this guy. Lenny didn't have that tattoo. I would've noticed.

Mal finished scribbling the receipt and handed it to me. I dragged my gaze from his tattoo and tried to keep questions out of my eyes.

"Have a look around, if you want," Mal said.

I glanced over to see if Lenny would follow, but he sat down with Queenie in front of the big fan and leaned against the wall, closing his eyes and clasping his hands over his stomach. It didn't look like he was worried about my safety with Mal, although that could have been because Mal was as old as my great-grandfather and on a good day I could go a round or two with The Rock, rather than that he thought Mal was a real upright kind of guy.

Seeing how I didn't want to interrupt Lenny's beauty sleep and I really was curious, I took Mal up on his offer to browse. Walking down the rows of bikes, Mal following, I marveled at the sheer volume of his stock and the amount of money the collection represented. I hoped his insurance was up to date. I stopped at a pretty group of white Harley Police Specials.

"Where'd these beauties come from?" I asked.

"Precinct was getting a fleet fitted with the new engine," Mal said. He took a swig of JD. "Parts on these are too old to fit the new bikes, so I got this bunch real cheap. Guy on the force owed me a favor."

He showed me a smile I was afraid to read too closely, and I moved on. I oohed and aahed over a beautiful Indian, laughed along with him at a Wide Glide with a naked woman painted on the tank, and took a test seat on a lovely Heritage Softtail before coming to a bike that was as ugly as the one Lenny had gotten for me.

"Sister to the one you got," Mal said, grinning. "Came from the same police sale. The Man took 'em from a coupl'a small-time drug dealers he busted a ways back. Good for parts or for a pinch like you're in."

"Yeah, it's real nice for Lenny to find me a scooter."

"Heart o' gold."

We were at the opposite end of the building from Lenny and the fan would drown out anything we said, so I took a chance and asked Mal how he knew Lenny.

"Rode together for years," Mal said. "Like a brother to me." He saw the look on my face. "Okay, like a son."

I figured I wouldn't push it.

He got a faraway look in his eyes, and a little smile creased his wrinkles. "Had me a sweet little lady then. Most beautiful gal I ever owned. Shame she didn't age as well as I'd hoped. Wife finally said she'd dump me if I didn't get rid of her."

I bristled, his attitude offensive, even for an old-timer.

"Shiny little Sporty," he said, sighing. "Red and black, just the right amount of leather and chrome."

I almost laughed out loud, but was afraid to break his spell.

"Had me a right good line of rides after her," Mal said. "But none came close to her place in my heart." He pounded the fist with the cigar gently on his chest.

"Lenny rode a real beast back then, as I recall," he said. "Chopped almost to the frame, it was." He shook his head. "Glad his taste has gotten better over the years."

"You guys ride with a local club?"

His head snapped toward me, and he came back to the present.

"Yeah, yeah." He waved his hand, scattering cigar ash. "A local club." He turned abruptly and started veering back toward the other end of the building. "We had a good time, while it lasted. You take your time, look at whatever you want."

He angled his way toward Lenny and eased down beside him. Lenny's eyes opened and I saw the same worry he'd had when we left the Biker Barn. His little snooze hadn't helped anything.

I meandered back toward them, taking my time, since they had immediately gotten involved in what looked like an intense and personal discussion. I hoped I hadn't caused it by inquiring into Lenny's background.

I was down to the front end of the building, checking out a scary-looking chopper and trying to ignore the guys, when Mal's voice echoed through the building.

"My God, Hammer, you're shittin' me!"

I glanced up sharply, only to see Lenny making gestures to Mal to keep it down. I frowned to myself. I didn't like Lenny keeping secrets from me.

I headed back down the aisle, keeping the guys in view, and Lenny shot me an uneasy glance. Mal's face had gone white, and his hand clenched around his bottle.

"Len?" I said.

He closed his eyes and shook his head, sighing deeply.

"Okay, brother," he said to Mal. "We gotta go."

Mal looked up at Lenny, his eyes blank. "What?"

Lenny enunciated very clearly. "We have to go."

Mal looked up at me then, and his eyes focused. "My goodness, where are my manners?" He pushed himself up from the floor and tried to smile, but his easygoing manner now seemed forced.

Lenny looked at the floor, running his hands through his mane. "You're never gonna die, are you, old friend?"

Mal smiled. "Lord willing, my man, I'll be around another fifty years." Again, the attempt at light-heartedness didn't work.

Lenny held out his hand and Mal gave it one of those shakes where you grab the other guy's wrist instead of his hand, and they looked each other straight in the eye.

"You take care, now, Sweetheart," Lenny said. "And thanks for helping out my friend here."

Mal saluted with his Jack Daniels hand. "Anything for you, buddy. I mean that."

Lenny went to the counter and hoisted the fork over his shoulder, heading for the door.

"Thanks, Mal," I said.

"You got it, baby."

I waited, but his eyes didn't rise to meet mine.

Chapter Twenty-two

"I need ice cream," I said.

"What?" Lenny gazed dully at me from the passenger seat. He'd been comatose most of the trip back, Queenie whining intermittently and sniffing his chin. I wanted to know what was going on with him, and if I took him back to work, he'd split as soon as we got there.

"And I need it here." I swung into the parking lot of an ice cream stand a few miles from the Barn. It had been around as long as I could remember, a popular spot, the surrounding grass peppered with picnic tables and overshadowed by big trees. A haven amid the hustle and bustle of suburbia.

"I don't want ice cream," Lenny said.

I hopped out of the truck, and Queenie bounded out behind me. I knew Lenny would follow if I ignored him.

I was right. By the time I picked a line—the shorter of the two—he was behind me, staring blankly at the placard listing 33 flavors.

The picnic area was filled with kids and moms, some more messy than others. A favorite hang-out after school, I guessed.

Moms to the front and side of us in the line glanced nervously our way, clutching their children to their khakis. I tried to shut them out, but it was hard, seeing as how they were leaving a circular hay bale's space around us.

Our order was finally taken and scooped by a sullen-looking teen with a ring through her nose—probably the reason our line was shorter than the other—and we carried our ice cream toward a picnic table. The table we headed for sat in the middle of three others filled with loud, sticky kids. Not ideal for a serious conversation, but it would have to do. It was too hot to sit in the truck to eat.

We were several yards away when I noticed the quiet. The shrieking of kids had stopped as moms directed wide-eyed stares our way. The children obviously felt the tension and studied Lenny and me with frank curiosity. The moms' looks weren't so innocent.

One mom in particular, situated at the next table over, pinned us with accusing eyes. Lenny hesitated, but I kept walking. I sat, watching the mom's face as she took in Lenny's beard, tattoos, and Harley shirt. She moved her gaze to me, and when we made eye contact you would've thought I'd threatened to rape her and eat her children. Never has ice cream been consumed so fast or such a mess left as remained in her wake.

We soon found ourselves alone.

Lenny finally continued toward the table and dropped onto the bench. I listened for sounds of wood splintering, but, miraculously, the wood held.

"At least it's quieter," I said.

Lenny looked at me with such puppy dog eyes I almost gave in and took him home. I contemplated my sundae while trying to think of something comforting to say. "Lenny—"

"I don't want to hear it."

"Fine."

We dug in, me eating my hot fudge sundae, Lenny devouring his five-dip banana split. For not wanting ice cream, what he'd gotten seemed more than adequate.

I'd put the last spoonful in my mouth when Lenny said, "You remember your dad?"

I swallowed. "My dad?" I rested my elbows on the table and thought about the man in the picture on my desk. "I have some vague recollections. Images. But I was only three when he died. Some of the stuff I don't know if I really remember, or have just seen pictures. You know."

Lenny smooshed some ice cream with his spoon and swirled it with strawberry topping. "How'd you get by?"

I shrugged. "Mom took over the farm. Dad had life insurance. We survived." Just like Lucy and Tess were learning to do.

"I don't mean money. I mean not having a dad while you grew up."

Queenie thrust her nose onto my lap and I traced my fingers around her eyes. "I had Howie."

"Well, yeah, but he wasn't your dad."

"Says who?"

He sat back. "Huh?"

"If Dad had lived, it would've been different. But he didn't. Howie kind of…took over. Taught me all the stuff my dad would've taught me. Introduced me to tractors and lawnmowers and wrenches. Gave me a hard time about boys…." My voice trembled. I swung my leg over the bench and walked toward the nearest waste can. I tossed my trash toward it, but it banked off the edge and landed in the gravel.

"Not enough arc," someone said.

Nose-ring girl smirked at me from about twenty feet away, then bent under a picnic table to pick up a dirty napkin. I glanced toward the building and saw that the lines had dwindled to just a few people.

She stood up and wrinkled her nose at the empty tables. "Don't let the asshole moms bother you."

I jerked my chin toward her nose. "They don't like you either, huh?"

"Not hardly." She laughed. "Only reason I got the job is my uncle owns the place. Said if I start losing him business, it might be good. Get some friendlier customers coming."

"Sounds like a good guy. If not the wisest businessman."

"Eh. He doesn't need the money. This is just a hobby." She tossed the wadded-up napkin at the wastebasket and made it in. She held up her arms. "Three points."

When I got back to our table, Lenny was staring at his melting ice cream.

"Why do you want to know about my dad all of a sudden?" I asked.

He started, like I'd scared him, then frowned. "Just wondered if you remembered him, that's all. I didn't mean to make you think about Howie."

I put my hands on my hips and rolled my neck, trying to ease out tension. "I think about him all the time, Len. Besides, talking about him's supposed to make me feel better, according to my doctor." I pointed at his sundae. "You going to eat that, or not?"

"Not." He pushed the bowl to the side. "Can we go now? Before more kids and moms come to make us feel like shit?"

"Tell me first. What's the deal with Mal? He went weird on us after you guys were talking."

Lenny's eyes flashed. "He didn't go weird. Whatever that's supposed to mean."

"You guys were talking, and he basically freaked. Come on Len, I want to help, if I can."

Lenny lumbered up from his seat. "It's nothing. Really. Besides, you're the one who needs a hand these days, not me."

I sighed and placed a hand on my ribs, watching as he walked back to my truck, Queenie at his heels. He was right. I definitely did need a hand. But thinking about his problems was one temporary way to make mine go away.

Chapter Twenty-three

"Hey," Abe said. "Guess you didn't get my messages last night?"

I looked up from the filing cabinet to see Abe framed by the office door. "Sorry. A cow calved late and I didn't hear the message till this morning. Thought we could talk this afternoon."

"Sure."

I swiveled my chair around and gestured to visitor chair. "Want to sit?"

He hesitated. "Well, I…uh…not really."

We stared at each other awkwardly until I realized I was sitting where he usually worked. I jumped up. "Here. Here's your seat. I'll get out of your way."

I scooted around the desk. Abe hesitated, then sat down in the chair I'd vacated. I felt like an idiot, playing musical chairs, but I wasn't sure how to act. Talking about kisses and romance wasn't something I was adept at, or really wanted to do.

"Um, sorry I didn't call you back last night," I said.

"That's okay. I understand."

We stared at each other some more. And I fled.

I rushed down the hall and into the parlor, where Lucy was making preparations for the evening milking. She looked up from where she bent over a bucket of soapy water, then bent back down.

I watched her without speaking as I tried to breathe through my Abe-induced panic.

"Tess home?" I finally asked.

"She's up in the apartment doing her homework."

"Homework? At her age?"

"I know, it's crazy." She kept her face averted, and I'd reached my small talk quotient. I took another step toward the barnyard to let in the cows.

"You don't need to help," Lucy said. "You did the morning. And Zach's around somewhere, so he can give me a hand if I need it."

"Oh," I said. "Okay." I stumbled out of the barn, almost running into Zach.

"You okay?" he asked.

"I'm fine," I snapped. "Shouldn't you be working?"

Always a smart boy, he simply raised his eyebrows and let me pass.

At a loss, I stood in the middle of the drive, my arms hanging at my sides. Lucy was milking, with Zach to help. All of the other cows had been fed and watered. Queenie snoozed in her usual spot in the parlor. Abe hid in the office, probably as freaked out as I was. What was I supposed to do with myself?

I could've messed around with my new bike, or taken it out for a ride, but it wasn't registered or insured yet. Besides, it was so ugly I was going to have to get immune to it before I actually used it.

I also could've hung the photos in my office, but I didn't feel up to the emotions that would produce. Plus Abe was in there, and I certainly wasn't going to subject either of us to that again. Someday, maybe in a few years, I'd get around to those pictures.

I had finally decided to get something to eat when a movement around the back corner of the feed barn caught my eye. I stiffened. Who was back there messing around? I watched for another minute, seeing some moving shadows. I wished Queenie were outside to let me know what her take was. I hoped it wasn't yet another person trying to mess with Lucy. I guessed I'd better check it out.

At least I had something to do.

I walked toward the feed barn, making as much noise with my boots as I could, with the hopes of scaring away whatever it was. But when I stepped around the corner Tess looked up with surprise. I stopped and took a deep breath to calm my nerves.

"What's up?" I said. "Your mom thinks you're in the apartment doing homework."

She looked at me fearfully. "You're not going to tell her, are you?"

"Depends."

"I was petting the kittens. Look."

She held up the gray one—the runt of the litter born about six weeks before. Tess looked so small and vulnerable I decided I'd keep her secret.

"All right," I said. "I won't tell your mom. This time."

She smiled and looked like she wanted to ask something else, biting her lower lip.

"What?" I said.

"Can I…can I have the kitten?"

"Have them all. They're never-ending."

"Just this one. I could keep it in the apartment."

Seeing as how Queenie came in my house, I couldn't see myself being a usual landlord, adamant about the "no pets" business. Besides, Lucy and Tess were the ones living up there. When Howie was in residence I didn't step through the door for a period of almost twenty years. So what did I care if they had a cat?

"Fine. But the kitten really needs to stay with her mom a couple more weeks. You can play with her, but she'll need to go back to her mom every day."

Tess pouted. "How come?"

"She's just a baby. She still needs her mom's milk. Give her a little time, then you can take her inside for good. If your mom says it's okay."

"She won't care!" Tess picked up the kitten and started to skip away.

"What's her name?" I called after her.

"Smoky."

"Very nice."

She left me behind the feed barn, feeling stupid and even more useless. I walked back toward the house, where I really was going to get something to eat. But this time I was stopped by a car pulling into the drive. I angled toward it.

A woman stepped out of the late-model Chevy, watching Tess skip toward the garage. Once Tess had disappeared, the woman turned toward me and held out her hand.

"Anita Powell," she said. "Bucks County Children and Youth."

I shook her hand, but could feel the confusion on my face. "What can I do for you?"

"Are you Lucy Lapp?"

"No. Stella Crown. Lucy works for me."

"Can you take me to her, please?"

"What's this about?"

"I'm sorry, I really need to speak with her."

I stared at her, trying to read her face, if not her mind. Successful at neither, I turned toward the barn. "Come with me."

I led her to the parlor, where Lucy was switching a milker from one cow to another.

"Lucy?" I said. "Someone here to see you."

Lucy stood up and came toward us, while Zach peeked up over a cow's back, his face alight with curiosity.

"Lucy Lapp?" The woman put out her hand again. "Anita Powell. Bucks County Children and Youth."

Ignoring the woman's hand, Lucy looked at me. I shook my head, knowing no more than she did.

"What are you doing here?" Lucy asked her.

The woman pinched her lips together. "We had a call at the department saying we needed to check out your circumstances."

"What?"

"The caller said they were concerned for your daughter's well-being. Her safety and health."

Well-being. The same word my anonymous caller had used.

Lucy's face flushed a mottled red. "Who called you?"

"I'm sorry, I can't tell you that."

"Can't *tell* me—"

I put a hand on Lucy's arm, and she quieted.

"What exactly did this person say?" I asked.

Anita Powell looked at Lucy. "Is it okay to discuss this in front of your employer?"

Lucy's head swung back and forth from the woman to me, her face a mask of anger and fear. "Go ahead. I have no idea what you're here for."

The woman frowned. "We received a call that your daughter spends a lot of time unsupervised, that you live in a garage, and…." She glanced at me. "That you're still part of an open homicide investigation in Lancaster County."

"What?" If steam really came out of ears, Lucy would've been a dying combine, ready to blow.

I looked at the woman. "Have you substantiated any of this?"

She held up her hands. "That's why I'm here. To see what the conditions are. I am legally bound to follow up any allegations of neglect."

Lucy was still fuming. "Let me give you a tour of our garage, and you can see just how neglected my daughter is."

She stomped out of the parlor. Anita Powell and I followed, right to the base of the garage apartment steps.

"That," Lucy said, pointing to the ground floor, "is the garage. This," she gestured up the stairs, "is where we live."

She continued stomping, so that I was afraid the stairs might crack and fall down, but we made it up without demolition. Lucy threw open the door to find a startled Tess on the floor of the apartment, Smoky playing on the papers strewn around Tess' crossed knees.

Anita Powell took in the apartment, stepping into the room and glancing around. "No, I wouldn't say this is a garage." She smiled. "This is actually very nice. Cozy."

Lucy's face and shoulders relaxed a little, until the woman crouched down by Tess.

"Hi, Tess," she said. "I'm Anita."

Tess glanced up at Lucy, who nodded. The girl looked back at Anita.

Anita smiled at her. "I'm here to see where you live and how you're getting along. Do you like it?"

Tess nodded, but didn't say anything.

"Is this your kitten?"

Again, Tess' eyes shot toward Lucy, who raised her eyebrows.

"It is," I said. "I gave it to her ten minutes ago."

Lucy looked at me, and I shrugged. "She was going to ask you. She just didn't have time yet."

Anita turned back to Tess. "You've started school?"

Tess nodded. "Yesterday."

"You like it?"

"I have some friends now. I met them today."

"That's great." She stood up. "Okay if I peek around a minute?"

Lucy's face reddened again, but she waved for the woman to go ahead. Anita took a few steps into the kitchen, and again into the bathroom and bedroom. She came back to us.

"You sleep in the same bed?"

"We've only been here three nights," Lucy said. "We slept there one of those nights, and the other two I slept on the couch."

Anita nodded. "Okay. We can go back out now. I just want to ask you a few more questions." She squatted beside Tess again and said, "Thanks, Tess. You enjoy your kitten."

Tess smiled shyly. "I will. Her name's Smoky."

Anita patted the kitten's head, then stood up. "Shall we?"

The three of us trooped downstairs and stood under the shade of a hickory tree in the side yard.

"Everything looks great," Anita said. "Do you leave Tess unsupervised often?"

"Never," Lucy said. "She plays by herself some while I'm working, but I've never left the farm. If I would, I'd certainly have someone watch her. I've already met a teen-ager who would make a great baby-sitter. Now who called you and said these things?"

Anita made a face. "I'm sorry. Like I said, I can't disclose that. Here's what you can do, though." She pulled a notebook out of her pocket and scribbled on it. "This is the address for the Office of Children and Youth, the Department of Child Welfare in Harrisburg. You can write to them, asking that the referent be disclosed."

"And they'll tell me?"

"Depends. They'll contact the referent, and if that person is willing to be named, they'll tell you. If after forty-five days the referent declines to respond, the Department will write you a letter to that effect."

"Forty-five days?" I said. "That's ridiculous."

Anita grimaced. "The government is a slow-moving monster."

"And how about this open homicide investigation?" I asked.

Lucy sucked in her breath. "There's nothing to it. At all."

Anita regarded her sympathetically. "I understand your husband passed away not long ago?"

"Yes," Lucy said through her teeth. "He died. After an accident which left him paralyzed. There was no foul play involved. Ask the police."

"I intend to," Anita said. "In fact, I already put in a call to the Lancaster police. The detective in charge of the case was absent, but I'm sure he'll call me back when he can, and get this all cleared up."

"And until then?" I asked.

Anita smiled. "Until then, I see nothing here to be concerned about. I doubt I'll be back."

"But you'll let us know when you close this report?"

"I will."

"And what will you tell your caller?" Lucy spat. "To mind their own business?"

"I actually won't tell them anything. This report is confidential. If they call back, and if I've talked to the Lancaster detective by then to clear that up, I'll simply say there will be no more activity on this report."

"And if they're not satisfied?"

Anita smiled wider. "They'll have to be."

Lucy crossed her arms and looked at the ground.

"I'm really very sorry," Anita said. "This is one of the worst parts of my job, upsetting people like you. On the other hand, it's a good aspect, too, because I get to see children like your daughter who look healthy and happy." She opened her car door and got in. "I'll be in touch." She closed the door, started the car, and drove out the lane.

"Lucy…" I said.

"Don't," she said. "I don't want to hear it. Now, I'm going to do the milking. By myself."

I let her go.

Chapter Twenty-four

Detective Willard answered his line on the first ring. I sat back in my kitchen chair and scratched my leg, which suddenly burned with itching.

"Hey, Detective, it's Stella Crown."

"Ms. Crown, sorry I didn't call you back about that graffiti. I've been running ragged. In fact, I just got back from teaching a class, and I'm off to interview a fraud victim in five minutes. Or as long as our call takes. Did something else happen?"

"Nothing criminal. How's Brady?" Willard's son was a recovering victim of last month's food poisoning scare. It was partly my doing that he survived, and I had a keen interest in how he was faring.

"Doing great, thanks," Willard said. "Glad to be back in school. Besides the fact he almost died, the summer bored him. What's up with you? How are you healing?"

"Better now I have a farmhand again."

He was silent for a moment, probably thinking about Howie's death, which he investigated. "So you found someone."

"Yup. She's great. But she's also why I'm calling."

"How's that?"

"It's kind of awkward. I like her a lot, but there are some questions about her past that need to be answered. The graffiti we had was directed toward her, and now we had a social worker here saying Lucy might be part of an open homicide investigation. While I'd like to believe Lucy, I need to get this cleared up."

"And where do I come in?"

"Her husband had what someone seems to consider a suspicious fall about two and a half years ago. He became a quadriplegic and died a year afterward. I was wondering if you might be able to check up on the case for me. Find out what really happened."

"Where was this?"

"Lancaster."

He clicked his tongue as he thought. "I know a guy there. Went to the FBI academy with him. I can give it a shot. Why don't you give me the particulars?"

I told him Lucy's full name, and Brad's, and read him her old address, which was on the financial information Abe had handed me a few minutes earlier. We'd been very careful our hands hadn't touched.

Willard's computer keyboard pattered in the background as I spoke.

"Okay," he said. "Not sure how soon I can get this for you, but I'll see what I can come up with. I'll do some work on your vandalism, too. Maybe tomorrow morning."

"Thanks. I sure appreciate it."

"No problem. How are you healing up?"

I grunted. "Other than itching like I've got an arm and leg full of poison ivy, I'm doing pretty well."

He laughed. "Bring on the cortisone."

"A truck load of it."

I hung up and took a deep breath before turning to dig in my fridge. I was famished.

While I ate I watched out the window for any activity. Lucy came out of the barn and trotted up to the apartment, then came back down a few minutes later, Tess in hand. Lucy carried a cooler, which she took with them into the barn. Supper, probably.

By the time I was finishing my own food, Abe was leaving the barn and heading for his car. I swallowed my last bite, wondering if I should go out to talk with him. He stood for a moment, looking at the house, and I held my breath, wondering if he could see me in the window. Eventually he opened his car door, got in, and drove away. Crisis averted. For the moment, anyway.

I thought back five weeks, avoiding the painful subject of Howie and dwelling instead on the painful subject of Nick Hathaway. A gorgeous man I'd believed to be a barn painter, who'd turned out to be the furthest thing from it. A man who made my blood run hot just by being in the general vicinity. Who left me standing alone in my drive after a ferocious kiss. I hadn't heard from him since.

I pushed myself away from the table and stood up, hating myself for feeling lonely. For wanting someone other than Abe.

I had to get busy, or I'd drive myself crazy.

I succeeded in finding plenty to do during the evening that allowed Lucy her space—washing and folding a couple loads of laundry, changing the oil in my truck, giving Queenie a good brushing—and that kept my mind from traveling down dangerous paths. This time, I was grateful that life on a farm offers a non-ending list of chores, and my sore ribs and itching skin were other welcome distractions to keep my thoughts on the moments at hand.

I was asleep on the sofa when knocking startled me awake. The weather babe was busy pointing out some swirly patterns on the TV screen I couldn't decipher, and the ice in my birch beer had completely melted, causing condensation to slide down the glass and make a puddle on my coffee table. I didn't want to get up.

"Who is it?" I yelled.

The door opened.

"Just me," Abe said.

"Oh." I yawned, too tired to react to the sudden tightening in my stomach. "Come on in."

He stood at the end of the sofa, looking down at me. I glanced at the clock on the wall. Almost ten-thirty.

"It's late," I said. "What are you doing here?"

He shifted on his feet, then sat beside me. "Couldn't sleep. Not your problem, apparently."

"I've been up since five, Mister Nine-to-Fiver."

"Hey. I'm at least an eight-to-sevener with all the hours I put in here."

"So sorry."

"Yeah, right."

I laughed, but it sounded sleepy.

"Watching the news?" he asked.

I blinked. "Didn't mean to. Meant to go to bed an hour and a half ago. Guess I didn't make it there."

The weather gal was talking about a tropical storm making its way up the east coast. Remnants of that would probably hit us by late the next day. Great. Yet another thing to worry about.

We sat in silence for so long, watching the weather report turn into sports, that I started to drift off again. I woke up abruptly when Abe's arm slid around my shoulders. I shifted in my seat and looked at him. He didn't take his arm away.

"Darn it," he said. "I feel like I'm in high school again."

Abe's ex-girlfriend, Missy, had gone back to New York five weeks ago, the same time Nick had left. While I wasn't sure I was ready to take things beyond Abe's and my best friend status—no matter I was the one who rashly initiated that kiss yesterday—it seemed Abe felt five weeks was long enough to wait.

"Try to relax," he said.

Relax. Right.

A minute later I felt Abe's face doing something in my hair.

"Abe."

"Shh."

His mouth found its way down my cheek to my neck, and I realized I was tilting my head to give him better access. The arm around my shoulders tightened, and he turned his hips to face me. His free hand began to ruffle my hair, then moved down my neck to my shoulders and continued down my arm.

"Abe," I said again, but he silenced me by moving his mouth to mine. I was aware of every millimeter of our skin that was touching, and my mind rattled on hyper alert. I tried to give in to the kiss, but each moment led me into greater and greater panic, until I pushed myself away.

Abe blinked with surprise, his lips shiny in the dim light from the TV.

"I'm…I'm sorry, Abe, I just…."

"It's okay." He brushed my hair back with his fingers and looked into my eyes.

I turned to sit facing forward on the couch, and leaned my elbows on my knees, holding my head. "I'm sorry. I'm really tired. Exhausted, really, and…."

"Stop, Stella. It's *okay.*"

But it wasn't. It wasn't okay at all.

He left without saying another word, the door clicking shut quietly behind him.

Chapter Twenty-five

I had finally fallen asleep, my dreams filled with a strange mixture of Abe and Nick, when the phone shrilled at my ear. I sat straight up, heard the phone ring again, and snatched the receiver off the cradle. Bart's frantic voice came on the line.

"Stella! The cops are at Lenny's. I don't know what's going on, but his neighbor called me, and I know you know some of the cops, so I thought—."

I shook the receiver, as if doing so would calm Bart. Realizing the futility—and stupidity—of that, I said, "I'm coming," and hung up.

I eased out of my bed, gingerly pulled on some clothes, and headed out to my truck.

◇◇◇

The groan I heard sounded human, so I figured Davey Crockett was at least alive, if not awake.

Halfway to Lenny's I'd had the brainstorm that he might need a lawyer, so I screeched into a Wawa, found the phone book, and got Crockett's home number.

"It's Stella," I said.

"Who?"

"Come on, man, I saved your life the other day, remember?"

"Oh, yeah."

I heard him shifting around, probably sitting up.

"It's twelve-thirty," he said.

"It is. Remember the big red-haired guy who flattened Big Trey?"

He chuckled. "How could I forget?"

"Well, he needs you. I just got a call that cops are at his house."

"What for?"

"Don't know. But I thought this would be a good time to trade in our chips."

He sighed. "Okay. Just tell me where to go."

I got to Lenny's first and on Crockett's orders informed the first cop I came to that Lenny had representation and all questioning was supposed to halt until he got there. The cop gave me a full once-over, taking in my tattoos, jeans, and Harley T-shirt.

"If you think I'm kidding," I said, "you'd better believe you'll be sorry."

He turned and trotted up Lenny's sidewalk.

The block of rowhomes pulsed with police lights, making it look like a dance arena, and it seemed as if every light in Lenny's house was on. People were strewn all along the sidewalk looking at the house, their arms crossed, unhappy expressions on their faces. I wanted to tell them they should be glad they were just awake and not being harassed by cops, but I kept my mouth shut.

I pushed my way through the grumpy crowd toward Lenny's house, stretching my neck to see what was going on. A hand on my arm stopped me.

"You're one of Lenny's friends, right?"

A middle-class mom type stood in front of me, a housecoat covering what looked like floral silk jammies, her face anxious. She reminded me of the mom at the ice cream stand and I hardened defensively.

"Yeah," I said.

"Well, I don't know what's going on, but I heard through the grapevine they think this is a gang thing. That's more bullshit than I've heard in years. And I have four teen-age boys."

"Of course it is," I said, once I got over the surprise of those words coming from June Cleaver's mouth. "Lenny's a straight act."

"That's what I told the cop who came to my door. But they didn't care what I said."

Other neighbors drifted toward our conversation, and I could see they were in agreement with Mom. A weight lifted from my shoulders as I realized they were upset because Lenny was in trouble, not because the cops had wakened them.

"Stella!" Bart was suddenly by my side. "Come on."

I followed him, the crowd parting for us, up the walk to the front door. Once there, a cop stopped us at the door.

"He won't let me in," Bart said, jerking his thumb at the cop.

I turned to the cop and he shook his head.

"Detective Willard in there?" I asked.

The cop blinked. "Yeah."

"Tell him Stella Crown's here and wants to see Lenny."

His brows puckered. "What?"

"Good lord," Bart said.

"Just tell him," I said to the cop.

He shrugged, gestured to another cop to stand at the door, and disappeared into the house. About two minutes later Detective Willard was in the doorway.

"Stel—Ms. Crown? What are you doing here?"

"Lenny's a friend of mine," I said. "What's going on?"

He rubbed his face. "Come on in, then." He glanced at Bart, who moved to follow me.

"He's with me," I said.

Willard checked Bart out a bit more, taking in the hair and tattoos, then moved back into the house. We took that as an okay.

Lenny sat on his couch in shorts and a T-shirt, looking like he'd been yanked out of bed. His left cheekbone was swollen and red, and his arms rested, handcuffed, on his knees. An officer stood at attention on either end of the couch.

"Good grief, Willard," I said. "What are the shackles and the Queen's guard for? And I'll assume the shiner wasn't your doing."

"You know it wasn't. As far as the handcuffs, we didn't know what situation we were walking into. We had to be careful."

"Well, I vouch for him. He's a big teddy bear."

Lenny glared at me, even as Willard had an officer unlock the cuffs.

"What the hell do you want, woman?" Lenny said. "God, Bart, did you call the whole world?"

"You're welcome," I said as he rubbed his wrists. "Now what's going on?"

"A crock of shit, that's what," Bart said.

I looked at Willard.

He frowned. "We got a call about loud noises and yelling. The caller even thought he heard some shots."

"Shots?"

"Apparently Mr. Spruce here had some visitors tonight. We were afraid it was a gang problem."

Bart exploded with some kind of sound.

"Lenny?" I said. "In a gang?"

I'd always known Lenny had a checkered past, which had been explained a little bit more that afternoon when I'd met Mal Whitney. But as far as I knew from my own experience Lenny was a good friend, an honest businessman, and a die-hard teetotaler. Sure, I had some questions, like what exactly his connection was to one-percenters and outlaw biker clubs, and why his nickname was Hammer, but I wasn't about to ask them. It didn't matter to me. It never had.

But now I had a strong feeling those skanky people at the Biker Barn, the ones Lenny wouldn't tell me about, had played a big part in why the cops were here tonight.

Willard looked at Lenny and Lenny stood up, pushing his hands into his pockets and turning away. The cops by the sofa tensed and moved their hands toward their belts, but Willard stopped them with an irritated gesture.

"Hello there, Detective."

We all looked up at the new voice, and David S. Crockett, Esquire, came into the room, decked out in a suit and looking like a different man than on Sunday. He'd even shaved. Impressive for having just rolled out of bed.

Willard stood and offered his hand. "Mr. Crockett."

They shook, apparently having met before, and Crockett glanced around the room, taking in everyone who was present. He nodded at Bart, put down his briefcase, and walked over to Lenny, where they had a conversation the rest of us couldn't hear.

"This your doing?" Willard asked me.

I forced a smile. "Couldn't leave Lenny to the wolves, could I? Just like you, I didn't know what the situation was."

He grunted and sat back down in his chair. Crockett and Lenny left the window and settled on the sofa.

"You may continue your discussion with Mr. Spruce," Crockett said.

Willard smiled slightly. "Thank you, counselor." To Lenny, he said, "Did you recognize the people who broke into your house here tonight?"

Lenny shook his head, not making eye contact with anyone.

"You have any idea who might be behind it?"

Lenny shook his head again.

"Did you tell him about the break-in at the Barn?" I asked.

Lenny glared at me, and Bart made another unrecognizable sound.

Willard looked at me, then at Lenny.

"Someone tried to break into our business yesterday," Lenny finally said.

"Why didn't you report this?" Willard sounded annoyed.

"Because they didn't get in."

Willard's forehead became a mass of wrinkles. "Any idea who did *that?*"

I stared at Lenny, hoping my brain waves would convince him to tell the truth to Willard. It had to have something to do with that nasty couple we saw.

But Lenny just shook his head.

"Okay," Willard said. "Anything from your past that might give credence to the idea it was a gang fight tonight?"

Crockett whispered something in Lenny's ear and Lenny closed his eyes, obviously not happy. When he opened his eyes, he was looking at me.

"What?" I said.

Bart shuffled his feet, then burst out with, "Who cares, Len? She's going to find out sometime."

"Find out what?" I asked.

Bart opened his mouth, but Lenny beat him to it. "About twenty years ago I was part of an outlaw club."

I waited for more, but none came. "And?"

"That's not enough?"

"It's not exactly a surprise. And who cares what you used to be, anyway? That was a long time ago."

"Ties are never completely severed," one of the cops said, earning another glare from Willard.

"Bullshit," I said. "Just because Lenny used to be tight with criminals doesn't mean he is one."

"I'd have to agree with that," Crockett said, a smile tickling his lips.

Willard thought for a moment, then looked straight at Crockett. "The person who made the call tonight is afraid, justifiably. It's well known that gang ties are still strong even after someone's left the club, and the neighbors don't want their street getting shot up by gangbangers. If Lenny is one, they want to know."

I threw my hands in the air. "So much for second chances. And what about all those neighbors?" I pointed out the window. "I don't see *them* worrying about their safety. They're out there wanting to make sure Lenny's okay."

"Stella," Lenny said.

"What?"

He shook his head. "It doesn't matter."

"Are you involved in any illegal activity in your present life, Mr. Spruce?" Willard asked.

Crockett bent to talk to Lenny, but Lenny brushed him off. "Not a thing. I'm not involved in anything illegal. You can ask my lawyer."

Crockett laughed at that, as did Willard.

"I respect your lawyer," Willard said. "So I'll bear his opinions in mind."

He put away his pad. "There's not much more we can do, I'm afraid. Since you can't ID your attackers–"

Or *won't*, I thought, irritated.

"—and you have no idea who it could be, we really have nothing to go on. They were wearing gloves, you said?"

Lenny nodded. "Leather ones."

"Then it's no good fingerprinting anything, either. So try to have a good night, Mr. Spruce. I'd make sure to lock all my doors if I were you."

Willard tilted his head at the cops, and they filed out of the room.

I rounded on Lenny. "Are you crazy? Why didn't you tell him what you're afraid of?"

Crockett looked at Lenny with raised eyebrows. "What's this?"

Lenny stood and walked to the far side of the room. "I'm not afraid."

"Then you're a moron," I said. "You just got attacked in your own home. Assuming that's true."

He glared at me. "Of course it is."

"Then tell us who it was. I know you recognized them. It was those two from the Biker Barn, wasn't it?"

He shut his mouth, stubbornness etching itself all over his face.

Crockett stood, too, and put his hands on his hips. He lowered his head and stretched his neck from side to side. "Come on, Lenny. Tell us what you know. We can't help you otherwise."

Lenny crossed his arms and looked out the window.

"Fine," I said. "I'm going home. If these people come back and put a bullet in your head, don't come whining to me."

Bart's eyes widened. "Geez, Stella, don't bother to mince words or anything."

"Hey. I came over here to help. You know I'd do anything for Lenny. But if he refuses to help himself, there's nothing more I can do."

Crockett looked at Lenny. "That's true, you know. We'll do what we can, but you've got to come clean."

Lenny remained silent, staring outside.

"Okay," I said. "Call me when you get smarter."

"Stella!" Lenny called after me. "Please. Don't tell Lucy."

Too angry to respond, I stalked out of the room.

Chapter Twenty-six

I didn't even bother going to bed.

By the time I got home it was four-o'clock, and as soon as I gave Queenie some good loving and walked into the house I poured myself a big glass of orange juice and whipped up a batch of whole wheat pancakes. If I wasn't going to be granted sleep, I might as well fortify myself for the day ahead. Although the rage in my chest was enough to keep me going for a while.

I turned on the TV to keep me company and was brought up to date on the tropical storm headed up the seaboard and probably our way. I glanced out the window at the still-dark sky. Couldn't tell today's weather at this point, but at least it hadn't started raining and blowing yet. We'd see what the day brought.

By the time I'd eaten, the clock on the stove said it was four-fifty. Since I was tired and moving in sticky slow-motion, I got ready for milking, even though in reality I had a few minutes more to rest. If I started early I'd probably have things in order when the time came to pump the girls. The way my brain was working, I was afraid even with all my years at the job I might forget some part of the process.

Somehow I stumbled through work, and when Lucy showed up in the parlor after getting Tess on the bus I tried to keep my face hidden so she wouldn't see my exhaustion.

"What's up with you?" Lucy asked. "You look like you spent the night in the back of your truck."

So much for hiding.

"Couldn't sleep," I said. It wasn't a lie.

"Anything I can do?"

"Not right now, thanks."

"Sure you don't want me to finish up here?"

I looked at the vacant but dirty milking stalls and the cow pies on the concrete and decided I'd much rather take a break than shovel manure.

I jerked my chin toward the pitchfork and sank onto a bale of straw. "Thanks. You can change the station if you want. Don't know if classic rock is your style."

She smiled. "I'll listen to just about anything. And I love CCR."

I pushed myself off the straw and left her listening to "Around the Bend." Queenie seemed as tired as me since she had waited up the night before. She didn't bother to rise from her usual spot to follow me up to the house.

Before I knew it, I was awakened by a knock on the door for the second time in twelve hours, although this time I wasn't lying comfortably on the sofa. My neck felt like someone had sat on it, but at least I had pushed my orange juice out of the way before my head crashed onto the table.

"Yeah?" I croaked. I cleared my throat and called again.

Lucy came into the kitchen and raised her eyebrows. "Don't tell me this is where you've spent the whole morning."

She was dirty and sweaty, and when I looked at the clock I was shocked to see it was lunchtime.

"Sorry," I said. "Didn't mean to leave you out there on your own."

"No problem. Are you sure—"

The phone interrupted her. Afraid it was Abe, I let it go while Lucy and I stared at it. My voice mail clicked on and Bart started talking, his voice tinny through the machine's speaker. Trying to look nonchalant, I snatched the phone off the hook in the middle of a sentence mentioning last night and the police, and turned my back to Lucy.

"I'm here. What's going on?"

"Lenny's home sleeping, which is where I'd like to be, too, but somebody has to run the store."

"Poor baby."

"Oh, shut up. Anyway, I called to say thanks. I know Lenny appreciated what you did, even if he acted like a butt."

"I'll forgive him someday, I'm sure. Any idea when he'll be in?"

"He said after lunch. But I don't know if he'll want to see anybody."

"Even me?"

"Especially you."

"For heaven's sake, Bart, I don't understand why he's being so weird about—" Remembering Lucy, I clammed up.

"I know, I know. Just give him a little time."

"Whatever. Thanks for calling."

"Sure. Later."

I hung up the phone and took a second before turning back toward Lucy. She stared at me, hands on her hips, her eyes steely.

"Couldn't sleep, huh?" she said.

"It was the truth."

"What happened? Bart mentioned the police."

I shook my head. "Nothing I can tell you about."

She spun around and stomped toward the door.

"Come on, Lucy," I said. "You've only known the guy two days."

She paused, her back stiff, then continued out the door. I watched out the window as she ran up to her apartment, then back down. She pushed up the garage door and got in her car.

After five unsuccessful minutes of key-turning, she flooded the engine and laid her head on the steering wheel. I know this because I walked out to the garage and watched during the last bit of her swearing and beating the poor Taurus.

I went up to the driver's side door and leaned down to the window, not saying anything. Her face rested on her hands, and rivers of tears streamed through the dirt on her arms. I closed my eyes and said a small prayer. I'm not real good with crying females.

"You…you don't trust me," she snuffled. "All this stuff with Social Services, and that phone call, and the graffiti…you're starting to believe it."

I stood up and took a deep breath, feeling suddenly guilty about my call to Detective Willard. "Lucy…."

"I mean it," Lucy said. "I thought I was fitting in here. I thought you liked me. And I thought…I thought Lenny liked me."

"That's exactly what the problem is."

She looked up, her face blotched and red. "What do you mean?"

"I can't tell you what happened last night because Lenny needs to tell you himself, if he wants you to know. He'd kill me if I spilled the beans, because he cares too much what you think."

Her face brightened, and she sat back. "Really?"

"He's embarrassed. And afraid." As I said it, I realized that was why he was upset with me, too. It wasn't because I was butting in, but rather because he didn't want me to think less of him. Ridiculous.

Lucy sniffed and wiped her face with her T-shirt. "Should I go see him?"

"Bart said Lenny'd be in after lunch. Why don't you wait till then, and give a call. If he wants to see you, I'll drive you over if your car still isn't working." The thought flashed through my mind that she could take Howie's truck, but I wasn't ready to relinquish the last of his possessions to her. Besides, if I drove I might get to see Lenny, too.

"Okay." Lucy left the key in the ignition of the car, which didn't seem too risky, seeing as how it wasn't starting, anyway.

"Come on," I said. "Let's get back to work."

Chapter Twenty-seven

When Lucy called, Bart didn't even bother asking Lenny if he'd see her—he knew the answer would be no. Bart said she should just come to the shop, and once Lenny saw her it'd be too late for him to do anything about it. So Lucy took a shower and I taxied her over to the Biker Barn. I went into the shop first, after I'd introduced her to Bart.

"Len?" I said.

He looked up from behind a beautiful blue and silver 1996 Road King and several emotions flashed across his face.

"It's me, Lenny," I said. "Not the Christian Women's League."

He went back to work, not saying anything. But two could play that game. I sat on a stool and waited him out.

Finally, he looked up and sighed. "You're not going away, are you?"

"Eventually. Want to tell me anything?"

"You already know more than I like. You want to tell *me* anything?"

"Oh, come on, Lenny. What do you think I'm going to say? That I feel differently about you? That I don't want to ride with you anymore? Is that what you want?"

He studied his hands, his face like a little boy's.

"Cut me some slack here, Len. I'm not the ice cream mom. I don't care about twenty years ago. Any checkers in your past are off the board as far as I'm concerned. So stop this shy schoolboy routine. It makes me want to barf."

He looked at the floor some more, then finally grinned. "I wasn't sure. But seeing as how you're mouthing off as usual, I guess I haven't scared you too much."

I rolled my eyes and got off the stool. "You're about as scary as my newborn calf." I headed toward the door and pushed it open. "And now you've got another visitor."

He looked apprehensive. "Who?"

"And don't bite my head off. I didn't tell her a thing."

His eyes narrowed, then widened as Lucy slid in the door. He shot me one last desperate look and I left them alone.

"Okay, Bart," I said. "They're all yours."

"That's a joke, right?"

"Sure. You guys just make sure she's home sometime before evening milking, okay?"

He made his hand into a gun and pointed it at me, cocking his thumb. I had just decided to ask him if he knew Lenny's friend Mal Whitney when a couple of guys from our HOG club came in the door. It didn't seem right to talk about Lenny's problems in front of them, so I swung out the door, promising myself I'd check up on the guys later.

<><><>

I had assured Lucy it was okay if she wasn't home when Tess got off the bus, so at three-fifteen I whistled for Queenie and went out to the end of the lane, wondering what to tell Tess about her mother's whereabouts. I wasn't sure how Tess would feel about Lucy being with Lenny.

When the bus pulled up I immediately flew back fifteen years to before I had my license. I had started driving to school as soon as I could because I didn't have a lot of friends on the bus. I was never sure if that was because I was a farm girl or because the Granger boys had made it clear what would happen to people who messed with me. But then, my personality isn't exactly the homecoming queen type, either.

My mother was still around during my school bus days, her breast cancer not claiming her until I was a legal driver, and she would often have something wonderful and unhealthy to eat when I got home and trudged up the lane. Nice big cookies and fresh milk, or maybe a warm loaf of bread drenched in real butter.

The bus' door made its usual whooshing sound as it opened, snapping me out of my memories, and Tess jumped with both feet off the bottom step. The driver waved and turned off her flashing red lights once Tess was safely in the drive.

"Where's Mom?" Tess asked.

"Um, had to go somewhere."

"Okay. I had orange pudding for lunch today."

I blinked. So much for coming up with an elaborate excuse about Lucy.

"And a hamburger made out of *beans*."

I laughed and watched as Tess skipped up the lane. Queenie yipped and did her own little trot, keeping up with the girl, who was still talking.

"We played kickball at morning recess, then in the afternoon they taught me four-square. You ever played that?"

I opened my mouth to reply, but she continued.

"A fourth-grader named Belinda said I have a long lifeline. She could tell just by looking at my hand. And I'm going to have lots of kids."

"Wow."

We got to the garage, where Smoky was waiting under the stairs. Tess scooped Smoky into her arms, nuzzling the kitten's neck, then set her on the steps. She jumped with both feet onto the first step, which scared the kitten so badly she sprinted to the landing, her tail expanded to twice its normal size. Tess took her time jumping, holding onto the railing, and finally made it to the top.

Once inside the apartment, I helped her cut some chunks of cheese to eat with crackers, poured her a lemonade, and settled her on the sofa.

"Okay," I said. "I have to get back to work. I'll check in once in a while. Promise to be good?"

She grinned. "I promise."

"Okay." I wondered if there was something else I should do, but figured she was old enough to stay out of trouble if she wanted to. Besides, with her snack and her cat she had the next few minutes filled, at least.

I left her, and spent the next while trimming hooves on a couple of cows who needed a manicure. I tied them to a silver maple in the side yard where I could work in the shade and they could lie down while waiting their turn. The sky had turned overcast, and I hoped I could finish up the job before the rain started.

Zach soon came riding in on his bicycle and after parking it sat down on the grass with Queenie.

"What's going on?" he asked.

"Lucy's at the Biker Barn, Tess is in the apartment, I just got started here. You want to take some hay around to the heifers?"

"Sure. In a minute."

After finishing the first cow, I left Zach and Queenie tussling and meandered toward the garage to check on Tess. She wasn't in the apartment, so I headed back out to see where she was hiding.

I found her around the side of the garage in the long grass, playing with Smoky. The only reason I could locate her among the weeds was that I heard her crooning to the kitten. On either side of her, outdated and unused equipment sat rusting in the tall brush, looming over her.

"Doin' all right?" I asked.

She smiled up at me. "Isn't she the greatest?" She held up her kitten, who looked like any other barn cat to me.

"She's gorgeous. Be careful of this old equipment, okay? Don't go climbing around on it."

She glanced up at it like it had never crossed her mind. "I won't."

We both turned as Queenie started to bark, and a huge pick-up drove in the lane. I was surprised to see the brand-new-shiny Silverado pull up beside Zach, and even more surprised to see the well-tailored and handsome man who got out of it. He looked about six-three, a hundred eighty, and none of it bulged where it shouldn't. His dark hair was trimmed into a sharp GQ cut, and he had a deftly trimmed mustache to match. I sighed and wondered what lawyer needed something from me this time.

"Uncle Scott!" Tess shrieked.

His head jerked our way, and Tess bounded out from the long grass toward the man. He reached out and she leapt into his arms, laughing. His smile grew wider as he spun her around, and when he finally stopped, he aimed the smile at me. It was a nice smile, but it stopped before it reached his eyes. The sadness there overtook any joy.

"Hi," I said. "I guess you're Uncle Scott."

"That's me. So you've heard the name?"

I shook my head. "Just now."

His face dropped. "I see."

"But then, they have only been here a few days. We haven't talked about a whole lot of personal things yet."

This seemed to appease him a little, and he set Tess gently on the ground, ruffling her hair.

"So how are you an uncle?" I asked. "You Lucy's brother?"

His face contorted briefly. "No. Brad's."

"This is Queenie!" Tess chirped, standing by the collie. "Isn't she great? And I have a kitten, too! And this is Zach."

"Really?" Scott's smile emerged again for a moment, but disappeared quickly, his eyes darting toward Zach, who sat with a look of confusion on his face. Scott stood, hands on his hips, and looked around at the farm. He pointed at the garage. "So that's where Tess is staying? In the garage?"

I grunted with frustration. What was this bizarre fixation with Tess and Lucy's living arrangements? "There is a full apartment on the second floor. Indoor plumbing and everything."

He seemed to miss the sarcasm in my voice as he nodded gravely. "And where's my dear sister-in-law?"

I frowned. I didn't like his tone of voice. "She's not here at the moment."

"And she left Tess alone?"

I stared at him. "Does it look like she's alone? Last time I checked I was capable of taking care of an eight-year-old."

He glanced at me. "Sorry. Just want to make sure everything's good for my niece."

"Everything's fine."

"I hear Lucy found a church already," Scott said.

"They attended one on Sunday. Seemed to like it."

"Sellersville." It was a statement, made with feeling.

"You have a problem with them?"

He blew air out his nose. "Several. So you don't go there?"

"When I go anywhere."

He looked at me. "You're not a regular church-goer?"

I gave a small smile. "And that matters because...."

"Just wondered what kind of environment Lucy chose to work in."

"I can assure you we don't go in for raucous parties and fornication."

He gaped at me, then at Tess, mortified. Like Tess would understand the word "fornication."

I glanced out the lane, hoping to see Lucy coming down it. "Lucy should be home before too long, if you want to wait."

He shrugged. "I really can't stay. I was in the area doing business at Hatfield Meats, but I have to get back home to my own kids."

"You're in the hog business?" I knew there was no way a pig was getting within a mile of his fancy truck.

"Administrative."

Ah. "Well, I'll be sure to tell Lucy you stopped by."

"Yeah. You do that." He knelt and spoke to Tess. "You come home and visit soon, okay pumpkin? We miss you."

She flung her arms around him, tears filling her eyes. "You're leaving already?"

"Gotta go, sweetheart. But I'll be back." This last statement he said to me, and I wondered at its meaning.

"You're welcome anytime," I said. "I'm sure Lucy will be sorry she missed you."

He grunted a laugh. "Yeah, I'm sure."

With one last kiss on Tess' head, he climbed back into his truck and left.

A tear made its way down Tess' cheek.

"You miss your old home?" I asked.

She nodded and wiped her face on her sleeve. "And Gramma and Grampa."

"The ones that were here the other day?"

She shook her head. "Not them. The other ones."

Lucy's folks. I was surprised we hadn't seen them yet, seeing how the in-laws kept popping up.

"You seem to like your Uncle Scott."

She nodded. "I was at his house a lot."

"With your cousins?"

"Yeah." This was a whisper.

I sent Zach a desperate look, and he stood. "Hey, Tess. Want to help me take hay down to the heifers?"

She bit her lip, stemming the tears. "Yeah."

"All right. Come on. You too, Queenie!"

The three of them headed off toward their chores.

"Zach," I called after them. "Thanks."

He looked back. "Anything for you. Remember? You're my only woman."

Chapter Twenty-eight

A half hour later I finished up with the cows and let them loose in the paddock. When I stepped into the office the light on my phone was flashing again. I pushed play, and heard Detective Willard's voice telling me to call him. I got him at his desk.

"Found out a few things about your employee," he said. "I was able to get a hold of the lead investigator in Lancaster, a Detective Collins, for the case. He said he was never quite sure what to make of Mr. Lapp's fall. He didn't have enough to call it foul play, but he never came up with a satisfying answer as to what happened. Your employee and her husband were quite vague when they were questioned afterward. Both said Mr. Lapp was carrying some big boxes and tripped. Neither one offered any more, or any less. Like they had planned out exactly what to say."

"Or like that's what really happened."

"Sure. Except there was nothing to indicate there'd been anything to make Mr. Lapp trip. Unless it was just his feet, which we all know is a possibility. When the medical people arrived they weren't concerned about preserving the scene—they were concerned about preserving Mr. Lapp's life. From what they observed, his body position backs up a fall, but could give no indication whether or not he was pushed."

"So the cops didn't blame Lucy, or try to prove a case against her?"

"They checked out every avenue. The most suspicious thing was the large life insurance policy taken out on Mr. Lapp only seven months before. But your employee got a policy, too. From talking to family and friends they found there were certainly some disagreements over religion. Mrs. Lapp had actually stopped going to church with her husband, and tried to keep their daughter at home, as well. She also was fighting to take their daughter out of her private school."

I remembered Lucy's face when I'd mentioned Mennonite schools. She had no love for them. At least the one in Lancaster.

"What about other people?" I asked. "Either Lucy or her husband involved in any affairs?"

"Nothing they could find at the time of the accident. When Mr. Lapp died, however, there was some talk of another man."

Noah? I wondered.

"But," Willard continued, "Mr. Lapp's death was pretty straightforward—no talk of foul play there. So Collins couldn't in good conscience go after Mrs. Lapp's current relationships."

An affair while her husband was confined to a wheelchair? Unseemly, but understandable. And not something I really wanted to know.

"The papers mentioned drugs," I said. "Like Brad had been under the influence when he'd fallen. Any truth to that?"

"None. They ran blood tests right after the accident and found nothing suspicious. He was totally clean. And he had no history of drug use at all. Didn't even drink."

At least they had sure answers about something.

"Well, thanks. I appreciate your looking into it."

"You're welcome, but I'm not quite done."

I froze at the sound of his voice. "What?"

"There were some people who made no bones about trying to throw suspicion your employee's way."

"What? Who?"

"Her in-laws. They were quite adamant about getting the real story. Brad was hiding something, they said, and they were positive Lucy was, too. They were convinced Lucy had pushed him, but Brad wasn't about to turn her in. Of course he wouldn't, they said. He knew she could finish him off in a heartbeat, if he told. A pillow, an overdose, whatever she wanted.

"So the cops were relentless in their investigation. They looked at the families, too—Mr. *and* Mrs. Lapp's. The only friction they found was over their church. You know how I mentioned your employee had stopped going? Seems she grew up in a much more progressive Mennonite environment, and Brad grew up old school. They'd been attending Brad's church, and the family—Brad's and Lucy's—knew there were some very hard feelings about the way some issues were handled."

I thought about Uncle Scott, who I'd just met. Tess surely loved him, and the affection in his eyes was plain. Affection for Tess, but not necessarily for Lucy. Brad's folks I wasn't so sure about, but just because they were conservative didn't mean they didn't have Tess' best interests at heart. And the woman from Children and Youth had shown up the day after their visit.

"The complaint to Social Services—any way you'd know if Brad's family initiated it?"

"Not something I could find out. But Detective Collins didn't sound surprised when I mentioned it."

"And telling the Children and Youth agent there's an open homicide investigation?"

"Bunch of hot air, really. Collins told me the case has been closed for two years. When Brad died, his family tried to bring it all up again, claiming Lucy made out very well financially, and that had been her goal from day one."

I bristled. "Ignoring, of course, the full-time nursing she'd done for her husband for a year since he fell."

"Grief can make people ignore a lot of things."

I swallowed.

"But," Willard said, "Detective Collins knew the investigation was going nowhere. Basically informed the Lapps they needed to salve their grief another way. Looks like they then took the avenue of trying to gain custody of Tess, saying now that Brad had died Lucy would want to move on to other things."

I thought back over the last few days. A call from the Lapps' minister saying Lucy was a trouble-maker, a visit from the in-laws to check out the place, and an investigation by the Bucks County Children and Youth. Now today, another visit from Brad's family. It couldn't be a coincidence. Whether or not they'd stoop to the offensive graffiti was another matter.

I looked out the window, hearing the rumble of Lenny's bike.

"Thanks for checking this out for me," I said. "I really appreciate it."

"No problem. I'm glad to help. About that graffiti, I was hoping to swing by this afternoon. That work okay? Your farm-hand will be around?"

"Getting home right now."

"I'll see you later, then, assuming this incoming storm doesn't give me too much extra work. By the way, did you talk with your friend Mr. Spruce today?"

I hesitated, glancing out the window to see Lenny parking the bike. "Yeah. Went and saw him at his shop."

"He okay?"

"Seems to be."

"Good. But why don't you see if you can get him to come clean with me? I know last night was a true break-in, but if he would tell me the truth, I might be able to prevent anything worse from happening."

I closed my eyes. So Willard had seen through Lenny's story. I should've known.

"I'll do my best, Detective," I said. "But I can't make any promises."

Chapter Twenty-nine

I glanced at the sky as Lenny stopped the bike to let Lucy slide off, and noticed the wind had risen dramatically since I'd gone inside. I was glad to see Zach and Tess coming up from the back field.

"Better get on home, Len," I said, "unless you want to weather the storm here."

He shook his head. "Promised Bart I'd be back soon. He has some church meeting this evening, and I said I'd cover for him at the shop. Open till eight, you know."

"Okay. Well, be safe."

He roared off, and Lucy watched him, a slight smile on her face.

"Had another visitor," I said.

She blanched. "Not Noah?"

"Nope. Uncle Scott."

She closed her eyes briefly, then glanced toward Zach and Tess, still fifty yards away. "Tess see him?"

"Sure. Gave him a huge hug, and cried when he left."

Lucy dipped her head, rubbing the back of her neck. "Sorry he came. My in-laws take every opportunity they can to cause me trouble."

I shrugged. "It was no trouble. Seemed like a nice enough guy."

I was hoping this might pull some information from Lucy, but she just shook her head and forced a smile when Tess got close.

"So you got to see Uncle Scott?" she asked.

Tess bobbed her head up and down. "For a few minutes. He had to go."

"He said he'd be back," I said.

Lucy's mouth formed a straight line, but any reply she was going to make was drowned out by a sudden gust of wind, accompanied by the beginnings of a rain shower.

"I'm going in to listen to my weather radio," I said. "This looks like tornado weather. I don't like it. Make sure the barn doors are closed and the windows are latched. Zach, help her out."

Lucy jogged away, but Zach stayed, Tess standing so close to him I was afraid he'd trip when he turned around.

"What about the cows?" Zach asked. "Should we get them inside?"

"They're fine. They'll naturally find the safest place. No reason to panic them by herding them in."

"And aren't we supposed to leave windows open in tornadoes?"

"A myth," I said. "Now go help."

He hustled off, Tess in tow, to do my bidding. I hurried into the kitchen and turned on my radio.

After a couple of irritating minutes of reports about tides and winds at the Jersey shore, the newscast got around to the local forecast.

"A tornado watch has been issued for the following counties until eleven-o'clock p.m.: Northampton, Lehigh, Berks, Montgomery, Bucks—" I snapped the radio off at the mention of our area and trotted back outside to help get things battened down. Queenie pranced around anxiously, yipping at the strong winds and spotty rainfall, and I reached down a hand to soothe her. I couldn't see Lucy and the kids, so I jogged to the feed barn on my own, making sure the windows and doors were latched. The garage was shut, as was Lucy's front door, but I noticed a few of her windows stood open. I still didn't see her, so I ran up the stairs, ribs aching, and entered the apartment.

Once I'd shut her windows I let myself out, only to find her coming up the stairs. She stopped short at the sight of me.

"Sorry," I said. "I didn't know where you were, and the windows were open."

Silently, she turned back around and waited at the base of the stairs. Zach and Tess both stood with Queenie, their hands entwined in her fur. The rain had stopped, and while the sky directly above us and to the southeast mulled black and threatening, the horizon shone with eerie pinkish-gray sunlight. The air went deadly still. A chill rushed through my body, and just as I took the first step down the apartment stairs the town's siren began to wail. The tornado watch had been upgraded to a tornado warning.

"Everybody inside!" I shouted. "Down to the basement!"

We ran.

The musty cellar was damp and chilled, and while Lucy hustled the kids to the far corner, I quickly emptied the canning shelves of the few fermenting bottles stored there so they wouldn't crash onto our heads. I stashed the jars on the floor and pulled a wooden table over to where the kids stood.

"Get under," I said.

"But Smoky's still outside," Tess said, her eyes filling.

"He'll be fine," Lucy said. "Cats are smart. Besides, his mama will take care of him."

Still anxious, Tess hunkered down beside Zach. The two of them fit snugly under the table, and Lucy and I huddled as close to them as we could. Queenie pressed against my legs, her whimper high and frightened. The wind outside began again, and rose in ferocity as we waited. I wished I had thought to bring my weather radio down with me. Zach trembled beside me, and I put out my hand to rest it on his back. Shrill whistling through the basement's windows added to the melee, and just when I thought it couldn't get any louder, something that sounded like a train came overhead, and smashes and booms reverberated as things hit the house.

We scrunched together, arms over our heads. I'm sure I wasn't the only one praying.

A long minute later the locomotive was gone, and I relaxed my grip around Zach's waist. Cautiously I stood and walked toward one of the windows. I peered out.

Thank God we were all okay and the house over our heads was still standing. But the feed barn and the garage—along with Lucy's apartment—were gone.

Chapter Thirty

We stood outside. None of us said anything. There was nothing to say that would have been meaningful. Where the garage and apartment had been was now a pile of wood and concrete. Lucy's car was somewhere underneath it.

The mature trees in my yard had been thrashed, huge limbs ripped off the thick trunks, branches falling onto other smaller trees, destroying them, too. My beautiful hickory, under which Howie's truck was parked, had been demolished, Howie's truck taking a good bit of the wood in its windows and now dented roof and hood.

The yard was littered with debris—branches, glass, leaves, roofing, downed wires. A disaster site.

I sank down to the step, afraid my legs would give out. Queenie huddled in front of me, but the other three remained where they were.

Fifteen minutes later Jethro and Belle came barreling in the drive, skidding to a stop at a wire that lay menacingly across the gravel. Jethro jumped out of the truck, careful not to touch the potentially lethal cord.

"You'se okay?" he yelled.

Zach made to run to him, but Lucy grabbed his arm. "Those wires, honey. Can't go over there just yet."

It took a few moments for my voice to work enough to respond to Jethro. "We're fine."

Belle rolled down her window. "We couldn't get through on the phone. Now we see why. I've got our cell. I'll call the electric company."

I put up a hand in thanks, and while she called, Jethro stood surveying the destruction. I rested my head on my forearms, a sudden sweat breaking over my body. It had been too close.

A half hour later I was still sitting on the step. Lucy had taken Tess into the house, Smoky in her arms, and Zach sat beside me. His shaking had stopped, but he was pale and quiet.

"Why don't you go in?" I said. "Get some water. Or something to eat."

He shook his head. "Not hungry."

I took a deep breath and let it out. "Me either."

The PP&L truck soon arrived, and the moment the workers declared the wire dead Jethro and Belle ran over to scoop Zach up in their arms. Jethro turned to hug me, but I threw my arms up, desperate to stay out of his crushing embrace.

"Oh, we're just so glad…" Belle said, her voice tapering off.

"But Lord," Jethro said. "Look at this place."

I couldn't look anymore, but I needed to check on the herd. I got up and walked away.

The milking cows were fine, having avoided any flying debris by huddling together in the long barn. The heifers, hunkered under the only tree in the back field, wandered around, mooing. But they were fine, too. And thanks to the protection of sturdy hutches—which thankfully hadn't blown away—the calves were all unhurt.

But once again I had been struck. All blood-fueled creatures were alive, but my trees….My yard….My feed barn and garage….

I stood dully staring out across my field when I felt a presence beside me.

"You okay?" Abe asked.

I shook my head. "Not really."

"Want to come home with me?"

"Can't. Got to milk the cows."

He was silent. "Guess that's right. Want some help?"

I closed my eyes and concentrated on my breathing. I had lost so much. Again. But Abe was still here, no matter how awkward things felt between us.

"Yes. I'd like some help," I finally said.

Together, we walked toward the barn. Zach, seeing where we were headed, made to follow, but I stopped him.

"Go home, Zach. You deserve a break after that."

"But—"

"We'll be okay. Abe'll stick around to help."

Zach glanced at Abe doubtfully, and Abe grinned. "I may not know the job like you, but I can follow orders as well as the next man."

Zach had to laugh at that.

By the time Lucy, Abe, and I got the cows clipped into their stalls and eating, the electric company had rigged up power to the barn. They know how vital electricity is to farmers, and seeing as how my generator was in the garage when it went, I was dependent on PP&L. Thank God they came through.

Halfway through milking Abe got a call on his cell phone. He handed it to me. "It's Lenny."

"Heard about the tornado and tracked down Abe's number," Lenny said. "You're all okay?"

"Yes."

"I'll be down in a jiffy."

"Not really anything for you to do," I said. "It's almost dark. We can't start cleaning up today anymore."

"It's not all about things," Lenny said, and he hung up. Ten minutes later, he was at the farm.

Lucy, who had shown no emotion whatsoever since I'd told her about Scott's visit, burst into tears as soon as Lenny dismounted his bike. He held her in his arms, and once she let it out she got back to business and we finished up the milking. Tess sat quietly in the corner, stroking Queenie.

"Come on, everybody," I said. "I think I have some frozen pizza."

"Uh uh," Abe said. "I'm getting Mexican. Anybody want to ride along to El Cactus?"

He and Tess were soon back with an array of chips, beans, and burritos, as well as some two-liter bottles of birch beer and Vernor's. By the time we had inhaled every bite I was feeling a bit more human, although I couldn't bear to look outside. Even in the dark I could see too much destruction.

We sat around the table, no one quite sure what to say.

"Well," Lucy finally said. "I guess I can't blame *this* on my in-laws."

We laughed too loud, for too long.

When we'd quieted, Abe said, "What now?"

"All I want to do," I said, "is go to bed."

Lucy stretched. "Sounds good."

And we stilled. Lucy no longer had a bed, and I'd been too dense to even consider what that meant.

Everyone stared at me, and my insides crumbled.

"Okay," I said. My voice cracked, so I cleared it and drank a few sips of soda. "Okay. I guess Lucy and Tess will just have to move in with me."

◇◇◇

Moving in took only the time we spent making the spare beds, seeing as how all Lucy and Tess owned had been destroyed. The two extra bedrooms took up almost as much room in my house as the entire apartment had encompassed above the garage.

Belle stopped by a little later, thrusting a bag of Mallory's hand-me-downs into Lucy's arms. "They might be a bit big," she said, "but they're clean."

Lucy hugged Belle, and when they separated, both women's eyes were shiny.

"How's Zach?" I asked.

Belle smiled, wiping her eyes. "Resilient. Went off to MYF."

"That's right," I said. "It is Wednesday, isn't it?"

"Willie—Zach's MYF sponsor—called when Zach hadn't shown up by seven, and when we told him what happened he thought maybe Zach would like to share his experience with the rest of the kids."

"Smart man. I bet Zach's feeling pretty important about now."

"Probably so."

"Tell him goodnight for me."

Belle left, and Tess was soon asleep. Lucy stood in the living room, shuffling her feet, Lenny beside her. I was sitting at the table, Abe in the chair next to me. My brain reeled. *What in the world was I going to do with housemates?*

"Come on, Lucy," Lenny said, earning my everlasting thanks. "Let's sit down in the other room for a bit, take a load off."

She looked at me. I could tell she was wondering how far to take feeling at home.

"You heard the man," I said. "Go put your feet up. Abe and I weren't going in there anyway."

Lucy gave me a grateful look and I watched them meander into the living room, as opposite a pair as you can get.

Abe cleared his throat. "Want me to stay?"

I closed my eyes. I had a girl upstairs in my childhood bedroom, a woman who would be taking yet another space, a friend who was there to see Lucy, not me, and a man who occupied a huge part of my heart, but not the part I had hoped.

"I don't think so, Abe," I said. "I really need to be alone."

Alone.

"I understand," he said. He leaned over to kiss the top of my head. "I'm glad you're okay." He walked toward the door.

"Abe," I said.

He stopped.

"Thanks."

He opened the door. "Anytime, Stella. I'll help you any way I can."

And he was gone.

I sat there, feeling sorry for myself, wondering why my decisions always came around to bite me in the ass. I had hired Lucy, feeling some kind of kinship with her, and now here I was, the epitome of independence, with two semi-permanent roommates. Wouldn't Howie be laughing now.

On the other hand…Tess was asleep, Abe was gone, and the two lovebirds were probably necking on the sofa. Or, more likely, collapsed out of exhaustion.

Nobody for me to cater to. I liked that.

I gave a long, audible sigh of something as close to contentment as possible under the circumstances, took a nice long shower and went to bed.

But not for long.

Lenny came slamming into my room sometime in the middle of the night, scaring the bejesus out of me.

"Holy crap, Lenny," I said. "You're in the wrong room."

"They got Bart," he said. "You gotta go."

He stumbled around the room like a drunk, wringing his hands. I shook my head to clear it.

"Who has Bart? And where am I going?"

"The hospital! And it's them, I know it is!"

He grabbed me by the armpits and hoisted me out of bed in my T-shirt and underwear. I batted his hands away and went searching for some jeans. Once I had them on, I turned on the light.

"Sit down," I ordered, pointing at the bed.

Surprisingly, he complied, the bedsprings screeching with protest.

"Now tell me what's going on," I said.

He let out what sounded like a sob. "Bart. Some of the guys from the club found him at the Barn. He was lying out back and he…he's not doing very well." He looked at me with pain in his eyes. "They *stabbed* him, Stella."

My heart skipped a beat. "Is he—"

"He's alive, but barely. The guys called the ambulance and he's in surgery right now. You've gotta go down there."

I had pulled on some boots while he was talking, so I was as dressed as I was going to be.

"Okay," I said. "Come on."

"I can't."

I stopped in the doorway and turned on him. "What do you mean, you can't? Your best friend is at death's door and you won't *go?*"

His face crumpled. "It was *me.* They were after *me.* The only reason they did Bart was because I wasn't there."

The door to Lucy's room opened, cutting off my reply, and she shuffled out, her face swollen with sleep. "What's going on?"

"I'm not sure. But stay with Len, will you? I've gotta go to the hospital and check on Bart, and Lenny's not doing so good."

She nodded, and after one last look to see if Lenny was following, I raced down the stairs and toward the hospital.

◇◇◇

Walking in the door of Grandview Hospital's emergency room took all the guts I had. Just five weeks before, I had entered only to find out Howie had died on the operating table. I prayed it wouldn't be the same this time.

Besides feeling traumatized because of Howie, I had to wonder if Bart's attackers were watching. Lenny was afraid to come because he thought they were after him, so he must think they would lure him here by getting at Bart.

The woman at the registration desk told me Bart was still in surgery and that someone would be out to let me know when he was finished. I didn't think that sounded good, the way she put it, but I took it at face value.

When I walked into the waiting room I had to push down a hysterical laugh when I saw Detective Willard camped out on one of the sofas. He was sleeping, snoring softly with his mouth hanging open. A couple of regulars from our HOG club were sitting in a corner playing cards. Thankfully, no creepy, suspicious-looking characters were hanging around. And the skanky couple from the Biker Barn was nowhere to be seen.

"Hey guys," I said.

My biker friends looked up guiltily, hands shielding their game.

"I don't care you're playing cards, you jerks," I said. "You saved Bart's life." I tried to keep my voice even, and I think I succeeded.

"Want to join us?" one asked.

"Nah. But thanks."

"Actually," the other one said, looking at his watch. "Now that someone else is here, I gotta get goin'. My shift starts in forty-five minutes."

For the first time, I glanced at the clock. One-fifteen. No wonder my head felt like it had been caught in a vice.

"That's fine, guys," I said. "I'll take over from here. I'll let you know when Bart can have visitors. Thanks again."

"Hey," one said. "He's a brother."

They gave me some kind of thumbs-up sign, but I couldn't seem to coordinate my hand to do it back. I parked myself on a chair somewhere close to Willard and leaned my head against the wall.

"We've got to quit meeting like this," Willard mumbled.

I opened my eyes and knew from the taste of my mouth that I'd been asleep. Willard still lay on the couch, but he was looking at me now, and he had stopped snoring. I glanced at the clock. Two forty-five.

"Heard anything yet?" I asked.

He shook his head. "This is the same guy that was at Lenny Spruce's house the other night, isn't it?"

"Bart Watts," I said.

"Bart Watts." He closed his eyes and sighed.

"Doesn't anybody else work for the police department?" I asked.

"Not in the borough I cover. I mean, there are officers, but I'm the only detective."

"How come you were at Lenny's the other night, then? That's out of your jurisdiction, isn't it?"

"Wouldn't you know their guy was on vacation? Disney World with the kids. And since nothing big ever happens in Perkasie, I figured I'd be safe saying yes."

"Guess you learned."

"Guess so. But if this is in any way connected, it's probably a good thing I caught both cases. Good for my job. Not good for my health."

Double doors at the end of the room swung open and I sprang to my feet. The surgeon saw us—the only two people in the waiting room—and came over, quiet in his little booties. I could tell by the look on his face that the news was different this visit, and the weight of a feed sack slid off my chest.

"Detective," the doctor said, nodding. He turned to me and pinched his lips together, taking in my tattoos, bed head, and Harley T-shirt. "Family?"

"Practically," I said.

Willard nodded. "She deserves to know."

The surgeon looked skeptical, but talked anyway. "He's going to be okay."

I hit my fist into my palm, making the doctor jump a few inches backward. Then I remembered Bart's religion and crossed myself on his behalf. The surgeon swallowed and kept talking, looking only at Willard.

"Most of the damage is non-life-threatening. Broken nose, a few broken teeth, lots of bruising and split skin. We put in multiple stitches, but we'll wait for a plastic surgeon until the patient can express his own wishes."

"He'll love some scars," I said.

"The worst injury," the doc continued, ignoring me, "is the knife wound. Missed his heart and aorta both by about an inch. He'll have quite a time recovering, but we're going to be able to put him back together most satisfactorily. We've still got some work ahead of us, but I wanted to let you know as soon as possible what his prognosis is."

Most satisfactorily. Quite different words from when Howie had been in the same ER.

"If I didn't have sleep breath," I said to the surgeon, "I'd kiss you."

He took a step away, then scuttled back into surgery. I squinted at Willard, who was grinning like a kid.

"What?" I said.

"Nothing." He grinned some more. "Nothing at all."

Chapter Thirty-one

When I got home, my headlights flashed across the drive, revealing Lenny's bike in the darkness. So he was still there. I hopped down from the truck, wincing slightly at the pain in my side, and walked briskly up the walk, eager to tell Lenny that Bart was going to be all right.

I remembered just in time not to slam the side door. It would take some getting used to, having to be careful about noises at night. I was sure Tess and Lucy would have to suffer through many mistakes before I got this living-together thing right. I hoped it wouldn't last long enough I'd get too used to it.

I found Lenny in the living room, crashed on the sofa. His mouth hung open, and he emitted soft snores. The blinds were all drawn and the room was shrouded in darkness. I turned on a lamp to see his arms crossed over his chest protectively.

"Len," I said. I shook his shoulder.

He started, his eyes opening wide and fearful. When he focused on my face, he sat up. "How—"

"He's okay, Len. Bart's going to be fine."

Tears welled in his eyes, and his face tightened, his mouth quivering. I patted his shoulder until he got himself under control. He pulled a handkerchief from his pocket to wipe his eyes and blow his nose.

"Thanks, Stella. Oh God, I never would've forgiven myself."

"I know. But now maybe it's time to tell Detective Willard what you know." I didn't add that a few words the other night might have saved Bart this attack.

"I don't know, Stella. We'll see."

"See what? How soon they come after you? Don't be an idiot. At least tell me. Who are these people? Why are they after you?"

He turned his face away, and I fought the desire to slap him. "Fine," I said. My voice sounded wooden. "What now?"

Still looking away, he asked, "What time is it?"

"Quarter after three."

He rested his head on the back of the couch, and his face, gray from worry and fatigue, sagged.

"Just stay here, Len," I said. "No reason for you to make the ride to your place. What's one more person in this house, anyway?" I tried out a laugh, but it didn't quite work.

He lay down on the couch, resting his arm on his eyes. I couldn't imagine the guilt he must be feeling.

But I could feel the anger building in me. Anger at Lenny—he should've told Willard what he knew; anger at the assholes who plunged their knives into Bart; and anger at myself. I knew a lot of what Lenny knew. I should've told Willard the night those jerks entered Lenny's house. And now, because of my silence, Bart lay bleeding and broken in the hospital.

I vowed that the next day I would either convince Lenny to spill his story to the detective, or I would do it. So to hedge my bets, I'd do some investigating to find out what Lenny wasn't telling me. It's not like one or two hours of sleep were going to do me any good, anyway.

I grabbed my keys from where I'd tossed them on the counter, and headed back out to my truck.

When I got to Lenny's house I did a ride-by, checking out the vehicles parked along the road. All foreign jobs, and no bikes. If his biker enemies were there, they hadn't ridden. And no outlaw would drive anything but American. My stop at the curb was far from graceful, and I hoped my tires had survived the bump.

I strode up the walk, but when I reached the front door I remembered I didn't have a key.

"Dammit," I said out loud.

I had to walk around the entire block to get to Lenny's garage, and I hesitated before entering the alley that ran behind the row-homes. For the second time that night, I broke out in a sweat. The alley would be a prime spot for someone to hide.

I made a fist around my keyring, arranging the key points between my fingers, so anyone jumping me would get a face full of metal. I took my first step in, wondering if I should go back and get the wrench from the glove compartment of my truck, when a gate from a backyard flew open. A man in an undershirt flung a garbage bag into a can, rattling it loud enough to wake any sleeping neighbors. He didn't see me, and turned right around and went back into his yard, his gate slapping closed behind him.

Once my heartbeat returned to normal, I eased through the rest of the alley. I made it to Lenny's garage without further incident, and found the house key in the nail drawer. As long as I'd known Lenny I'd never had to use his key. I couldn't even remember why I knew it was there.

The house was silent and smelled stuffy, as if it had been closed for weeks instead of part of a day. For a moment I felt guilty invading his home, but then remembered somebody was out to get him, and was hurting others in the process. It was time to find out what was going on, and if Lenny wasn't going to tell me, I was going to hunt it down myself.

I wandered into his living room, not sure what I was looking for. Where would Lenny keep details about his past or whatever was haunting him? I couldn't imagine him keeping a journal, writing secret, innermost thoughts every night before going to sleep. I also couldn't imagine an address book listing potential enemies. If he wanted to find somebody, he'd probably just start a chain reaction by telling one person, and soon the sought-after would show up at his door.

The room looked like any bachelor's living room. A TV and DVD player at one end, a stereo surrounding it, and a very sat-on sofa taking up most of the space. At one end of the sofa was a little table for necessities—a lamp, and a coaster for cold drinks. All that hung on the wall were a Harley-Davidson calendar—the kind without the bimbos, thank God—and a few photographs of Lenny and Bart at the Biker Barn.

I drifted into the next room, which was a kind of office. He didn't have a computer, but there was a desk and a filing cabinet, and not much else. I got through the top drawers of the filing cabinet—utility bills, insurance information, mortgage papers—and sensed I was looking in the wrong place. This was just paperwork, not anything meaningful. I stood up, stretched, and went back into the living room.

I dug around the entertainment center, finding only the things that should be there—DVDs, CDs, TV schedules from the newspaper—and turned to the end table, which had a cabinet in the bottom part. I opened the door and sucked in my breath. Just as in Howie's safe, here was a stash of photos. I pulled them out and sat on the sofa.

The first print on the pile showed Lenny with a woman and a little girl, probably about two years old. Lenny and the woman were standing on opposite sides of a bike with the little girl on the seat between them, looking terrorized by the flash. The woman, giving something resembling a smile, sparked some feeling of recognition in me, but I couldn't place her. It kind of gave me the creeps, though, looking at her.

But the person that was supposedly Lenny gave me the biggest shock. He was scraggly and unkempt, his bulk looking more like the unhealthy kind than just the big kind, his current build. He wore black jeans, an unrecognizable black T-shirt, and a jean jacket with the sleeves cut off, which looked like it had never been washed. The hair on the back of my neck rose. Outlaw clubs were notorious for their unwashed colors. Initiation into the ranks was accompanied by a mess of vomit, urine, and other disgusting things, and washing your vest was a serious enough offense to cause expulsion from the club.

What really got me was that underneath the filth and grime there was something I hadn't seen in him before. Something I wasn't sure I would have recognized if I hadn't seen Howie's picture of me with my father and mother when I was a toddler.

Family pride.

I sat back, feeling lightheaded. Lenny was a father?

Shaken, I took away that photo to look at the one beneath it. This photo was again of the woman and girl, but without Lenny this time. They were sitting on the steps of a front porch somewhere. It didn't look like this row home. While Lenny's current house was stone, the one in the picture was clad in what looked like dark, shabby asbestos siding. The picture was a little overexposed, so details weren't very clear.

After that there were several pictures of Lenny and his biker buddies, surrounded by a surprising amount of beer bottles. Surprising because as far as I knew, Lenny never touched the stuff. But in these pictures his hand often clutched a cold one, and he didn't look real steady.

I recognized a face halfway through the stack and realized it was Mal Whitney—Sweetheart—looking twenty or so years younger, about Lenny's present age. His left arm was draped around a woman, presumably the wife he had mentioned, with his right arm cranked up and around Lenny's neck. The guys grinned like crazy people, but Mal's wife could've been a poster child for endurance. Huh.

At the bottom of the stack lay another picture of Lenny and the woman. This one was close and clear and made a shiver run down my spine. I sucked in my breath, and suddenly realized why the woman looked so familiar. She looked exactly like the nasty biker chick Lenny and I saw at the Biker Barn the other day.

Holy cow. That chick was Lenny's daughter.

Our conversation from the ice cream stand suddenly came back to me, and I felt like an idiot for not putting it together that day. Lenny had been asking if I remembered my father. He wasn't concerned about me. He'd been remembering his own daughter, and wondering if she ever thought of him. She obviously hadn't been a part of his life for many, many years.

I looked back down at the picture of Lenny and the woman. The photo cut off the woman's right arm at the biceps, but I saw what was probably the very top of a tattoo. A familiar one. My pulse pounded in my throat as I scrabbled back through the piles of photos until I came to one that showed her whole arm. I turned on the lamp, stuck the picture in the bright light, and squinted. The shiver in my spine came back.

I closed my eyes, picturing where I had last seen the fierce snake with the blood red tongue. It didn't take me long to remember. The nasty chick's boyfriend had a tattoo exactly like it.

I stood up. There had to be something else in the house to give me some answers. Lenny wouldn't have just these few pictures and nothing else.

I walked back into the office and pulled open more file drawers. Perhaps I was wrong about this room. Perhaps there would be something helpful.

All I could find in the files was business stuff. Nothing to do with Lenny's personal life. Just taxes, work expenses, and other boring papers. The drawers of the desk were just as fruitless, and there wasn't any other place in the room to hide anything. I abandoned the office and headed up to the second floor.

When I got to the landing, I hesitated. This was getting really personal now, violating the man's bedroom. But I stepped into the room anyway, and looked around. The bed was unmade, the sheets tangled and the blanket thrown onto the floor, along with a ratty comforter. The one pillow was scrunched into a little ball. Drawers on the dresser were half open, socks and underwear fighting for space, while the closet revealed a couple of shirts on hangers and several pairs of boots in a heap on the floor. A nightstand held an actual ticking clock, and a pile of change lay scattered across its top. The floor was a black and white mess of laundry—clothes, towels, and handkerchiefs.

"Good grief," I said out loud.

I stood for a moment longer before wading through the mess to his closet. The shelf was a big fat zero, as was the wall at the back. I had to check, seeing as how Howie's closet had produced the wealth of family pictures. I picked through the boots and came up with nothing except some disgustingly smelly socks.

His dresser was just as unhelpful—nothing but what should be there. I shoved the clothes into the drawers and somehow got all the drawers to shut.

It was in his bedside table I found what I'd come looking for.

A mess of yellowed newspaper clippings occupied the drawer, and I stared at them, not sure I wanted to know what was in them. The first headline I saw screamed, "Two Bikers Die, Two Injured, in Fatal Blast." I forced myself to read the whole article even though I felt like throwing up.

The article detailed how the clubhouse for the Serpents motorcycle club had exploded the night before, killing the president and the secretary/treasurer. Lenny Spruce, along with Mal Whitney and a guy named Scott Simms, had been taken in to "help the police with their inquiries," being prominent members of another local club. The Priests.

I shoved the entire stack of clippings into one of Lenny's pillowcases, and practically ran out of the house.

I was ready to climb into my truck when a woman stepped out of the bushes holding a rolling pin.

"Hold it right there!" she said, waving the implement. Her flowered housecoat flapped about her legs, and wild, sleep-flattened hair ringed her head.

If the situation hadn't have been so serious, I might have laughed. But the last thing I needed was a dent in my head, and I recognized the woman as a friendly face.

"Whoa, lady," I said. "It's Stella Crown. Remember? Lenny's friend? We talked the other night when the cops were here?"

She shone a flashlight in my face and I covered my eyes.

"Take your hand away from your face," she said.

"Lower the flashlight, then."

She tipped it so it lighted up my stomach, and I looked at her. She dropped it the rest of the way.

"Sorry," she said. "I heard your truck out here, and wanted to stop whoever it was. Lenny's been through enough the past few days."

I gestured toward the house. "Just checking on things for Lenny. His partner was…in an accident, and Lenny's crashed at my house right now."

"I'm sure it's fine you're here. But I've seen those bikers out back a couple of times this week and I figured you were them again."

I froze. "What bikers?"

"A guy and girl, if you want to call them that. Scummy folks. Not like you and Lenny."

"When exactly did you see them?"

"Well, let's see." She crossed her arms and the light from the flashlight played on the side of my truck. "A couple days ago. I guess it would've been Sunday night. I figured they were friends of Lenny's, so I didn't say anything. Then I saw them again yesterday while Lenny was gone. They went into the house and came out again after just a few minutes."

"Did you tell anybody?"

"Sure. I called Lenny at the Biker Barn right away. They were here early, soon after he'd left for work. I saw them because I was cleaning up the boys' breakfast stuff."

"Did you tell the cops about this?"

"I told one of the officers last night, when they were here at Lenny's. He didn't seem to think much of it, though."

Detective Willard would be hearing it again from me, in case it had slipped by him.

"Well, thanks for telling me. I'll make sure the cops hear about it again."

She shrugged. "Lenny told me not to bother the cops. That he knew who the bikers were and he'd take care of it."

I didn't like the sound of that.

She studied my face and saw I wasn't happy. "Lenny doesn't deserve this," she said. "He never hurt anybody."

She turned to leave when I walked around to the driver's door of my truck.

"Hey, lady," I said.

She stopped.

"Next time you see someone going into Lenny's house you might want to call the police. I'm not sure how much good a rolling pin would do."

She looked down at it like she'd forgotten it was there, and gave a little smile. "You never know. This one has seen a lot of action. I make a mean pie crust."

I slammed the truck door, laughing in spite of the situation. Perhaps I'd finally found Ma Granger's match.

Chapter Thirty-two

It was quarter to five by the time I made it home, so I got a nice solid forty-five minutes of sleep before heading out to the barn. I would've just stayed awake like the morning before, except I fell asleep behind the wheel of my truck as soon as I'd parked it in the driveway. It was amazing I could even sleep, seeing how my yard looked like a bomb had exploded on it. My first sight upon waking was a board that had lodged itself in the side of Howie's truck.

Once I pulled my gaze from the wreckage and got my neck un-cricked I took time to run into the house and change my clothes, unfortunately catching a glimpse of my pasty skin and exhaustion-blackened eyes in my mirror. No wonder the surgeon had been afraid of me—I looked like I'd spent the last week hiding in a closet.

Lucy met me in the barn an hour later, where I was filling feed troughs. The cows were clipped in, crunching on hay.

"Gosh," Lucy said. "You look terrible."

"Gee, thanks."

"No offense."

I glanced at her, trying to judge if she looked any better than I did. She probably did, but that could've just been genetics.

"I'm betting you didn't get a whole lot of sleep, either," I said.

She shrugged. "I got a few hours. I'm not feeling too bad, if you don't count my head drumming a constant beat."

"Bed sleep okay while you were in it?"

"Sure. And I only woke up twice wondering where on earth I was."

She cracked a grin, which broke my reserve. I flicked grain off my jeans while I tried to keep myself from blubbering.

"Tess going to school today?" I asked. My voice sounded normal.

"I think so. She had some nightmares about the tornado early last night, but we talked about them and she seemed to sleep solid the last several hours." She glanced at the house. "I think it will help to keep her routine the same, especially since it's so new. Thanks to Mallory, she has some clothes to wear, and I'm hoping she'll share during show and tell."

"Shouldn't you be in there helping her get ready?"

"I set the alarm clock in her room, and I'll pop back in to make sure she's on her way."

Lenny's bike erupted in the still morning, and Lucy and I looked out the window.

"Where's he going?" I asked. To see Willard, I hoped.

"Said he wanted to visit Bart, and make sure everything's okay at the Barn."

"But what about the people that are after him? What if they're waiting for him?"

Lucy paled. "You think they'll be there? At the hospital? Or the Barn?"

I rubbed my temples, sighing. "I'll run after him."

A cow sneezed on my feet, her nose dusty with grain, and I did a quick side-step. I tripped over my boots and grabbed onto a water pipe.

"Just as I thought," Lucy said. "You're in no condition to be protecting Lenny. Isn't there someone else who could do it?"

I closed my eyes and tried to think. "I'll call somebody from the club. See if they can help."

Lucy's eyes were anxious. "If you can't find anyone, let me know."

I nodded.

"Now make the call and go to bed before you hurt yourself," Lucy said. "I'll take care of this."

"All right," I said. "Thanks."

In the house, I found the number for Harry, our club president. When I gave him the lowdown, he told me he'd get right on it. If he couldn't find someone in the next few minutes he'd go himself. Relieved to find backup so easily, I stumbled upstairs, where I tore off my boots and jeans and fell into bed.

I woke to a huge crash outside my bedroom window.

"What the—"

"Sorry!" I heard.

I stuck my face against the screen of the open window to try to get a view into the yard. My driveway was filled with trucks, a Harley-Davidson Fat Boy, and a full-sized Dumpster, while my yard teemed with big, sweaty Granger brothers.

"Huh," I said. I couldn't believe I'd slept through all the noise.

I pulled my jeans back on, glanced at the clock, which said it was now late morning, and gulped a Motrin before walking carefully down the stairs, feeling ten times better than I had on my way up several hours before.

"Well, well, if it ain't the princess," Jethro Granger said. "Looks like you could use a few more hours of beauty sleep."

I glared at him. "How come your son's so much nicer than you? Zach at least treats me with some respect."

Jethro laughed. "He knows you could beat him up. I figure I'm pretty safe."

"Just because your gut would smother me."

"Okay, kids, break it up."

An even huger arm than Jethro's draped across my shoulders and I looked up into the face of Jermaine, Ma's adopted son and the owner of the bike that sat in the shade of one of my surviving trees. His beautiful skin was the color of a perfect mug of hot chocolate, and the sun reflected brightly off of his shaved head.

"What are you guys doing here?" I asked. "Welding business slow today?"

"We're the clean-up crew," Jermaine said. "You don't think we'd be letting you sit by yourself with all this crap?"

I looked around, startled again by the destruction.

"Good lord," I said. "You'd think Somebody could give me a little slack one of these days."

"Not gonna happen you keep taking His name in vain," Jethro said.

"Uh oh. You becoming Ma?" We all knew better than to blaspheme in Ma's presence, for fear of the dreaded "hot sauce on the tongue" routine. Even at our age.

"Nope, I just can't have a sister-in-law with such a potty mouth."

I stared at him.

"Whoops," he said.

"I don't know what Abe's been telling you—"

"Oh, let it go," Jermaine said. "Abe's been saying nothing. Jethro here's just got a wild imagination. And a big mouth."

"I call what I see," Jethro said.

"And what you're going to see soon is the sole of my boot," I said.

Jethro looked at Jermaine. "Try to do a little charity work and what do I get?"

Jermaine put up his hands and stepped back. "Don't put me in the middle of you two psychos. I'm just here to help."

Jethro winked at me. "I'm just joshin' ya. You know that."

"Uh-huh. Anyway, I appreciate the help. You guys happen to know where Lucy is?"

Jethro hooked his thumb over his shoulder. "Took my truck down to that new Home Depot there on Bethlehem Pike. Need a few things to do some patching up, so she went to get 'em. Told her to put 'em on your tab. Hope that's okay."

My tab. Not something I liked thinking about. "Sure, that's fine."

"What I want to know," Jermaine said, "is what that piece of trash bike is doing in your yard."

We all looked at the Beast where it sat alongside the drive, bringing down my land value.

"Present from Lenny," I said. "Till my bike's back on the road."

"Too bad it wasn't in the garage when it went," Jermaine said.

Talking about the bike made me wonder where Lenny was, and who was with him, but my thoughts were interrupted by the milk truck pulling into the lane. Doug, the driver, jumped out and looked at the carnage, his mouth open.

"Holy crow," he said, walking over to me. His mouth dropped a little further as he sized up Jethro and Jermaine. "What happened?"

"Tornado."

"Nobody was hurt?"

"Thank the Lord, no."

"Well, that's good, anyway." He looked uncertainly at me. "Anything I can do?"

"Don't think so." I jerked my chin at the Granger boys. "I've got some good trash haulers at the moment."

Jermaine and Jethro grinned and introduced themselves. Doug closed his mouth long enough to smile back and shake their hands. He took another look at the destruction and slowly shook his head.

"I'm glad everybody's okay." He glanced toward his truck. "Should I get started?"

"Be my guest. Luckily nothing here should interfere with your job."

He tipped his hat and wandered, still awestruck, to his tanker.

I turned back to the guys. "Any luck with Howie's truck?"

Jethro winced but put on a brave face and led me toward the battered Ford, with me stopping to say hello and thanks to the other Grangers and Sellersville Mennonite members who had found their way to the farm. The Grangers were easy to spot: Jordan patching up a hole in my house, Josh pushing trash around with the Bobcat, Jacob busy hauling pieces of charred lumber to the Dumpster, and Belle doing her best to get glass shards out of the driveway. Abe was nowhere to be seen.

Peter Reinford, along with a good handful of volunteers from Sellersville Mennonite, traipsed back and forth from the yard to a wood chipper, hauling downed branches. Willie, Zach's MYF sponsor, leaned on the machine, wiping sweat from his forehead.

"Thanks for coming out, everybody," I said.

Peter straightened and flexed his shoulders. "Can't say I'm used to this kind of work, but it feels good. The usual Mennonite Disaster Service folks from church are already down in Florida with the hurricanes, so you have to take us leftovers."

"Hey, now," one of the other men said with a laugh. "We're doing the best our old bones can manage."

"And I appreciate it," I said. "You don't know how much."

"We're glad to be here," Peter said. "Just leave the cleaning up to us."

He turned back to his task of feeding downed branches to the chipper.

I gestured to Willie, and he stepped away from the machine, pulling ear-protectors off his head.

"I hear Zach got to regale you with his tornado story last night," I said.

He grinned. "Boy, did he ever. He's a good storyteller."

"I'm sure he didn't leave out a detail. I'm also sure telling about it was the best thing for him."

Willie grew serious. "I was afraid he wouldn't be able to sleep, otherwise. I went through a tornado as a kid, and every time there was even a little storm after that, I'd lie in my bed sweating and shaking."

"It was pretty terrifying."

He smiled gently and his eyes radiated kindness, reminding me of Dr. Peterson.

"Thanks for looking out for him," I said.

"I look out for all my kids."

He slipped his ear protectors back on, and I continued after Jethro and Jermaine.

Howie's truck sat looking like a broken old man on a park bench. One of its side windows was shattered, and it leaned to the right on a flat tire, reminding me of Lenny's friend Mal Whitney. The side had several deep dents, caused by flying lumber, I supposed, and the paint had been scratched to the metal at some points. Like everything else in the yard, it sported a splotchy coat of debris.

I sighed. First my bike, now Howie's truck. Completely trashed.

"Don't despair, girlie," Jethro said. "We can fix 'er up good."

I looked at the truck, wondering if nostalgia alone was enough to force a vehicle out of almost certain retirement.

"Is it worth it?" I asked.

Both brothers looked shocked.

"You're not serious," Jethro said. "Howie's truck?"

I shrugged and looked away, stuffing my hands into my back pockets. I could feel the guys' eyes on me.

The quiet was broken when a trio of vehicles pulled into the lane, Ma Granger in the lead at the wheel of her old Mercury. She and several ladies from church piled out of the cars, and I had to smile.

"Kitchen committee?" I said to Jethro.

"You got it, babe."

I met Ma on the driveway and she put her arms around me. "Thank the Lord you're safe," she said. "You can replace the garage and barn. Even the trees. You we couldn't do without."

I hugged her back. "Thanks, Ma. I'm glad to be here, too."

"Okay, ladies!" Ma stepped back and gestured to her crew. "Let's set up." To me, she said, "You care where we put things?"

"You can have the run of the place. Need tables?"

"Abe's coming with those. I sent him over to the church to bring back a few from the fellowship hall. He should be here any time."

So that's why he was absent.

"I sure appreciate it, Ma."

She clucked her tongue. "We can't have people starving, can we? They're working hard. Now, Jethro and Jermaine, stop standing there with those smirks on your faces. Get back to work."

"Yes, ma'am," both men said, and immediately did their mother's bidding.

"And you," Ma said to me. "I don't want to see you working out here. Abe told me how you've been killing yourself. Now that you have that nice girl Lucy working for you, you need to take it easy."

"Yes, Ma."

"I mean it. Don't you try to sneak it past me."

"Yes, Ma."

"Now come here a second."

I followed her to her car, where she pulled out two garbage bags.

"I don't know what kind of bed covers you have for those two, but here are a couple quilts. Before you know it, these evenings are going to get chilly, and without heat in your upstairs—"

I held out my arms and took the bags. "Thanks, Ma. You're the best. Where are these from?"

She pulled back the top of one of the bags. "This was made by my grandmother Myers. And this," she pulled back the next one, "was given to Pa and me on our wedding day."

I opened my mouth to protest, but she cut me off.

"We got two, and besides, Pa's not around to lie under it with me anymore, is he? So you give it to that girl of yours."

"Yes, Ma. Thanks."

"Now go on. I have things to do."

I carried the quilts into the house and laid them on the sofa before sinking down beside them. I wasn't quite sure what to do with myself. I hated to leave the volunteers cleaning up the place, but I wasn't in any condition to be heaving heavy objects into the Dumpster. I certainly would only get underfoot of the food preparers, and wasn't anywhere near wanting their wrath—or their spatulas—to descend upon me.

I decided I might as well make myself useful and work on Lenny's problem, while I could. I hadn't heard back from Harry, so I assumed Lenny was in the good hands of someone from the club. I pushed myself off the couch and limped out to the truck, where I grabbed Lenny's pillowcase. I'd just shut the truck door when yet another car drove in the lane and Queenie went crazy.

The two people who got out of the familiar dark blue Buick stood speechless, their eyes wide. They apparently weren't expecting a natural disaster. I walked toward them, my blood boiling and my hand on Queenie's collar. The man took a step back as I neared, his eyes boring into me with a silent request.

I ignored it.

"Noah, it seems to me Lucy was quite clear when she told you to leave and never come back. What was it about those words you didn't understand?"

The woman standing beside the passenger door turned slowly to stare at Noah, her jaw jutting out to a dangerous angle. "You said you hadn't been here. You said you hadn't talked to Lucy for weeks!"

Noah's eyes darted from side to side. "Oh, yeah, well. I guess I forgot I stopped by the other day. I was in Souderton on business. You know. For the church. Just thought I'd come for a minute."

"Is that so?" Her voice could've shattered it was so chilly.

"And that's how long you're staying today," I said. "A minute."

"And who might you be?" the woman said.

Noah looked like he wanted to die.

My smile felt as cold as the woman's voice. "I might be the one who owns this farm. I'm Lucy's boss."

She crossed her arms and pouted. "So where is Lucy? I didn't come all this way to be turned out."

"That's too bad, because Lucy's not here."

"Out gallivanting around already?"

I wanted to slap her. "And just who are you? Seeing how you're trespassing."

She rolled her eyes. "Lucy's sister-in-law. Shelby. I'm sure you've heard all the horror stories."

I smiled some more. "Actually, she's never mentioned you."

Her mouth twitched. "I'm Brad's sister. I hope she's at least mentioned *him*."

I'd had enough. "What do you want? I'm not really in the mood for visitors."

They looked at the throng of people in my yard.

I clarified. "Unwelcome ones, I mean."

Shelby turned to Noah. "Well, this is just great. I'm so glad you convinced me not to call ahead of time."

Noah blushed fiercely.

"We all know why he did that, don't we?" I said. "Now why don't you folks head back to Lancaster. There's nothing for you here." I looked at Noah. "Unless you really want to wait for Lucy. I'm sure she'd be ever so happy to see you."

Shelby stomped the gravel. "I'm not leaving till I talk to her. You go on home if you want, Noah. I'll call Scott to come get me."

Noah shook his head. "He'd love that for sure."

I tuned out their bickering and thought. My very being wanted to heave them out on their cans, but having Lucy tell them to take off would probably be more effective in the long run.

"Okay," I said. "Here's the deal. You get back in your car and wait over there." I pointed toward the end of the lane where there was a graveled side spot. "When Lucy gets home you may get out." I smiled at Noah. "If you dare." I wasn't envying him his time in the car with Shelby, who looked ready to pop him one. But that was his own fault, for disobeying Lucy's direct orders.

I kept smiling until they got back in the car and pulled it to the side. Then I found Jermaine and Jethro.

"See those folks?" I pointed toward Noah and Shelby.

"Sure," Jermaine said.

Jethro nodded.

"Why don't you give them a wave, let them know you see them."

They did as I asked, and I tried not to laugh at our guests' shocked expressions.

"If they even try to get out and snoop, could you discourage them?"

Jethro smiled. "It would be our pleasure."

I patted his right biceps, appreciating the hard muscle underneath his T-shirt. "I owe you one."

Feeling more secure about my uninvited guests, I slung Lenny's pillowcase over my shoulder and continued the trek to my office. With a groan I settled in my chair and pulled the newspaper clippings from the bag. I ignored the headlines of the articles and stacked them according to date. Several area newspapers were represented, the *Philadelphia Inquirer* being the most prominent, and there were a few pictures mixed in with the prose.

The first article was innocent as far as I could tell. Mal had shown his bike at Lansdale's Bike Night, held in mid-August of 1976, and had won first place for the original paint job. A very young-looking Lenny stood smiling beside Mal, who sat astride his fancy Sportster. Probably the bike he had told me about—the red and black one his wife was jealous of. I wondered if Lenny had done the painting or if Mal was just as talented.

The next article was a study of motorcycle gangs in the area—namely the Pagans, the largest outlaw club in the nation other than the Hell's Angels—including what their different personalities and businesses consisted of. The Priests were mentioned—Lenny's club—as well as a few other small groups. The InSex, the Wild Ones, and the Serpents.

I sucked in my breath. The Serpents. The mother of Lenny's daughter and his daughter's boyfriend had serpents tattooed around their biceps.

I skimmed the article and understood why the Mrs. Joneses of the world were afraid of bikers. If I thought these folks comprised the whole biker world, I'd never sleep at night, either. Drug smuggling, prostitution, Mafia connections, production of methamphetamines. Just to name a few stellar contributions to society. For being only one percent of the biker world they sure did a lot of nasty stuff.

The Pagans are some of the worst, and they hang out all along the Eastern seaboard and beyond. There are a lot of Pagans in the Philadelphia area, and probably in my northern suburb, too, but they keep to themselves. If you need to compare them to something, I'd say they're kind of like sharks. You leave them alone and don't spread blood in their water, they'll most likely ignore your very existence. Unless, of course, you accidentally cut them off with your truck and they decide to pull out their sawed-off shotguns. But that's about as likely to happen as Jaws showing up in your swimming pool.

Lenny's name popped up again in an article, and that familiar chill ran down my spine. The Priests and the Serpents both figured in this article. Seems the two gangs were having disputes over who owned what territory and things were getting a bit out of hand. Lenny, Mal, and that guy named Scott Simms had been brought in for questioning after a bloody fight broke out at a bar in Hatfield. No one had been killed, but several people had been treated and released at the North Penn Hospital ER.

I took a moment to stand up and pace, shaking my hands and doing some deep breathing. Nothing I was reading was making me feel any better about Lenny's present predicament. And seeing what Lenny's life had once involved, I was really wondering what had sent him toward his current law-abiding lifestyle. Perhaps it was the simple fact that he had acquired a family, and had decided they deserved something better.

Chronologically, the next article was the one I had already read at Lenny's. The one detailing the explosion and deaths at the Serpents' clubhouse. I read it again, making sure I hadn't missed any details.

After digesting that article again, I didn't want to read more, but knew I had to. And the next story clinched the bad feeling that had been growing in my gut.

It seemed the Priests finally took over the Serpents and their territory after the explosion. From what law enforcement officials could make out, the Serpents had been storing weapons and explosive devices—illegal, of course—in the back room of their club. Something had caused the materials to ignite during a supposedly secret meeting of the club's officers. The president and the secretary/treasurer had both been killed, while the enforcer and vice president hovered in critical condition at the hospital. The sergeant-at-arms had somehow escaped with no more than minor injuries.

Police didn't have much hope of clearing up what had happened, seeing as how the Serpents weren't willing to help much. The little the club members told the police led the investigation nowhere, and while nothing overt was said about the Priests' part in the killings, law enforcement was waiting on pins and needles for retaliation to begin.

A spokesman from the Priests said none of their members could have been responsible. The entire club had been at the Reading Beer Bash, and no one wanted to miss that—it was their biggest annual outing. Besides, who ever said they were involved in criminal matters? Needless to say, law enforcement was skeptical about such a vague and unprovable alibi.

"Let them kill each other off, as far as I'm concerned," said one officer, who for obvious reasons wanted to remain anonymous. "I just hope they do it somewhere innocent people won't get caught in the cross-fire."

Kind of like how TV preachers—and churches like Yoder Mennonite—thought about gays and AIDS until they learned better.

But even though law enforcement couldn't prove anything, Lenny, along with Mal and Scott Simms, had been dragged in to "help the police with their inquiries." All had been released with no further questioning that had been reported.

Had Lenny really killed people? My stomach contracted, and I hoped I wouldn't have to make use of my wastebasket. The nausea eventually eased, and I forced myself to take a look at the last article.

This announced the birth of Kristi Rochelle Spruce to Lenny and a woman named Vonda Dane. I swallowed. Vonda was the name tattooed on Lenny's arm. I had never known who was behind the design, and certainly had never imagined she was the mother of Lenny's child. I still couldn't believe Lenny was a father and had never told any of us. I wonder if Bart even knew.

Which led to another big question: Why had Kristi—and her mother, apparently—disappeared from Lenny's life? And why had Kristi suddenly reappeared?

I hoped Lenny had a good explanation for all of this, because murder was something it would be hard to look beyond, even for someone who loved him as much as I did.

For the second time that week, I turned to the Internet. AskJeeves.com pointed me toward several articles about the Priests and the Serpents—some the same ones I had in hard copy—and a few more about Lenny. An award he'd gotten for a paint job, another scrape with the law, nothing that shed any light on our present situation.

Mal was just as elusive. An article about his business selling bikes, the clip from way back about Lansdale Bike Night, and not much else.

It was with Scott Simms I hit pay dirt.

There were the same articles mentioning Lenny, Mal, and Simms, several more for various law-breaking activities—assault, bar fights, DUIs. But the one that made me stare slack-jawed at my screen was only a few days old.

It seemed Scott Simms had died the weekend before in a motorcycle accident. The accident Abe had brought to my attention, where the guy was riding to work and was broad-sided at an intersection.

Scott Simms' nickname was The Skull.

Chapter Thirty-three

"What are they doing here?"

Lucy stood in my office doorway, her face a mask of anger. I shook myself out of my shock over The Skull and glanced out the window to see Noah and Shelby standing uncertainly behind their open car doors. Do they get out, or don't they? Did Lucy see them, or not? Was this ferocious-looking collie going to rip their faces off, or just bite them in the ass?

"Hey, she's your sister-in-law," I said. "And he's your...whatever."

"Don't remind me." She went to the window and peeked out above the air conditioner, groaning. "Why did I ever do it?"

I froze, wondering if I was actually hearing something important. She didn't continue.

"You guys date?" I asked.

"For a bit. I thought it would be good for me. He was Brad's best friend, an MYF sponsor at the church—I mean, he's a good guy. It started out okay, but geez, he's just too much. And my sister-in-law—the head case out there—about had my hide. Besides betraying her brother, I was taking the man she'd been after ever since Brad started hanging out with him in elementary school."

What was she telling me? She'd had an affair with Brad's best friend? While Brad was confined to his wheelchair?

"I broke it off a couple months ago when I realized I had to get out of Lancaster. You'd think we'd been dating a couple years instead of a couple months the way he freaked out."

So no extramarital shenanigans. I was relieved.

"You think he's behind the graffiti?" I asked.

"Noah? He doesn't have the guts."

"He had the guts to come here again today. In her presence. And he's about the right size. Whoever was here that night was no Arnold Schwarzenegger."

She wrinkled her nose and backed away from the window, bending over and touching her toes. When she straightened, she blew out a sigh. "I guess I'll go send them away before one of the Granger brothers eats them." She brightened. "Or maybe I can get Peter to talk to them about church and how teenagers should be taught. They'd love that. Noah gets very defensive of his oh-so-perfect MYFers." She walked out, slamming the door behind her.

MYFers, I thought. High schoolers. Not old enough to go after custody of Tess, but just the right age for spraying obscenities on garage doors.

I watched as Lucy strode across the driveway. She stopped several feet from her visitors, her hands on her hips. I couldn't hear what the three of them were saying, but I could certainly read their body language. Noah's face fell further and further toward shame, while Shelby looked ready to explode.

In the end Lucy stalked into the house while Shelby and Noah got into their car. They drove away, not looking back. So much for our daily soap opera.

When I turned back toward my computer, the newspaper article about The Skull had not disappeared. I needed some huge answers from Lenny.

I picked up the phone and called Harry.

"You find somebody to hang with Lenny?" I asked.

"I tried. Couldn't find anyone, so I went myself, caught up with him at the Barn. Thanks a whole helluva lot."

"What?"

"Lenny about ripped me a new one. Told me he didn't need a baby-sitter, and I'd better take off fast or he'd make me wish I did."

I sat back. "That doesn't sound like Lenny."

"Tell me about it. I told him you were concerned about his safety, and that just made him madder. I had to respect the man's wishes, as well as my own safety. Sorry."

"Me, too. He still at the Barn?"

"Was there when I left him. Can't say more than that."

"Thanks, Harry. I'll make it up to you."

I should never have left Lenny's well-being to someone else, no matter how tired I'd been. I grabbed my keys and went out to my truck.

The Biker Barn was dark and empty. I put my hands up to the door and peered into the show room, but couldn't see anything but silhouettes of the iron horses and their accessories. Lenny's bike was absent, and if Harry hadn't told me, I would have never known that Lenny had even been there.

I tried the hospital and was informed visiting hours had not begun. The guy at the front desk assured me there was no way a huge, red-bearded biker could've made it past his radar.

I drove to Lenny's house. Same luck. No lights. No open doors. A quick walk-through, using the key from the garage to let myself in, produced nothing of use. It didn't even look like Lenny had returned since I'd snooped the night before.

I put the key back and sat in my truck, staring at the row of homes stretching the length of the street. I hoped desperately that Lenny had gotten himself somewhere out of harm's way. We knew without a doubt these people meant business.

And besides Lenny's safety, he owed me an explanation. Owed Bart. Where in the hell was he, and where could I get information if he'd disappeared?

The answer struck me suddenly, and I wondered why it had taken me so long to consider it. Mal Whitney. I put the truck into gear and drove toward Route 663 and Mal's place.

The warehouse was closed up tight when I arrived, but a light shined through a little window cut into the siding. I pounded on the door. When there was no answer, I pounded again.

"Mal!" I called. "It's Lenny's friend, Stella!"

I heard footsteps, then about five locks being undone. Soon the door was opening a fraction, a heavy chain keeping me outside. Mal peeked out and his eyes widened.

"You?"

"Yes, remember? Can I come in?"

The door closed and the chain scraped in its casing. Mal opened the door, peered nervously behind me as if expecting to see someone else, then roughly pulled me in. He slammed the door shut and threw all of the locks before turning to me. The light hit his face and I sucked in my breath.

"Geez, Mal, you look like hell."

Basically the same thing Lucy had said to me, except Mal's condition was much, much worse.

His face was a shade of gray I didn't know people turned while they were alive, and his eyes, besides looking like someone had used them for punching practice, were bloodshot and watery above his swollen nose. His hand trembled as he pulled the familiar bottle of Jack Daniels against his chest, and his mouth worked like he was going to say something.

Instead, he veered around me, toward the back of the warehouse, where light illuminated one small corner of space. He was limping, and I saw now that the hand holding the bottle was also supporting his right side. I recognized the posture, having been doing a lot of it myself over the past several weeks. What the hell?

I took my eyes off him long enough to squint into the darkness, the bikes offering many forms of shape and shadow. I couldn't tell if anyone else was there or not, but when I looked back at Mal he was sinking gingerly into a sagging, overstuffed chair. He wouldn't be sitting if the people who did this to him were still around.

"What do you want?" he asked, not looking at me.

"What happened to you?"

He struggled out of his chair and paced around the lighted space, stopping when he reached the darkness to turn and stumble back the other way.

"Mal," I said.

He lurched to a stop, his fingers picking at the one-percenter tattoo I had seen the other day. His eyes shone, glassy and terrified.

"Three can keep a secret," he mumbled. His words barely reached my ears.

"Sweetheart," I said.

This time he looked at me, and his eyes cleared.

"Sweetheart, please tell me what's going on. I want to help."

He put up his hands, sloshing whisky onto the floor. "Oh God, what a mess." A sob escaped his throat, and his mouth trembled.

I put my hand on his shoulder. His shirt felt stiff and sticky and I wondered if he'd changed since whoever pummeled him had left. I leaned back so I wasn't casting a shadow and tried to see what I was touching. In the dim light I couldn't tell if there was blood or what on his black shirt, but I did see the tattoo of a skull with a clerical collar on his arm—just like Lenny's. The mark of the Priests.

I talked as quietly as I could and still have Mal hear me. "Mal, please, *please* talk to me. Before someone else gets hurt."

A shaky sigh leaked from his mouth, and he straightened his shoulders.

"Twenty years ago," he said. "Twenty long years."

"When the Serpents' clubhouse exploded? When their leaders died?"

His eyes moved to my face. "So you know?"

"About the explosion. That you were hauled in for questioning. That's it. Is that what this is all about?"

He felt behind him for his chair, and slowly lowered himself to the cushion. He stared at the far wall for so long I thought he'd zoned out on me.

"Mal—"

"We were ordered to blow up the clubhouse. But there weren't supposed to be people in it." His eyes, rimmed a harsh red, filled with tears. "There weren't any bikes in the parking lot, so we went in the back. We knew right away somebody was there. We took off like we'd already lit the match.

"Lenny and I were done. We said no way were we igniting the place with people in it. We thought The Skull felt the same. We all left." His lips trembled, and he bit them together. "But The Skull went back. Blew up the place with the guys in it. He didn't care. Didn't care about the people."

My stomach, at risk of rebellion since I'd first seen the article at Lenny's, suddenly relaxed. Lenny hadn't killed those people. He'd seen them, and decided against the violence.

"We knew he'd done it," Mal said, "and we confronted him the next day, as soon as we heard. He just laughed. Said we were chickenshit thumbsuckers, that we obviously weren't cut out for the outlaw life if we couldn't do our jobs. And then he threatened us."

Mal erupted from his seat and resumed his panicked pacing.

"Threatened you?" I asked. "With what? That he'd kill you, too?"

Mal stopped. "No. Our families. My wife. Vonda and Kristi. Said if we breathed a word to anyone, he—or any number of the guys in our club—would make us sorrier than we'd ever been."

I dropped my head into my hands, now thoroughly confused. "But The Skull's dead. Why is someone coming after you now?"

Mal spun around, his face anguished. "Not just someone. Lenny's *daughter.*"

"But *why?*" I pictured the tattoo on Vonda's arm, and the arm of Kristi's boyfriend. Vonda was obviously a Serpent who came over to the Priests after the explosion. But Kristi was Lenny's daughter, at least half Priest. "Why is Kristi trying to kill her own father?"

His mouth twisted. "Because after all this time…she thinks Lenny did it. She thinks he killed those people, and then four years later he abandoned her."

Chapter Thirty-four

The surgeon must have told the nurses on Bart's floor about me, or else they figured Bart's visitors would look like him. I didn't have any trouble getting in to see him, although they told me to make it quick.

Bart opened his eyes when the chair screeched as I pulled it closer.

"Well, well," he mumbled. "If it isn't…the princess."

"In the flesh. So how much like crap are you feeling?"

"Like a small pile. How do I look?"

I couldn't see much since his face was swathed in bandages and his body was covered with a sheet.

"Like the Mummy," I said. "At least they didn't cut your braid off."

"Shaved the…goatee, though. And…they won't let me… smoke."

"Well, damn them."

He laughed, then winced.

"Sorry," I said. "I'll try not to be funny. You see Lenny today?" I tried to make my voice casual.

"He stopped by this morning. Snuck up the back way."

I let out a breath of relief. At least he'd been alive a few hours ago.

"He tell you anything?" I asked. "Give you any idea what's going on?"

"Just that…it was supposed to be him. Lot of good that does me…now." He closed his eyes and his head fell to the side. I thought he was asleep, so I started to get up. His eyes snapped open. I sat back down.

"I can't believe…I actually got…stabbed," he said.

"Do you remember anything? See anybody?"

He shook his head slightly. "Got me from…behind. You know who it was?"

"Got a good guess." I hesitated. "Did you know Lenny has a daughter?"

Bart's eyes got wide. "Sure didn't."

"It seems she's back. And majorly pissed off."

"Jesus."

When Bart says this, he means it. He slowly crossed himself.

"So she's…out to get him? Why?"

"A couple of reasons. It's a mess. But I think she's behind the attack at Lenny's and the break-in at the Barn. And, of course…." I gestured at his face and chest.

He didn't say anything.

"Remember that customer you had—skinny guy, shaved head, nasty serpent tattoo around his arm?"

"Sure. Just…a few days ago."

"Lenny's daughter's boyfriend."

"Jesus," he said again. His eyes shut once more, but I waited this time. He soon opened them. "I wonder…."

"What?"

"You know how Lenny started getting all…cranky last weekend?"

"Yeah." No forgetting that.

"Well, I finally…got fed up and…asked him what his problem was. He mumbled…something about skulls and then… clammed up. I have no idea…what he meant. Do you?"

"You know a guy who went by the name The Skull?" I asked. "Scott Simms?"

"He was talking about…a guy?"

"A guy who got himself killed Friday morning. Got T-boned by a truck on his way to work." Bart stared at me. "Twenty years ago The Skull killed some rival gang members. Lenny knew, and The Skull made it clear that if Lenny told anyone, The Skull would kill his family—Vonda and Kristi. I bet you anything that when The Skull got killed on Saturday Lenny saw that as his pardon. He called me and asked if I'd introduce him to Detective Willard. I'm sure he was ready to tell what he knew. But now it's his family that's after him, and I just don't get it."

"Damn," Bart said. His skin was even paler than it had been when I'd arrived, and I regretted bothering him with Lenny's problems.

"And here I am," Bart said. "Useless as a baby."

"You just rest. These jerks have messed you up enough."

His face was stony. "So what's going...on now?"

"I'm going to talk to the cops. If Lenny's not going to do anything to stop this from happening to someone else, then I'll have to do it myself."

"Lenny's gonna be mad."

"Then he should've talked to me—or the detective—when he had the chance."

Bart's eyes closed and this time he really did start to drift off.

"I'll be in touch," I said.

He nodded without opening his eyes. He looked like hell. But at least he was alive.

Chapter Thirty-five

A light rain had started when I walked to my truck. I climbed inside and sat for a moment, listening to the tapping on the cab. I glanced at the sky, hoping it would hold only regular gray rain clouds. It did. My arm itched, and I scratched at it while I thought. Lenny had said he wanted to talk to Willard last weekend. Had it been the break-in at the Barn that had changed his mind? I drove into town, mulling this over.

Willard was pulling into the municipal parking lot as I arrived. I got out and waited while he locked his car.

"Got a minute?" I asked.

"Sure. I need to talk with you anyway." He opened an umbrella and held it toward me. I scooted under it and together we walked toward the police building.

Inside, Willard gestured toward the locked inner door, and the receptionist buzzed us in. He set his umbrella on the floor of the squad room and led me into his office, where he hung his suit coat on the back of his closet door.

"Sorry I didn't come around yesterday, like I promised." He sat in his chair and pointed toward another one. "That storm caused several car accidents I had to take care of. I hear you got clobbered, too. I'm sorry."

I shrugged, not sure how to answer without my voice betraying my fatigue.

He changed the subject. "Is this visit about your employee again? Or your friends Mr. Spruce and Mr. Watts?"

I sat down, rubbing my arms against the chill of the air conditioner. "It's about Lenny."

His face emptied to a blank, listening expression. "Okay. Start talking."

So I did. I told him about Kristi, The Skull, and the explosion twenty years before. I expressed my anger and frustration with Lenny, along with my fear that something would happen to him now they'd gotten Bart by mistake. And I gave him the stack of news clippings from Lenny's bedside table. I didn't stop until I'd told him everything I knew, down to the last detail.

Willard sat quietly, shuffling through the articles, shaking his head. "So he was going to tell me himself?"

"I think so. But then things started happening. Someone tried to be The Barn, Lenny saw his daughter, and Bart was assaulted. I can't even find Lenny today, although I know he was up to see Bart. I'm not sure if he's scared or just avoiding me."

"Probably both. But there's not much I can do if he's not in any of his usual haunts. We'll just have to hope he comes to see me before he gets into trouble. Again." He patted the papers into a pile and set them in the middle of his desk. "Now, on another subject, is your farmhand home? I was thinking of coming by, talking to her about the graffiti."

"She's there. At least she was when I left."

"Care if I follow you home?"

I sighed, exhausted. "You might as well. Something else is bound to happen that I'll need you for."

He almost smiled at that.

◇◇◇

The Grangers and Peter Reinford's crew were packing up when we arrived. The rain would make cleanup messy and dangerous. Ma and her kitchen ladies had already cleared out, leaving, I was sure, plenty of leftovers in the fridge. I hopped down from the truck and walked over to where Jermaine was suiting up for his bike.

"You be okay in the rain?"

"You're kidding, right? I've ridden through tidal waves on this thing."

"Just checking. You know I'll run you home if you want."

"And leave my bike? No thanks. Even if it doesn't get destroyed by a tornado it might make friends with your new Beast. Don't want to chance that."

I rolled my eyes. "Thanks for your work today."

"No problem." He swung his leg over his bike and started turning switches. "By the way, I moved your ugly bike into the tractor barn. Figured it didn't need any more rust."

I thanked him and walked over to Jethro's Chevy Dually where he stood in the bed, shutting a large, attached toolbox. Belle was bent over beside the passenger door, brushing dirt off her clothes.

"Thanks, guys," I said.

"Hey, we're here for you." Jethro walked toward the lowered tailgate and somehow got down without flattening a tire.

I looked around the farm and was dismayed not to find Lenny's bike. I hadn't realized how much I'd been hoping to find him there, safe. A headache that had been threatening since morning suddenly began pulsing behind my temple.

Belle put a hand on my arm. "You okay?"

"Sure. Yeah. Thanks again."

Willard walked over, his umbrella opened over his head.

"Mr. and Mrs. Granger. Nice to see you."

Jethro put out his hand. "Detective. How's that boy of yours?"

"Doing great. And yours?"

"Can't complain, can't complain."

They smiled at each other, bonded in the knowledge that their sons had survived the previous month's epidemic.

"Here to check out the destruction?" Jethro asked.

"Some of it."

"Well, you take care of our girl, here."

Willard laughed. "You think she needs watching over?"

Jethro glanced over and caught me pushing on my temple, trying to ease the throbbing. "Sometimes I wonder."

Belle patted my arm and climbed into the truck while Jethro headed around to the driver's side. Before climbing up to the seat, he took a moment to look around at my destroyed garage. He opened his mouth to say something, but ended up shaking his head and getting into his truck. He and Belle were the last to leave.

But not the last to arrive.

A familiar Chevy pulled into the lane, and my spirits sank even lower, if that was possible. Anita Powell, from Children and Youth, got out of the car and opened an umbrella.

"What now?" I said.

She stared at the destruction on my property, her mouth agape. The rain dripped in rivulets off her now off-center umbrella, splashing onto her shoes. Willard eased his umbrella over my head.

"I...I got a call about the garage," Anita said. "They told me it had been damaged by the tornado, but I had no idea...." Her voice trailed off.

"So what did they tell you? That Lucy and Tess were in the apartment when it went?"

She shook her head. "No. They knew no one was hurt. They're concerned Lucy and her daughter now have no place to live." Her glance went to Willard.

"Detective Willard," I said. To Willard, I said, "And this is the lady from Children and Youth I told you about."

Anita looked puzzled. "Why are you here, Detective?"

"We're not on the same mission, I assure you."

I wasn't sure she believed him.

The screen door to the house slapped open, and Lucy barreled down the stairs, oblivious to the rain.

"What?" she said. Her voice was the loudest I'd heard it since she moved in. "What now? I'm not feeding her right? Her homework isn't getting done?"

Anita's eyes widened and she gestured toward what used to be Lucy and Tess' home. "You don't think that deserves a little consideration?"

Lucy's combative stance only heightened. "We're obviously okay."

"You are, anyway."

Lucy's eyes snapped with fire. "Fine. You want proof? Tess!" She shrieked the name toward the house, and I flinched. Willard stared at Lucy, surprise coloring his face.

"Tess!" Lucy yelled again. "Come out here!"

Tess soon appeared at the screen door, her face frightened.

"Come here, honey," Lucy said, her tone softening. "Ms. Powell needs to see that you're whole and undamaged."

Tess eased the door open and peeked around. She stepped out, then back in quickly when raindrops splattered off the awning onto her head.

"Hi, Tess," Anita said.

Tess peered at her from behind the screen.

"Good enough?" Rain ran down Lucy's face from underneath her hair, but she didn't move to wipe it away.

Anita tightened her grip on her umbrella. "But what about a home? A place to live?"

"I'd think my house would stand up to your requirements," I said. "It's been good enough for me my whole life."

Anita blinked. "They're living with you?"

I could feel Willard's gaze on me.

"Where else?" I said. "They moved in an hour or two after the tornado."

"And we each have our own bedroom," Lucy said, her voice filled with fake sweetness. "That should make you happy."

Ignoring her tone, Anita asked, "Is this a long-term situation?"

My breath caught, but I managed to say, "Until we have the apartment rebuilt. They'll stay with me as long as they need to."

"Good enough?" Lucy asked.

Anita looked like she was debating whether or not to demand a tour of the house. I crossed my arms and hoped she understood how unnecessary that would be.

Her shoulders finally relaxed and a ghost of a grin lit her face. "So my caller will have to deal with yet another rejection."

"And you still won't tell Lucy who it is?" I asked.

Lucy snorted. "She doesn't need to."

Anita looked interested in that. So did Willard. I knew what she was going to say.

"There aren't a whole lot of people who doubt me that much. People who care about Tess, that is. The general tabloid-focused public doesn't count."

"So who do you think it is?" Anita asked.

"Who else? It's got to be my in-laws."

Anita didn't disagree.

"So she's right?" I asked.

Anita shrugged. "I've already told you I'm not at liberty to say. But…let me just acknowledge that if Mrs. Lapp looks closely at the people in her life she most likely will come up with the right candidates for the referent. Now, I think I'm done here. And you, Mrs. Lapp, need to get inside."

Lucy's shirt—a new one from a quick trip to Kohl's—had soaked through, and it sagged dispiritedly across her shoulders. Her hair hung in wet clumps, fringing her pale face.

Willard and I followed Lucy into the house and sat in the kitchen while she went upstairs to change. Tess lounged in front of the TV, watching "Zoom." She looked tired, like the previous night's bad dreams were catching up with her.

"No sign of Mr. Spruce, I take it?" Willard asked me.

I glanced at the phone. "No messages, so either he's incommunicado or Lucy got the call. And no sign of his bike."

Willard's concerned expression did nothing to ease my own anxiety.

Lucy soon came down the stairs and leaned down by the sofa, ruffling Tess' hair and talking to her quietly. After kissing her daughter's head, Lucy joined us where we'd settled at the kitchen table. She met Willard's eyes. "Are you here to talk with me?"

"First," I said, "did you hear from Lenny?"

She shook her head, her eyes wide. "I thought you were with him this afternoon."

"Couldn't find him."

She gripped her hands together so tightly the knuckles went white. "What if something's happened to him? What if they got him, too?"

Willard's nostrils flared. "So you know all about his troubles, and the people involved?"

She glanced at me. "Just that Lenny used to be in a gang, and he thinks some outlaw bikers are after him. Why?"

Willard shook his head briefly. "I wish Mr. Spruce would've told *me* some of these things." He blew his hair off his forehead. "Anyway, on another subject, I have a few questions about the graffiti."

The concern on Lucy's face didn't change, but she focused on Willard.

"We were unable to get anything off the blanket, forensically," Willard said, "but is there any chance you recognize it?" He'd carried a familiar-looking garbage bag into the house, and now he reached into it and pulled out the ratty brown blanket I'd last seen subduing Queenie.

Lucy shook her head. "Looks like any old blanket."

"Yes," Willard said, "unfortunately, it does. Now, for a few more questions about who you think might be behind it."

"Your in-laws?" I said.

Lucy bit her lip. "I really can't imagine them going to such lengths, but I guess it would fit."

"Fit what?" Willard asked.

Lucy leaned forward. "How well do you know Mennonites?"

Willard smiled. "I think pretty well. Why?"

"Mennonites—well, other than people like Ma Granger and her brood—are not good at confrontation. It's much more common to keep everything inside or to talk to everyone but the person you have an issue with. Like my in-laws. Everyone knows they've tried to take Tess away from me. Obviously, they're still trying. My in-laws think I killed their golden boy, Brad. But guess what? We've never talked about it, in all the two and a half years since his accident. Not once. Everything I've heard has been through lawyers or newspapers. Or an occasional friend. But when I'm with my in-laws, it's like nothing has come between us. We all miss Brad, so we have that in common, and we all love Tess. But that's it."

"They've never actually confronted you about trying to gain custody of Tess?" I asked.

"Nope."

"And you've never talked to them about Brad's death?"

"They don't want to hear what I have to say. They'd rather pretend to my face that Brad is just gone. That there's no controversy about it."

"So as far as the graffiti?" Willard asked. "You say that fits somehow?"

Lucy nodded. "Sure. Yet another way to cast doubt on me without having to do it face to face."

"So you think they're behind it?" I wished I'd gotten a better look at the vandals. There was no way I'd recognize them again.

Lucy shrugged. "I'd hate to think who else it might be. I mean, no one else has any reason to say those things about me."

"Noah?" I asked.

Willard perked up. "Who's that?"

"A guy I dated briefly," Lucy said dismissively.

"Noah Delp," I said. "He's shown up at the farm. Twice. And he's an MYF sponsor at Yoder Mennonite."

Lucy's head snapped toward me. "What does that have to do with anything?"

"I told you the vandals weren't big. What if they were teenagers?"

Willard looked interested. "Their motive?"

"Exactly my question," Lucy said.

"Loyalty to Noah. You said you dated him pretty recently and broke up with him a couple months ago. And now you moved away completely."

"So?"

"So what if the kids saw how much it hurt him, and they want to get you back? What if he went home after seeing you here, and somehow they found out you banished him from the farm?"

Lucy stared at me. "You really think that's possible?"

"Teenagers are the obvious people for graffiti," Willard said. "It's not something adults usually do." He scribbled in his notebook. "I'll check it out."

Lucy's hands were back to their kneading. "Do you have to? Can I try?"

Willard put his pen in his pocket. "It's a criminal mischief charge if they did it."

"What would that mean for them?"

He shrugged. "Depends. Some kind of restitution."

"Jail?"

"Not necessarily. Especially if you don't press charges."

Lucy looked at me.

"I'm up for our own restitution," I said.

Willard groaned. "Ms. Crown—"

"Nothing criminal, I assure you."

Willard studied the tabletop for a long moment. "If that's the way you want to work it, I can't do anything about it. But I've got your report from the other night, and I'll keep this blanket."

Lucy's expression relaxed a little.

"Great," I said. "We'll be in touch."

He met my eyes gravely, then stood and walked over to the door. I followed.

"I appreciate your work," I said. "Thanks for coming over."

He pursed his lips, looking me in the eye again. "I'm serious about being careful. Don't do anything...well, anything dumb." He picked up the umbrella he'd left in the entryway and held it over his head as he walked to his car.

I closed the door and turned to Lucy, who still sat at the table, her back stiff.

"So," I said. "Let's go after these folks. Your in-laws, the MYFers. You Mennonites may not like confrontation, but it works for me. Let's put the fear of God into all of them. They deserve it."

Lucy smiled coldly. "They do. But that's not the way I handle things."

"Fine. What do you want to do?"

She hesitated. "You know that family fun fest I've been considering?"

I leaned back against the counter, my headache still hammering away. "Yeah. What about it?"

"I'd like to have a trial run. Saturday work for you?"

I glanced at the calendar. "That's the day after tomorrow. Doesn't give us long."

"I can pull it together."

I shrugged. "Okay. But what exactly is that going to accomplish?"

"I'll invite them all here. They'll have a great time."

I stared at her. "Now you've completely lost me."

She smiled, more frigidly than before. "I'm going to do this the Mennonite way. I'm going to kill them with kindness."

Chapter Thirty-six

The night passed slowly. As soon as I'd start to drift off, I'd have nightmares about Lenny in the hands of the enemy. They got him. Or were chasing him. Or he was hiding out. It made me furious that I had no way of knowing where he'd gone. No way to help him.

When dawn finally crept up the horizon, I gave up on the sleep idea and got out of bed. A hot shower did its best to wake me, but I couldn't honestly say it did much. At least I'd start the day out clean.

I waited until I was done milking to call the police. Willard wasn't in, but the cop who answered the phone said there hadn't been any calls about Lenny during the night. I thanked him and hung up, both relieved and worried. Calls to Lenny's house and the Barn were just as unproductive.

"No news about Lenny?" Lucy stood in the office doorway, her eyes blackened from lack of sleep. The past week had kept our nights busy, and I was sure Lucy had been dreaming, like I had.

"Nothing. And I've run out of ideas."

She stared out the window, hugging her arms around herself. "I wish I'd have some for you."

"Until we get some, you need to work on your plans for tomorrow. How can I help?"

"I made a bunch of calls last night. We should have a good group here tomorrow. So now we need to set up."

We spent the next hour lugging bales of straw to the back yard. Well, she lugged them to the Bobcat and I used it to dump them in a pile. Lucy arranged them in a circle around what would be a campfire. Even though the days were hot enough to roast marshmallows without a fire, the evenings cooled off enough we could enjoy it. We found kindling and firewood and Lucy placed them within a circle of cement blocks. Finally, she clapped her hands together and brushed bark and dust off her pants.

"Now what?" I asked.

"Now I head to Landis' Supermarket for party supplies."

I grimaced.

"Don't worry," Lucy said. "I'll pay for them myself." She hesitated, looking uncomfortable.

"What?"

"Um, can I use your truck? It's going to be a few days till my insurance money comes in."

Once again, I'd forgotten her car was demolished. I would've offered her Howie's truck, except it was still on the disabled list. I dug into my pocket and tossed her my keys. "Grab me some scrapple, will you? And apple butter?"

She raised her eyebrows. "Should I get a funny cake, too, to make the gorge fest complete?"

I groaned with exaggerated pleasure. It had been too long since I'd had that Pennsylvania Dutch treat—white cake in a pie crust, with a gooey layer of chocolate at the bottom.

"And meanwhile," Lucy said, "you need to get some rest. You're looking mighty pale."

I was feeling mighty pale, so I went in to recharge my Motrin and get some lunch, breaking up the time by making unsuccessful phone calls to Lenny's house, the Barn, and the police station. I saved room for the funny cake.

The rest of the day passed slowly. Lucy, having reverted to the quiet, private person I'd first hired, worked on her party, and I did what I could to help. We did the milking together, Tess in the corner with Queenie, and finally retired to the house to enjoy a macaroni casserole Belle had brought. We heard nothing from Lenny.

A call to Bart assured me he was still on the mend, but he hadn't heard from his errant partner, either. The anxiety would do nothing to help Bart heal, so I decided I wouldn't call him again until I knew something for certain.

Another night of nerve-driven dreams slogged by, and Saturday morning lasted forever. By afternoon I gave myself over to the plans for the evening and worked on auto-pilot, helping Lucy pack a trailer with straw, to be pulled by a tractor at the party. We cleaned the calf hutches, knowing people would want to pet the babies; Tess brushed Queenie to within an inch of the dog's patience; and Zach rode his bike over and mowed the lawn. Most of the tornado debris was cordoned off at the foundations of the garage and feed barns, the clean-up crew having gotten the majority of the yard cleared off the other day. The farm looked as good as it was going to get.

Still no word from Lenny.

At five-o'clock Lucy fired up the grill and Tess—excited beyond words that her relatives were coming—helped me set the picnic table with condiments and picnic foods. Two huge drink coolers, borrowed from Sellersville Mennonite, sat at the end of the table—one with water, one with lemonade.

Now all we needed were the people.

Lucy waited out the last few minutes in stone silence, cracking her knuckles, her neck, her back—anything that would pop. Tess danced around, eager and happy, oblivious to the tension permeating the air. I sat on a picnic table bench, my elbows resting on the table, trying to look nonchalant. I'm not sure it worked.

Abe was the first to arrive, heralded by Queenie's barking. Ma sat in the passenger seat of his Camry, and Mallory, Zach's sister, opened the back door. I looked at them with surprise. I hadn't bothered to ask Lucy who all she'd invited. I guessed I'd find out soon.

Tess went running for the lane, Queenie at her heels, when an older model Accord drove in. The smiling couple that emerged had to be Lucy's parents. The woman was an older version of Lucy, and the man really did look like the guy on the Herr's potato chip bag.

I walked toward them. "Somebody's sure glad to see you."

They laughed, Tess giggling in their three-way embrace.

"We wanted to come earlier this week," Lucy's mother said, "but Lucy asked us to wait a while, until she felt settled, and we wanted to respect her wishes. I'm Lois Ruth. This is Ron."

I shook hands with both of them, glad to finally see people from Lucy's past with nothing but gentleness in their eyes. Lucy, finished welcoming Ma and Abe, ran toward her parents. She joined in the multiple-person hug, and I swallowed the envy that clogged my throat.

I stepped back, irritated at the stinging of my eyes, and watched as another car parked alongside the drive. Detective Willard, casual in jeans and a polo shirt, stepped out, followed by his son. I walked toward them.

"Hey there, Brady," I said. "Good to see you."

He waved at me shyly, ducking his head.

"Detective," I said. "Didn't know you were on the invitation list. Glad you could make it."

He smiled. "My wife and daughter planned a shopping trip to the King of Prussia mall. Brady and I were glad for an excuse to get out of it."

"I bet."

"Besides, I might get to see some interesting alternative law enforcement."

I shrugged, hoping things worked out the way we wanted them to.

"By the way," Willard said, reaching into his car. "Here's the blanket. Not sure what Lucy had in mind, but she asked me to bring it along."

I took the garbage bag and stashed it under one of the picnic tables, already thinking of ways to use it.

Queenie was going nuts, now, as the in-laws' powder blue Buick, Uncle Scott's truck, and a van—from Yoder Mennonite

Church, according to the logo on the driver's door—drove in. I smiled when I saw Noah's face peering at me from behind the windshield. I crossed my arms and watched as the teenagers poured out the side door. Noah's MYFers, I assumed. Any number of them fit my recollection of the vandals from the other night. I wondered which ones would actually be the guilty parties. If, of course, I was right about that.

I also couldn't help but notice that while Yoder folks were self-proclaimed conservatives, their kids didn't hesitate to wear the latest fashions. The girls exposed way more of their abdomens than most parents would like, and I was afraid the boys would soon lose the long shorts that threatened to slide down their backsides. The girls hadn't skimped on makeup, either, from what I could see. Yikes.

Uncle Scott's kids jumped down from the back doors of the Silverado, and his wife—a pretty woman wearing a yellow sundress—held onto his hand to make the big step to the ground. Tess ran shrieking to her cousins, Queenie following and wagging her tail bravely amid the onslaught of pats and good-natured prodding. Mallory, baby-sitter extraordinaire, went directly to the parents, offering her services for the party. Looked to me like Scott and the missus were glad to accept any help they could get.

Elsie and Thomas Lapp, along with Shelby, occupied the Buick. I was surprised Shelby hadn't finagled her way into the van with Noah. Maybe she was still mad at him for lying about visiting Lucy.

Lucy and her parents walked over to welcome the Lapps, who stood beside their car, seemingly unsure what to make of it all. I blinked as Lucy reached out and hugged Elsie, a move I wouldn't have thought possible a few days ago. Lucy's dad and Thomas shook hands, and when Lucy released Elsie, her mom took Elsie's arm and led her toward some lawn chairs, situated in the shade.

Lucy caught my eye from across the yard and I lifted a shoulder. She swallowed and straightened her shoulders, walking toward the center of the crowd.

"Welcome to all of you," Lucy said. "I'm so glad you could make it at such short notice. My boss, Stella, over there—"

I waved.

"—has given me the job of putting on a fun fest to raise a few extra dollars this fall. I thought what better way to try things out than on people who I know would enjoy it, and people who would be interested in where Tess and I are living these days. So relax, eat, play…we're at your service. Supper will be served shortly, and until then feel free to pet the calves and take a look around. After supper we'll have time for hayrides and good ol' roasted marshmallows."

As Lucy talked I watched the people. I didn't bother with those I knew. But the MYFers were interesting. A few of the boys couldn't help but look over at the place where the garage had stood just a few days ago. I wondered how disappointed they were that their work had been obliterated in such a drastic way.

A half-hour later I was putting a milker on a cow—milking waits for no woman—when I heard it. The faintest of rumbling. I shoved on the milker and trotted outside.

There he came, riding his Harley right into the fray. I walked toward him and waited till he'd killed the engine.

"What are you doing here?" I asked.

"Lucy left a message. She needed me, so I came."

So simple. "Well, I don't know whether to hug you or slug you for keeping me in the dark the last few days."

He closed his eyes, then looked at me tiredly. "How 'bout neither? Don't want to embarrass either of us."

I studied the bags under his eyes. "I'll let it go for now. But I'm glad you're all right."

I turned and went back into the barn, afraid my emotions would boil over one way or another. The cows wouldn't notice, but the folks in my yard just might.

Zach soon joined me.

"How's it going out there?" I asked.

He shrugged. "Nobody's quite sure what to make of Lenny, but he's handling it okay. You want to get something to eat? I think people will be ready for a hayride before too long."

I stood up and stretched my back. "That'd be great. Thanks."

I stepped out of the barn only to see Noah staring at the picnic table, where Lenny was filling his plate. Probably for the third time. I walked over to the food and grabbed some plasticware.

"Meet Lucy's old flame yet?"

He looked up at me and I tipped my head toward Noah. Lenny turned toward Noah, who blinked before putting his hands in his pockets and walking away.

"She doesn't still like him?" Lenny asked.

"Why would she? With you she gets much more to love."

Lenny laughed and took his plate to join Lucy, who sat on a straw bale, talking with her mother. Lois' face showed nothing but warmth when Lenny sat down. Elsie, seated across the circle, didn't reveal much of anything, but I couldn't help but wonder if she was thinking about her son. Lucy's husband had been quite different from the man sitting next to her now.

I was piling macaroni salad onto my plate when I stopped, spoon in the air. Anita Powell was walking up the lane, having left her car down toward the road. She smiled at me and crossed to the table.

"She's really doing it, isn't she?" I said. "You, the detective...."

She popped a baby carrot in her mouth and spoke around it. "And I thought, a free meal, why not? And help a woman who can use it?" She looked across the yard at the cluster of Lapps, deep in conversation, uncertainty painted on their faces. "Could that possibly be Lucy's in-laws?"

I grinned. "Want me to introduce you?"

"It would be a pleasure."

We walked casually over to Brad's family, Anita cool and professional. The Lapps glanced at me as I broke into their circle.

"You folks having a good time?" I asked.

They looked at each other, eyes wary.

"Sure," Scott said. "You have a nice place. Oh, this is my wife, Deena."

"Hi, Deena. Nice to meet you." I gestured toward Anita. "I thought you all might like to meet one of Lucy's new friends."

Anita stepped forward and held out her hand. "Hi, I'm Anita. Anita Powell."

Thomas, caught at the very moment his and Anita's hands met, turned beet red. Elsie's face froze.

"How did you meet Lucy?" Deena asked. She obviously had no clue what was going on.

"Well," Anita said, "I work for the county's Children and Youth Services. I came out to check on Lucy and Tess' new home. We hit it off right away. I've been back a couple of times to see them."

I tried not to smile at this stretching of the truth.

The Lapps—now all performing a deer in the headlights routine—stared at Anita. Well, all but Deena, who was looking at Scott, her nose wrinkled in confusion.

"So nice to meet you all," Anita said. She turned to look toward the tractor, where Lucy was talking with Willard and herding people onto the trailer. "Is that Detective Willard over there talking with Lucy? I need to speak with him." She left, walking with a purpose.

"Detective—" Thomas said. He stopped as Willard threw back his head and laughed at something Lucy was saying.

"Sure," I said. "He's a good friend of the family. In fact, he's been helping Lucy out by looking into some things for her, trying to finally bring closure to her husband's death. Would you like me to introduce you?"

The Lapps failed to respond, so I took that as a no.

I left Lucy's in-laws in their collective shock and headed toward the trailer, where Scott and Deena's kids, Tess, Brady, and the MYFers were settling in for a hayride. I couldn't help but notice the Yoder boys showing definite interest in Mallory, who was busily tucking the smaller children onto her lap. Smiling to myself, I made a detour and grabbed Willard's garbage bag from under table.

"Hey, kids," I said when I reached the trailer. I pulled the blanket out from the bag. "It might get a little chilly during the ride. Any of you need this?"

A gasp from the rear of the trailer turned my head, and I looked into the stunned face of one of the teenage girls, her eyes wide. Noah sat beside her, his shoulder pressing against hers in the close quarters. Innocently, on his part, I was sure. Not so innocently on hers. Noah was talking soccer with a boy sitting catty-corner from him, oblivious to the drama suddenly taking place. I stared at the girl for a long moment before thrusting the blanket toward her.

"Want it?"

She jerked her head back, speechless.

"We'll take it." A girl sitting on the other side of Noah raised her chin and met my eyes defiantly. "You're right. It might get chilly."

I walked to the back of the trailer, poking Lucy in the back on my way past, and stood behind Noah and the two girls. I flapped the blanket, spreading it out, then swung it over their heads, yanking the two ends together and pulling the blanket up under their chins.

"What—?" Noah said.

I leaned forward so only he and the girls would be able to hear my words.

"I think you need to counsel a couple of your…well, your closest MYFers, Noah. Ask them how come I have their blanket. Ask them where they were during this past Sunday night. And while you're at it, you might want to think twice about letting yourself get placed in a tight little Noah sandwich in things like this trailer. I have a feeling these girls have more on their minds than church."

He jerked upright, but I snapped the blanket backward, smashing him against the side.

"And the next time I catch any of your little lambs on my property, spray-painting obscenities or no, I'll do more than sic my dog on them. Who," I said to the girls, "is just fine, no thanks to whichever of you kicked her in the head. I hope her teeth marks took more than just a dab of Neosporin."

"But—" Noah said.

"And you might want to inform them, Noah, that while your break-up with Lucy might not have been mutual, that doesn't mean you want people thinking she's something less than what she appears. Just because someone isn't hot for teacher doesn't make her a fallen woman."

He stopped fighting his restraint now and leaned back against the trailer, his face white. He looked up to find Lucy staring at him.

"They came here?" he said quietly.

"And painted some nasty words about Lucy on the garage."

His eyes flicked toward the rubble, then back to Lucy's face.

"God, I'm…I'm sorry. I didn't—"

She smiled gently. "I see that, Noah. It's okay."

Silence spread over the group as everyone realized what was happening. Kids all around the trailer stared at Noah, their faces reflecting his discomfort.

Noah cleared his throat. "Stella. Could you please let go of the blanket now?"

I released it. Noah pushed the blanket off his legs and stood up. Not looking at either of the girls, he turned around, put a foot on the side of the trailer, and jumped to the ground. He walked away, not looking back.

I stuck my head between the two girls and put my arms around their backs, my hands resting on the trailer. "Have a nice ride. I'll try not to hit too many bumps." I took a step, then stopped. "And while you're busy pointing fingers at other people, you might want to check if the words you use just might apply to yourself." I looked pointedly at the low necklines on the girl's shirts, then walked away.

Lucy stood beside the tractor, her back to the trailer and her hand covering her mouth.

"You okay?" I asked.

She nodded, removing her hand. I saw she was smiling. "I can't tell you how relieved I am that Noah didn't do it."

"I'm glad, too. Now, are you going to drive this tractor, or should I?"

She sighed, sliding her hands into her back pockets. "Do you mind? I'd really like to spend a little time with my folks."

"Be glad to. Can you take a peek in the barn, though? I'm sure Zach's fine, but just make sure everything's okay."

I jumped onto the tractor and took the group on a nice twenty-minute ride. I missed most of the potholes.

When we returned to the farm Lucy, Lenny, and Lucy's father were at the campfire, roasting marshmallows. I took a seat on one of the straw bales, next to Lucy's mom.

Lois turned to me. "Elsie tells me their quilting group sent twenty-seven comforters to Iraq for the refugees there. Isn't that wonderful?"

Lucy's mother-in-law, seated next to Lois, twitched her shoulders with embarrassment. "It's not that many."

"It is to those twenty-seven people," Lois said. "Isn't that right, Stella?"

"Um, sure."

Lois sat back and sighed contentedly. "Isn't this just a beautiful place? I'm so glad Lucy found you, Stella. I'm sure she and Tess will be very happy here."

I looked at Elsie, whose eyes shifted away.

"I'm very glad to have them," I said.

"Gramma!" Tess bounded up and threw herself onto Lois' lap, almost upsetting the straw bale. Queenie trotted right behind her and sat at Lois' feet.

Lois laughed. "Hello, sweetheart. And hello, Queenie. Did you have a nice ride?"

Tess reached down to pet Queenie's ears. "It was great. And isn't Queenie great, too?"

Lois laughed again, the sound open and inviting. "It's all great."

I looked at Elsie some more, and she finally met my eyes for a brief, revealing moment.

Elsie held her arms out to Tess. "Come here, honey."

Tess hesitated, but Lois pushed gently on her back, sliding the girl off her lap. Tess stood stiffly at Elsie's knees. Elsie reached out and hooked a wisp of hair behind Tess' ear.

"You really are happy here?"

Tess looked at her, confused. "Yes."

"You like the farm? Your school?" She hesitated. "Being with your mom?"

"Yes. Where else would I want to be?"

Where, indeed.

Elsie placed her hand on Tess' cheek and left it there for a moment before leaning over to kiss her granddaughter's forehead. She stood and walked over to her husband, who sat in a lawn chair, quiet and alone.

Lucy's head jerked my way from across the circle. I nodded to her.

"Something's happening," Lois muttered.

"Finally," I said. "I think we might be getting to the heart of things."

Lois reached out and pulled Tess toward her, her eyes betraying her nervousness as she watched the Lapps confer.

Elsie and Thomas looked over toward Willard's car, where the detective and Anita stood talking. I got up and walked casually in that direction, figuring things were about to heat up.

"What?" Willard said when I joined them.

"I think you're about to become involved."

A throat cleared and Thomas stood at Willard's elbow, Elsie close behind him.

"Detective...Willard, is it?"

Willard turned. "That's right."

Thomas shifted his feet. "I understand you have been looking into my son's death."

"Yes, sir. And his accident."

"Can you please tell me what you have found?"

Willard's face went "professional," and I marveled at the change in his demeanor.

"First off," he said, "I am very sorry for your loss. I almost lost my son last month, and I can't imagine how it would've changed my life."

Thomas swallowed, and Elsie gripped his elbow, biting her lips.

"Thank you," Thomas said.

"I understand, from talking with the Lancaster detective," Willard said, "that you have had questions about Brad's accident. That you weren't sure it even was one."

"That's right," Thomas said. "We think—"

"But I couldn't find any reason to doubt your daughter-in-law's innocence. There is nothing to point to foul play. From all investigation, everything points to a tragedy. But it's a tragedy for everyone. For you, for Lucy, and for Tess. No one did anything to cause your son's death. It was just one of those unfortunate things that sometimes happen to good people."

Elsie let out a little cry and brought her fingers to her lips. Thomas stood stoically beside her, not reaching out in comfort of any kind. Lucy, however, who had come over during the last part of Willard's speech, stretched out her hand and put it on Elsie's shoulder.

"But there was another man," Thomas said. "The papers said—"

"The papers were wrong." Lucy's voice was calm. "There was never anyone else."

Thomas didn't look at her, but kept his gaze on Willard.

"So I'm to believe," he said, "that Lucy, for all her hedging and unwillingness to talk about the 'accident,' is innocent?"

Lucy looked at her father-in-law, her eyes dry, but deep with grief. "You can believe it, Thomas. You have to. Because I am."

Elsie burst into tears, her shoulders shaking, and Lucy wrapped her in a warm embrace.

Thomas watched the two women with disgust, then turned and stalked toward his car, where he opened the door and got in.

"It might take him a while," Willard said.

Anita nodded. "But I doubt I'll hear from him anymore."

"Thanks," I said to Willard.

He smiled gently. "I just told the truth."

Lucy met my eyes over Elsie's shoulder, and I couldn't help but wonder if anyone but she actually knew the whole truth.

Elsie and Lucy were soon joined by Scott and Deena, and I drifted away. Shelby was busy trying to wheedle her way into the van with Noah, where he sat with the driver's door open. The MYFers had already filled the seats, and I couldn't help but notice the girls in the back, far from their sponsor. Noah finally said something to Shelby that made her step away, and he slammed the door. The van came to life, and he backed down the drive and out onto the road.

Once he was gone Shelby, her face resigned, re-entered the rest of the world and saw her family huddled together. Alarmed, she trotted over to them.

Willard joined me at the picnic table, where I was filling a cup with lemonade. He leaned against the table and crossed his arms. "I guess I'm done here."

We watched with interest as Brady approached Mallory, where she sat wiping chocolate and marshmallow off the faces of Scott and Deena's kids. Mallory glanced up at Brady, a smile lighting her face.

"Not sure Brady's done, though," I said.

Willard smiled. "I suppose I can wait a few more minutes."

◇ ◇ ◇

Lucy, Lenny, Abe, and I stood in a small half-circle, watching the fire as it burned hot and red. Lucy's parents had just left, and Tess had retreated to the house, exhausted but happy with the memories of a fun evening. She had no idea of the enormity of what had actually taken place.

Thomas' anger notwithstanding, the rest of the Lapps had seemed to make their peace with Lucy, and I hoped the tentative cease-fire would last. Lucy acted hopeful, and when her in-laws—former in-laws, actually—had headed out the lane, the tears had finally come. Lenny wrapped his huge arms around her shoulders and let her cry until there were no tears left.

Mallory and Ma got a ride home with Willard so Abe could stay and help clean up. I had to grin when Mallory climbed into the back of the car with Brady. If the teenagers had their way, it looked like Willard would be getting to know Mallory pretty well within the next weeks and months.

Now, Lucy's tears were over, and Lenny rested his arm on her shoulders. "Well, darlin', you done real good."

She smiled. "You think?"

"I can't imagine they'll be giving you any more trouble," I said. "What could they say?"

Lucy was quiet for a moment before letting out a giggle. "Did you see Noah's face when he realized what those girls had done, and how they feel about him? I thought he was going to faint."

I smiled. "Talk about dense."

Abe frowned. "What those girls did deserves—"

"They're kids, Abe," I said. "Well, they're pain-in-the-ass kids, but they didn't really hurt anybody. Lucy can take it, and I have to wonder if Noah might inform their parents. And you know they won't be back."

He looked uncertain.

"I'm fine," Lucy said. "It's nothing. What really matters is that I'm sure the in-laws won't be trying to take Tess away anymore. I don't know what I'd do without my sweet baby girl."

Lenny reddened, and dropped his arm.

"Speaking of daughters," I said. "What's going on with yours, Lenny?"

He cleared his throat. "Actually...."

"What?" Lucy said.

"Kristi contacted me. I'm supposed to meet her at Cloud Nine tonight. At ten-thirty."

Lucy looked at her watch. "It's about nine-thirty now."

"What does she want?" I asked.

"To talk."

I shook my head. "And you believe that?"

"Why wouldn't I?"

Lucy put her hand on his arm. "She—or somebody—gave you this at your house the other night." She touched the yellowed bruise on his cheek. "And they would've done more if they'd had the chance."

"They did do more to Bart," I said.

"But she's my daughter."

I looked up at the stars, at least the ones not drowned out by the lights of the nearby developments. "You can't, Len."

He bristled. "Why not?"

"At least you can't go alone."

"Oh, no," Abe said. "You're not going to Cloud Nine."

I leveled my eyes at him. "Lenny needs me."

"Stella—" Lenny said.

"There are at least two of them," I said. "Kristi and her butt-less boyfriend. You're not going alone."

"Stella—" Abe said.

"Would you guys stop with the 'Stella' routine?" Lucy said. "She's a grown woman. She can make her own decision."

"Thanks, Lucy," I said. "At least someone knows me."

Both guys scowled at that.

"We can clean up tomorrow, Lucy," I said.

"I don't mind—"

"At least call Willard," Abe said to me. "Get some backup."

"He's driving your mother home," I said. "Remember? And we'll be fine. We're going to a public place."

"A strip joint," Abe said hotly.

I stared at Abe, and he stared back. Finally, he turned his back to me. "So Lucy," he said. "You want some help cleaning up?"

I punched Lenny lightly on the arm. "Give me five minutes to change. And you know what? I don't even have to hitch a ride with you. I've got the perfect bike for a night like this."

Lenny shook his head. But he agreed to wait.

Chapter Thirty-seven

Cloud Nine was hopping when we arrived. A good number of bikes were lined up alongside the bar, most of them representing more than half a year of my wages. It was easy to pick out Kristi's ugly chopper and the few near it. I slid the Beast into a close spot, and it looked right at home with Kristi's group.

"Sure you want to go in?" Lenny said.

I made a face. "Not exactly where I'd choose to spend a Saturday evening, but hopefully we'll be out quickly. What about you?"

He picked at his riding gloves. "Gotta do it."

We walked up the steps and pushed open the front door. Smoke wafted out, and I fought a coughing fit. Lenny paid our cover charge while I looked around the room. Kristi and her group weren't anywhere we could see them, so we found an empty table and sat, trying not to be conspicuous.

Mercifully, there was a break between dancers, so I didn't have to be subjected to some poor girl gyrating for tips. I spied a waitress coming toward us, and I put up a finger to request a Coke.

Several feet from our table the waitress stopped, looking over my shoulder. One glance at her face, and I knew we'd found what we came for.

"So, you finally came out of hiding?" someone said.

I whirled around, but Lenny didn't move, his eyes fixed on some unseen vision. I guess even after twenty-some years you know your daughter's voice. Kristi stood behind us with the bald guy and several other scuzzy types. Kristi looked just as attractive as when we'd first met outside the Barn.

"Ah, Kristi," I said. "Lenny's told me so much about you."

"No shit? And what would he know? Seems to me the way the story goes is he abandoned me sixteen fucking years ago and hasn't looked back."

I remembered the photos I had found at Lenny's house and knew she was wrong. Lenny had never forgotten her. I looked at him, but he'd gone back to staring into space.

"Why don't you have a seat," I said, gesturing to the other side of the table. "Let's talk."

"I don't want to talk."

I stood up slowly, wanting to be at her eye level. She took a small step forward, challenging me.

"So what do you want?" I asked. "You want Lenny to say he's sorry for leaving you?"

She let out a bark that sounded kind of like laughter. "I'm not worried about losing him. What concerns me is what happened before he left. Before I was even born." She poked Lenny in the back with a dirty boot. "Why don't you just go on ahead and tell your friend here about that?"

Lenny still hadn't turned around. He finally looked at me, his eyes sad and deep.

"This isn't about my family," he said quietly. "Not completely. Or even about Kristi…my daughter."

I heard her snort. He jerked like he'd been slapped, then continued. "It's about the Priests and the Serpents."

"Your club," I said. "And their club." I looked to see if everyone in the gathered group had the tattoo, and I saw it on all of the arms that were visible.

"You know about the merger?" he said.

"*Merger?*" one of the bikers spat. I glanced at the man, and the woman beside him put her hand on his arm.

"I know the Priests and the Serpents were having turf wars," I said. "And the Priests took over after the explosion at the Serpents' clubhouse."

Lenny's eyes shot toward me. "You know about the explosion?"

"The explosion that killed three people," Kristi said.

"Three?" I said. "The article I read said only two."

"It took the VP two days to die. What do you think about that, *Lenny?*" Kristi said. She put her boot on his back again and pushed hard enough it rocked the table. I clenched my fists. I knew I could take Kristi, but not without backup in this crowd.

Lenny mumbled something.

"I couldn't hear you," Kristi said. She grabbed a clump of Lenny's hair and yanked his head back.

I lunged forward to grab Kristi's arm, and she turned and punched me in the ribs. Shocked by the sudden pain, I kept my grip on her arm and took her down with me as I fell to the ground, breathless. Kristi got in another punch to my side before I could roll out of her reach.

Kristi pushed herself up and lunged toward me. Reflexively, I grabbed her ankles and flipped her to the ground. I jumped on her and pinned her down, ready to fight, but a sudden movement made me glance to the right. Baldy's fist flew through the air toward me, and I ducked under it, narrowly missing the punch.

Lenny surged up, roaring, and I rolled away from Kristi and up onto my feet.

"Enough!" Lenny screamed. Then he quieted. "Enough."

A year passed while I caught my breath, and the Serpents helped Kristi up before settling back into a defensive stance.

A huge man with a spike through his nose came suddenly between Lenny and the group of Serpents. "Time to take it outside, folks. Don't want no fighting in here."

One look at his missing teeth and the bulge under his left arm was enough to convince even Kristi and her crew to vacate the premises. The guy watched as the Serpents filed past us, and as we followed. Only when the door banged shut behind us did he disappear.

We formed a ring in the parking lot, the lights creating more shadows than I liked. It was hard to tell how much people were moving without staring directly at them, and there was no way to keep an eye on all of them at once.

"I tried to stop the explosion," Lenny finally said.

"Sure," Kristi sneered. "You set off to kill the Serpents' leaders and got a sudden attack of conscience when you got to the clubhouse."

"No," Lenny said. "We went to get the clubhouse only. We didn't know anybody was going to be there."

"Oh, come on." She stepped sideways, her boot making a pebble crack like a gun shot. A sweat broke out on my scalp, but I tried not to show it. I had told Abe we'd be in a public place, but the parking lot was feeling way too private.

"We didn't know," Lenny said. "We thought everybody would be at the Reading Beer Bash, where our group was. The Serpents went every year. How were we to know there was a secret meeting of the officers? It's not like we had a spy in the club."

"So what stopped you?" Kristi asked. "Why didn't you just blow it up like you planned? It's not like the bikes would be outside. You don't advertise your officers are at the clubhouse alone."

"When we snuck around back we saw lights. We knew then that the place wasn't empty. But we couldn't convince him to let it go."

"Him?" Kristi said.

I knew. "The Skull."

Lenny nodded.

I continued. "And the third guy was Mal."

"Sweetheart," Kristi said nastily.

Three can keep a secret...

No wonder Mal had been so freaked when I found him the other night. He'd just been reminded that he knew who killed three men, and thought he was about to die for it.

"Mal and I told The Skull we wouldn't do it. We'd gone to destroy the clubhouse, but that was it." Lenny was silent for a moment. "We thought we'd convinced him."

"But he went back," I said.

Kristi's nostrils flared. "You practically lit the fuse yourself."

Lenny's breath caught. "I should've known. I should've stopped him."

Kristi's face was a mask of rage. "You've known all these years and you didn't tell anybody."

"I couldn't," Lenny said. "The Skull said if I told anyone he'd kill you. Your mother. My family."

Everyone stared at Lenny, and I realized I'd been right. "When The Skull was killed in that accident on Friday you figured you were free to talk."

Lenny closed his eyes. "I was finally going to come clean. The danger to Kristi and Vonda was gone."

Kristi's face paled, and for a moment I was afraid she might keel over on the pavement. When she steadied herself she said, "You really didn't have anything to do with it?"

Lenny shook his head, his eyes watery.

"Kind of makes you wish you hadn't gone after him, doesn't it?" I said. "Unless you're still mad he left you and your mom?"

Her eyes flashed. "I should be pissed about that, shouldn't I? Wouldn't you be angry if your father left when you were four?"

I swallowed painfully. Kristi had no way to know I'd lost my father before I was even that old.

"But who cares about that, anyway?" Kristi said. "I had a better dad than Lenny ever could've been." She gestured to the older couple. "Stan and Lorene took Mom and me in the day we got abandoned by this asshole." She jerked her thumb at Lenny, who looked like he wanted to disappear. "They'd come over to the Priests with Mom when the Serpents were phased out. Mom trusted them."

"But why go after Lenny now?" I said. "Haven't you known for years who was suspected in the explosion?"

"I never knew. But when The Skull died on Saturday, Stan and Lorene decided it was time I understood why I don't have a 'real' father anymore. All I knew before was that four years after the Priests took us over Lenny split. Didn't even tell Mom where he was going."

I glanced at Lenny, and he looked like he wanted to be any place but there.

"Why hadn't your mother told you about the explosion?" I asked Kristi. "And why isn't she here?"

Kristi stared at me. "Mom's dead. Lung cancer got her almost ten years ago."

Lenny made a strangled sound.

"But she hated Lenny," Kristi said. "She thought he'd killed those guys. You'd think he would've at least told *her* what happened."

Lenny exhaled forcefully. "It was too dangerous for you. Every day The Skull reminded me what would happen if I didn't keep my mouth shut. Every time he saw you with me he'd make a line across his throat, or point his fingers like a gun. I finally realized I had to leave you to keep you safe." Tears formed in his eyes, and I prayed he'd be able to keep it together in front of these folks.

"What a hero," Kristi said, sneering. "Giving up everything to save the girl he thought was his daughter."

Lenny's eyes snapped to her.

"What do you mean?" I said. "The girl he *thought* was his daughter?"

She looked at Lenny, her eyes reflecting steel in the artificial light. "My mom wouldn't have had a baby with a *Priest*. She joined with Lenny as soon as the Serpents were swallowed up because she knew she was already pregnant. She didn't want the Priests taking her baby away because it had been fathered by a Serpent."

Lenny turned a harsh red and then paled so abruptly I was afraid he was going to faint. I could see a question in his eyes, but knew he wouldn't be able to ask it. So I did.

"And your real father?"

She stared at me. "My *real* father died when Lenny's pal The Skull blew up the clubhouse. He was the Serpents' vice president."

Chapter Thirty-eight

Lenny sank down onto the bumper of a truck, never taking his eyes from Kristi's face. His face went through a startling series of expressions. The one he was left with was not surprisingly a mixture of betrayal and horror.

The silence of the Serpents was heavy and loud. I was afraid to breathe for fear I might trigger something and let loose the arsenal of hatred seething under their tattered clothes. Turns out I didn't need to.

Kristi's adopted father, Stan, broke the silence.

"I think he needs to learn a little lesson," he said.

"For what?" I said. "Trying to protect Kristi all these years?"

"You heard him. He could've stopped the explosion if he'd been smart enough. Besides, I've been waiting for this a long time." He reached into his pocket and came out with a knife, its blade about four inches long.

Skinny Ass followed suit, taking out his own weapon. I remembered his hand snaking into his vest at the Barn when Queenie had him cornered, and now I knew what he'd been going for.

The whole group moved of one accord toward Lenny. Lenny stood motionless, seemingly resigned to what was coming.

I wasn't.

"So which one of those blades sliced Bart?" I asked.

Half a dozen heads snapped toward me, including Lenny's. His face hardened when his brain caught up enough to put it together that these guys really were the ones who'd attacked Bart.

"Was it Stan's knife or Baldy's?" I asked.

"It was Raymond's," Kristi snapped.

I snickered. *"Raymond?"*

Raymond turned the knife toward me and angled it so it would catch some light.

"Probably still has some of his blood on it," he said. "Want a taste?"

Adrenaline rushed through my veins and I would've gone for his throat if Lenny hadn't gotten there first, his two hundred plus pounds carrying them both backward, tumbling over a truck hood and onto the dirt. Lenny emitted a horrendous noise, and Raymond slashed at the air with his knife, handicapped by Lenny's huge body pinning down his arms. Raymond was just as likely to be crushed as Lenny was to get the sharp end of the knife, and I watched for an opening to step on Raymond's hand like I had Big Trey's way back at the pig roast.

The Serpents stood frozen, except for Kristi, who shrieked at Raymond to kill the bastard, and Stan, who was looking for a chance to bury his blade in Lenny's back. I was getting ready to launch myself at Stan when a couple of police cars barreled into the parking lot, spilling cops in riot gear. Never had I been so happy to see a gun barrel pointed my way.

The cops screamed at everybody to stay where they were, which wasn't hard since Lenny and Raymond were the only ones moving. Raymond's blade was turning toward the ground when the cops got close enough to put guns to the guys' heads, and then the knife hung there, ready to be used in a split second of chance.

"Blades on the ground," one cop said, his voice shaky. "Everybody else stay still." Raymond lay face up, and the cop above him stared into his eyes while another had Lenny and Stan under his watch. Raymond hesitated, snarling, but when he saw the officer wasn't about to back down he mustered up enough brain power to know a knife was no match for a service revolver. With a disgusted grunt he dropped the knife onto the dirt.

By this time more cops had hustled over, the parking lot filling up just as it had at our HOG picnic, and I breathed much easier. They soon figured out Raymond and Stan were the only ones with weapons, so with two cops to a sleazeball they got them handcuffed and pulled them away from the group.

A small crowd had come outside the bar to see what was so exciting it needed police, and more cops arrived and asked the on-lookers to please step back. The guy with the spike through his nose caught my eye across the parking lot and nodded. I wondered if he was the one who'd made the call.

Stan and Raymond were several steps away when Stan stopped abruptly and turned to look at Lenny. Lenny straightened and stared right back at him, some silent communication passing between them that excluded everyone else. I don't know for sure what it was about, but I have to assume it concerned the pathetic girl they both thought of as a daughter. Stan eventually leaned toward Lenny, spat on the ground, and let the cops take him away. Raymond gave Lenny a stare, but it was nothing compared to Stan's venom.

Lenny made a half-motion toward Kristi, but stopped when she bucked backward into Lorene, Stan's wife.

"Kristi—"

"Save it, old man. Ain't nothing you can say that will change anything."

"But—"

She shook her head, not looking at him. His eyes went dead, and he slowly sank back down to the bumper, despair present in the sagging of his shoulders. This sad spectacle of a huge man with tears running down his face should've softened the heart of even the hardest female, but Kristi looked at him with something approaching revulsion, and her lip turned up in a sneer.

"You're pathetic," she spat, using the word I had so recently pinned to her.

He turned his head away.

"Pathetic and a disgrace to bikers. Go home to your fancy shop and your faggot partner."

"Then—"

"We're through. I never want to see or hear about you ever again. As far as I'm concerned, you never even existed."

He raised his head to gaze at her, like he was drinking her in, never wanting to forget her. I could see in his eyes that no matter what had happened during the past week, no matter how vengeful or disgusting she was, no matter that she hated him with passion and had almost killed his best friend, he still thought of her as his daughter. Finally, he wiped his face and got to his feet.

"Good-bye, Kristi," he said gently.

She spun on her heel and walked away.

◇◇◇

Several minutes later the crowd had dispersed, headed back inside to their booze and naked women.

Lenny remained on the truck's bumper, pale and shaken, not saying a word. I stood beside him, trying to ignore my throbbing ribs. I scanned the people going by to make sure none of the Serpents were coming back to finish what they'd started, and after fifteen minutes of it, I'd had enough.

"Okay, Len, let's go."

I had to say it twice to get it to register, and he finally swiveled his head toward me.

"There's nothing else for us here," I said. "Come on."

Lenny was still in a daze. I nudged him with my knee.

"Len?"

Finally, he moved. But it was to look at the ground, not get up.

"Go on home," he said. "I might as well stay here, where I belong."

"*What?*"

"You heard what they said. I basically killed three people by letting The Skull go back to the clubhouse. I abandoned my dau—the girl I *thought* was my daughter, along with her mother. It's a good thing I'm not really her father. Dads come from a lot better line than folks like me."

"Give me a break, Lenny."

He looked at me with big, watery eyes, like a newborn calf. "Just go on. I'm not worth worrying about. Look at me. I'm just what Kristi said—pathetic. Look around you. This is what I am. I'm dirty, smelly, and violent. I fit in here. No one runs at the sight of me, keeping between me and their kids. No one sees me and assumes I'm going to steal their purse. Or their car. I should be around my own kind."

Every inch of my being wanted to slug him, but from somewhere deep inside me some strange, foreign thing forced itself to the surface. Maternal instinct suddenly reared its unfamiliar head. I knelt in front of my friend.

"Lenny, those stupid moms at the ice cream place were afraid of me, too. And of the nose-ring girl who dipped our ice cream. Think about who those women are. They seclude themselves in their new developments with their two point five kids and brush their hair at five-thirty every afternoon to make sure they're ready for hubby to get home from the office and take over. They wouldn't know a friendly outsider if it bit them on their liposuctioned asses."

He looked over my head and I grabbed his hands.

"Lenny, I don't give a damn what 'society' says. Think about who you are. You're a good man. All your neighbors say so. Your customers say so. Bart says so. You don't produce drugs. You don't sell porn. Just because you wear black and ride a Harley doesn't mean you're an outlaw. Remember what one-percenter means? It means *one percent*. You're part of the ninety-nine now. You decided that twenty years ago."

I felt like I was talking across miles, even though I sat inches from his face. I reached up and grabbed his chin, forcing him to look at me for my final plea.

"Why would a woman like Lucy give a rat's ass about you if you're such a slime? Why would she trust you with her daughter?"

I finally saw a flicker of life in his eyes, and gradually the fog seemed to clear. I let go of his face and he didn't look away.

"Does she really care about me?" he asked.

"Oh, Lenny, you big dummy. Can't you see she's nuts about you? And her world—her Mennonite world—that's where you belong. Violence isn't your way. You proved that years ago when you walked away from it all." I smiled at him. "I told Willard the truth the night at your house. You're nothing but a big teddy bear."

He was showing a glimmer of a grin when a couple came barging out the bar's door. Laughing loudly and hanging onto each other for support, the girl's boot caught under my butt, sending her sprawling, her bottle of beer spilling all over my back and Lenny's jeans. The guy went crashing down with her, his beer splashing onto her face and saturating the front of her shirt. After a moment of stunned silence, they looked at each other and started on a new fit of giggles. It didn't take more than five seconds before they were pulling each other's clothes off.

"Let's get the hell out of here," Lenny said.

Chapter Thirty-nine

Lenny sped toward Perkasie, wanting to get cleaned up before talking with Lucy. I rode directly home and found my farmhand sitting at the kitchen table, a mug of hot chocolate in her hands. She looked up anxiously.

"He's okay," I said. "Sad, and a bit disillusioned, but okay."

As I sank to a chair Lucy jumped up, grabbing another mug from the cupboard and pouring some hot water from the tea kettle.

"Here," she said. "Have some cocoa."

I took it and breathed in the rich aroma. "Thanks."

Lucy sat back down, across from me. "Tell me what happened?"

I shook my head. "Lenny will be here soon. He'll tell you himself."

She nodded, understanding. We sat quietly, sipping our drinks.

"So, Lucy," I finally said. "There's something I'd really like to know."

I hesitated, and she looked down at the tablecloth.

"Go ahead," she said. "Ask."

"You didn't push Brad. I know that. You don't even have to say it. But why the secrecy? Why not tell everyone exactly what happened? You'd save yourself a lot of grief if you just told the truth."

"Would I?" A ghost of a smile appeared on her face, but it didn't reach her eyes. She stared into her hot chocolate for a moment, then lifted her eyes to mine. "The truth can be worse than rumors, Stella. And it hasn't been worth it to reveal it."

"But—"

"Nobody pushed Brad. We loved him. I did. Tess did. His family—no matter how annoying they are—loved him like no other family could've." Tears formed in her eyes, and fell. "You want to know why I can't tell the truth? It's because the truth would hurt the one person I love more than any other."

"Tess?" I said. "But how?"

Tears fell even thicker down her cheeks. "It was her tractor," she whispered. "She left it on the basement stairs. Brad didn't see it, because he was holding that damned box."

I took a breath through my mouth. *Oh, God.*

"I knew Brad wouldn't want her to live with that guilt," Lucy said. "And she would've. She would've lived with it till her grave. And I couldn't do that to my little girl."

We sat at the table together, watching as the steam from our cocoa drifted toward the ceiling, mingling with the patterns in the plaster.

Chapter Forty

"The one on the right's a little crooked," Abe said.

I hammered another nail into the plaster and hung the third picture, the one of Howie and me at my birthday party. I stepped back to look at the arrangement and decided Abe was right. I slid the crooked picture to the left and it straightened out.

I didn't turn around, but could feel Abe's presence as well as if he'd been standing right beside me. Neither of us spoke.

It had been several days since I'd seen him. In fact, the last time we'd talked was before I went to Cloud Nine with Lenny. He hadn't exactly been happy with me.

Now, Queenie stood up from where she was resting in the corner and walked behind me to Abe. I heard him scratching her head, and emotion clogged my throat.

We stood awkwardly in my office, speechless, and I didn't even want to turn around to look at him. I felt too guilty about what I was going to say. The silence, punctuated with contented grunts from Queenie, dragged out for several minutes until I spoke.

"It's ironic, isn't it? We've dealt with so many fathers this week, and the only person I've ever considered as a father for my own children has been you."

I heard Abe shift his feet, but he didn't say anything.

"Somehow I don't think that's going to happen. Is it?" My throat closed and I looked at the floor until I had control again. I finally turned to look at him, and almost lost my nerve when I saw his face.

"You know I love you, Abe, but I just…."

He leaned over and put a finger on my lips. "Stop, Stella, please." He took his finger off and moved away, looking out the window.

"I think we both know it," he said. "I mean, we should've known before, but it wasn't until the other night—" He cleared his throat. "It wasn't until then I knew it just wasn't going to work."

"I'm sorry, Abe, I—"

He waved his hands. "You don't have to be sorry. It's as much me as you. That kiss…it felt wrong, didn't it?" He turned to look at me. "I think we've both had kisses before that felt right."

My face burned as I remembered the two kisses I'd had from Nick Hathaway just weeks before. Kisses that still made me lightheaded, just thinking about them.

Abe smiled softly. "It's Nick for you, isn't it?"

I sighed and closed my eyes. "It could be. I don't even know him that well, but he's the one I'm picturing now."

"As your children's father?"

I shrugged, looking at him. "As something more than a friend."

He nodded, looking pained.

"And for you?" I asked. "Is it Missy?"

"Maybe. But you know what else it is? It's the city. I mean, I love coming here to visit. But I've realized it isn't home anymore."

"New York's home?"

"I sure miss it. So it must be."

I knelt to rub Queenie's head. "Does Ma know?"

He squatted beside me and fingered Queenie's silky ears. "You're the first. I thought you deserved that."

I let out a deep breath. "I was afraid you'd be mad."

"That I'm not the one for you?"

"Yeah."

"I was afraid of that, too, until I realized you were right."

We petted Queenie some more. She was getting more than her fair share of comfort in this uncomfortable situation, I thought.

"So we're still friends?" I asked.

He placed his hand on mine, then picked it up and kissed the back of it. "The best."

I smiled and turned to wrap my arms around him. We knelt there on the floor, hugging, and I prayed no one would burst in on us this time.

No one did, and eventually I let go and stood up. I walked back to where I'd been hanging the pictures on the wall. The pictures Abe had been thoughtful enough to frame for me.

"You know," I said, "Howie was everything I could ask for in a dad, and we weren't related by a drop of blood or any piece of paper." I put my hand out to touch the photo, then dropped it. "I found some other people this week that lost dads. Tess, even Kristi. She not only lost her biological dad, but she never even had Lenny. Not really." I smiled. "Maybe Lenny and Tess will get another chance. Together."

"That would be nice, wouldn't it?" Abe put his arm around my shoulders, and this time it didn't feel awkward. It felt right.

Abe put out a hand and tilted the photo a little more to the left. "I'm going to give my two-week notice at Rockefeller tomorrow. If they'll let me go sooner, I will. Want me to keep coming around here till I go? Get you back into the swing of your paperwork?"

I nodded, my voice gone again.

"Okay, then," Abe said. "I'll see you tomorrow." The door opened. "I do love you." The door shut. Abe was gone.

I stood there waiting for his car to leave and heard rumbling coming down the lane. But it didn't sound like Lenny's bike. It sounded like mine. My heart beat a little faster.

I looked out the window. Abe stood beside his car, watching Lenny drive in. Lenny stopped the bike—*my* bike—and sat for a moment, looking back at Abe.

Lenny nodded at Abe. Abe nodded back. Then Abe got into his Camry and drove away. When the dust had settled, I went outside.

"You brought my baby home," I said.

Lenny didn't ask about Abe, and I was thankful for that. Lenny stood between me and the bike, hiding the tank, which he must've gotten from the Grangers and painted during the past few days. He had wanted to spend every moment with Bart at Grandview, but with the demands of the Biker Barn he hadn't been able to be there as much as he'd hoped. I guess my bike was the project he needed to keep his mind off his best friend lying in the hospital.

"Hope you don't mind I came by and swiped the fork while you weren't looking," he said. "I wanted to get it on for you. It ain't polished, but it works."

"Looks great," I said. "How's it drive?"

"Like a gem."

"Can't wait to try it." I took a step toward the bike, but Lenny blocked me.

"Bart said I'm supposed to give you a big kiss." He looked at me skeptically.

"Let's say you did."

"Works for me. Anyhow, he's doing good. They'll probably let him come home in a day or two. He's gonna stay with me till he's feeling better."

"And Mal?"

"Sweetheart's doing okay, I guess. A little fried in the head, but physically nothing was hurt that can't heal."

Lenny glanced up, and Lucy peeked out of the house's side door. Lenny waved. "I'll be ready in a minute."

She smiled and stepped back inside, closing the door.

"We're going out for lunch," he said to me. "Need to try out Lucy's new Civic."

"Great."

We looked at each other.

"So what about you?" I finally said. "What's going to happen about the explosion twenty years ago?"

"Nothing. Would you believe it? Crockett and I went in and told Willard everything. I even took a lie-detector test. Willard said he'll look at things again, but seeing as how they didn't have evidence against me back then—well, except hearsay—he doesn't think they'll find any now. And he seems to believe me about the threats against my...against Kristi and Vonda." His face clouded, and I decided to change the subject.

"So why aren't you letting me get to the bike?"

He shifted on his feet. "I did something to the tank you might not like. I thought it was perfect at the time, but now I'm not so sure."

"So what's the worst that can happen?" I said. "If I hate it, I'll just make you paint it over."

He grinned. "Forgot about that. Okay. Tell me what you think."

He stepped aside, and I caught my breath. Tears stung my eyes and I looked away, not wanting Lenny to see them.

The design he'd painted wasn't something I'd have wanted a week before. In fact, I would have been annoyed if he'd done it. But now it was perfect.

The tank was black, like it used to be, but the Harley emblem was gone. Blue ghost flames started bright at the front, fading out three-quarters of the way back. The flames surrounded some words painted expertly in sparkling blue script.

The words read, "Daddy's Princess."